THE FAMILY TOMB
MICHAEL GILBERT

"The Family Tomb is everything one expects of Michael Gilbert and more. It's a fine tale of deadly intrigue; these modern Florentines could have taught Machiavelli a thing or two."

—Ogden Nash

"I thoroughly enjoyed *The Family Tomb*! Anything from Florence delights me, from Jacob Burckhardt to the flood to Michael Gilbert, who in spite of violence and threats, and three of the most sinister figures I've met in years, manages to keep it all fresh and bright. I guess it's the Etruscan sunshine that casts out the Mafia gloom."

—Bernadine Kielty

"To a Florentine aficionado like myself it conjures up all sorts of pleasant recollections. It is something of a cross between a mystery and a thriller, but none the worse for that; it is better written than four out of five mysteries, and it gives us a gaggle of interesting and raffish characters."

—Henry Steele Commager

*Also available in Perennial Mystery Library
by Michael Gilbert:*

The Crack in the Teacup

THE FAMILY TOMB

MICHAEL GILBERT

PERENNIAL LIBRARY

Harper & Row, Publishers
New York, Cambridge, Philadelphia, San Francisco
London, Mexico City, São Paulo, Singapore, Sydney

This work was published in England under the title *The Etruscan Net*.

A hardcover edition of this work was published by Harper & Row, Publishers, Inc. It is here reprinted by arrangement with the author.

First PERENNIAL LIBRARY edition published 1986.

Library of Congress Cataloging-in-Publication Data

Gilbert, Michael Francis, 1912–
    The family tomb.

    "P 795."
    I. Title.
PR6013.I3335F3   1986   813′.54   85–45197
ISBN 0-06-080795-4 (pbk.)

86 87 88 89 90 OPM 10 9 8 7 6 5 4 3 2 1

PART ONE

The Net Opens

1

Robert Broke
TUESDAY MORNING

It was worst, Broke had found, at the moment of waking. It wasn't that he dreamed much about Joanie now. But when he was asleep she was there, somewhere in the background, a comforting presence, as she had been in life; someone perfectly reliable, perfectly compatible, always available. She was in the chair on the other side of the fire. She was in bed. You had only to stretch out a hand to touch her shoulder. The moment you woke up was really the moment when you realized that she wasn't there anymore; that what had been one part of her was a fistful of ashes in a North London suburb, and what had been the other part of her had gone, like a flame blown out.

He could hear Tina moving about in the kitchen. She must have let herself in with her own key, while he was still asleep. That, in itself, was an improvement. Previously he had been lying awake by the time she arrived. Every little improvement was a fact to be noted, just as a man who has been very ill will record and treasure the infinitesimal stages by which he comes back to health.

He got up, washed and shaved carefully, brushed his teeth, and put on a clean white shirt for a new day, because those were things you clung to.

Breakfast was ready when he reached the living room: coffee in an old silver jug, milk, toast, and butter and marmalade.

Tina examined him closely. She did not like it when Signor Roberto fell into a gray mood. It was not that he was ever anything but courteous, but it made her uncomfortable. This morning it was all right. Some little thing had pleased him. He was not smiling. He very rarely smiled. But his face was not set in those marble lines that she dreaded.

She said, "They say that there are more visitors to Florence this summer than ever before. More, even, than came before the floods."

Broke had never discovered who "they" were. Only that they were omniscient and usually accurate.

"What else do they say?"

"There was a motor accident in the Lungarno Corsini. Some fool driving too fast. The price of coffee is going up again, by two hundred lire the kilo. Two hundred! How shall we live?"

"We shall manage," said Broke. "How is your father?"

"He is not well. It is his stomach. When he went to the doctor, the doctor told him, 'Drink no more wine and you will feel better.' How can people say such stupid things? It is, alas, true that he drinks too much. But if he drank nothing, instead of being miserable most of the time he would be miserable all of the time."

"Doctors have to say things like that. It's expected of them. Is your father too bad to finish those picture frames for me?"

Broke liked Tina to talk to him. He told himself that it was good for his Italian; which was very good already. But that was an excuse. The truth was that Tina now knew all about Joanie and had finished being sorry for him.

"The frames are nearly ready. He will bring them around to the gallery himself. Will you have more coffee?"

"No, thank you."

"You will be home for lunch?"

"At the usual time," said Broke.

He walked down to the gallery. His car, a fifteen-year-

4

old Sunbeam Talbot, was in the garage, but, unless it was raining, he preferred to walk. Down the broad Viale Michelangiolo to the Arno, across the bridge, its parapet rebuilt after the floods, and along the Lungarno to the bookshop and gallery, which was in the Via dei Benci.

The streets of Florence were full of boys and girls on their way to school, on bicycles, on mopeds, on foot in chattering groups. Italian youth seemed to him to be an improvement on their modern British counterparts; they dressed better, washed more often, and, because they were more sure of themselves, seemed to trouble less about the impression they were making on their elders.

He was so deep in thought that Commander Comber had walked beside him for nearly a minute before he realized he was there.

"Wondered when you were going to wake up," said Comber, a jaunty little figure, beard jutting. "Lot of people in town today. Should be good for business."

"Yes and no," said Broke. "Half of them just come into the shop to look. They leave sticky fingerprints in expensive books, and if they see me glaring at them, maybe they buy a guidebook for three hundred lire."

"I'm sure you don't glare at them. You fix them with that terrible blank look of yours, and they feel they're being turned into stone—like Perseus and the Gorgon."

"You talk a lot of nonsense," said Broke.

"Today I'm a cash customer myself."

"I didn't know you were interested in art."

"In a general way," said Comber affably. "In a very general way. What I want is a book that gives the names of all the artists and all their best-known pictures, but without a lot of waffle."

"That sounds like a dictionary."

"Is there such a thing? No, I will not get out of the way. Impudent monkey."

This was to a youth on a Lambretta who tried to edge past them in the narrow street and was baffled by the Commander's habit of walking in the middle of the road.

"Steam gives way to sail, my boy."

The motor scooter mounted the pavement and shot past with a triumphant toot. They emerged into the bustle of the Via dei Benci, turned right, and the Galleria e Biblioteca delle Arti was on their right.

The shop was already open. Francesca, a solemn girl, who wore round glasses and held Broke in awe, always arrived before nine, took down the shutters, took in the mail, and dusted around.

The bookshop portion of the establishment was a hexagonal room, with an overhead glass light. The walls were covered with shelves, and there was a display counter filling most of the middle. The larger and more expensive books were stacked on it.

"I've made up my mind," said Broke. "Any book selling at more than three thousand lire is to be covered in cellophane. Completely covered. If people are sufficiently interested in it, we will be happy to break it open for them."

"Sì, signore," said Francesca. "I will buy some cellophane and start now."

Broke was already on top of a ladder. He climbed down with two books. "This one's got illustrations," he said. "It's a bit more expensive. This one's just out. It's called *The Cosmopolitan Art Lover's Companion*. I should guess that most of it's been cribbed from other books."

"Exactly what I want."

"You're not interested in one particular field?"

"The whole world is my province! Who was it said that? Talleyrand? Sydney Smith?" The Commander peeled off two thousand-lire notes. "By the way, are you doing anything this evening?"

6

"Nothing that I can think of. Why?"

"Would you like to come to a party?"

"What sort of party?"

"The usual sort of party. Eating and drinking, and talking and being talked to."

"Where?"

"At the Villa Rasenna. Professor Bronzini."

The Commander felt in his pocket and pulled out a thick card. It was pale green, and the writing on it was in purple ink. "Like a frog menu," he said. "I gather he's a bit queer."

"Are you using queer in the technical sense, or do you just mean that he's odd?"

"Both, really. He's a fantastic old nut, but his food and drink's all right. Come along for laughs."

Broke was examining the card.

Professor Bruno Bronzini warmly invites all his friends and fellow enthusiasts for Etruscan art and the Etruscan way of life to join him at the Villa Rasenna, to eat, to drink, to listen to Etruscan music on pipes and zither, and to enjoy the beauties of a civilization happier and more cultivated than our own.

"Happier!" said Broke. "He might have something there. Do you know this chap?"

"I've been introduced. I believe he really is by way of being an authority on Etruscan art. Made some discoveries, on his own property out near Volterra, and written books about it."

"Yes," said Broke. He thought about it, and shook his head. "He can't want just *anyone* turning up at his party."

"Not just anyone. He wants to meet you."

"He doesn't know me."

"He knows you have taken over Welford Hussey's shop and gallery. What's happened to Welford, by the way?"

"He's gone to South America. To study the Aztecs. He'll be back at the end of the year. If I haven't lost all his customers for him by then!"

"I overheard two young ladies talking about you the other day. One of them said that you were not in the least *simpatico*. On the contrary, very strict. You reminded her of her father. It caused her a delicious frisson of terror every time she came into the gallery."

"And what did the other say? Something equally silly?"

"Shan't tell you," said Comber with a grin. "Our young ladies here are remarkably outspoken, not to say indelicate, about the opposite sex. Talking of the opposite sex, here comes Miss Plant. Better mind your p's and q's. I'm off." At the door he stopped, and said, "You will come tonight, won't you? I'll pick you up at your place about eight o'clock."

"All right," said Broke. He didn't sound very grateful.

Miss Plant was, in every sense of the word, the leading lady of the English colony in Florence. She had been there since around the beginning of the century. The accident that Italy had happened to be on the wrong side in the Second World War had not incommoded her at all. It had, in truth, served to emphasize her standing and increase her prestige. It was true that the Italian authorities, badgered beyond endurance by the Germans, and after exhausting every excuse for delay, had eventually agreed to take Miss Plant into custody as an enemy alien. The experiment had not been a success. She had allowed herself to be driven to the Questura, and had sat there, upright, unmoving, and unspeaking, during the remainder of that day and the night following, acknowledging the arrival of evening only by elevating the umbrella she had brought with her. She had refused all food and drink. The thought that Miss Plant might actually starve to death, under her umbrella, in his outer office had so unnerved the Questore that he had preferred to brave the wrath of the Germans, and had returned her to her villa

8

under very nominal house arrest. Even so, she had not forgiven him. She omitted his name from the invitations to her first garden party after the war, and the Questore had disappeared from public life.

Miss Plant sailed into the shop, ignored Francesca, who had sidled up to serve her, and brought her guns to bear on the man. "My name is Beatrice Plant," she said. "You must be Robert Broke." She pronounced the name in the correct English way, as "Brook." "You've taken on the gallery from that American. Why is it, I wonder, that Americans have such curious Christian names? Welford! It sounds like a telephone number. We had an American here, just after the war, whose Christian name was Shaftesbury. Your wife was a Temple-Hardy."

"She was," Broke agreed grimly. If Miss Plant noticed the hardening in his face she gave no sign of it. The feelings of others were of little interest to her.

"You've met Elizabeth Weighill, I believe." She indicated the young woman who had followed her into the shop. "Elizabeth very kindly gave me a lift down into town this morning. The traffic gets worse every day. It's time somebody did something about it. Have you met her father?"

"I've met Sir Gerald," said Broke. He caught Elizabeth's eye as he said this, and she winked at him.

"It's surprising," said Miss Plant, "that this government should have had enough good sense to send us out a baronet as our Consul. The last one was a terrible little man, with no birth or breeding."

"Oh, nonsense," said Elizabeth. "He was perfectly all right. He called on Miss Plant on a very cold day in midwinter, and kept his overcoat on in the drawing room."

"I once had a doctor," said Miss Plant, "who kept his overcoat on in my *bedroom*. He was a very well-known man, I believe. Of course, I never had him in the house again. Macchiaioli."

9

Broke assumed that this final word was a war cry, connected with what had gone before. When it was repeated, he realized that it was a question. He pulled himself together.

"Are you looking for a book about them, or for reproductions of their drawings? We've got some Telemaco Signorinis in the gallery, and at least one Cabianca."

"I want a book about the Macchiaioli. Gertrude Strozzi started a discussion about them the other day. I'd not the least idea what she was talking about. I just want to know enough about them to put her in her place if she tries it again."

Fortunately Broke was able to produce a volume dealing with these minor painters of the nineteenth century.

When Miss Plant had taken herself off, Elizabeth said, "You mustn't mind her. She's been eccentric for so long that what started as a pose has become a habit. There's no malice in it."

"It's rather refreshing when someone simply says the first thing that comes into their head."

"If she did that," said Elizabeth, "It wouldn't be so bad. The real trouble is that she says the first *three* things that come into her head. One after the other. When she was introduced to Daddy she said, "How do you do, Sir Gerald. A second-generation baronetcy, ent it! Your father was Lord Mayor of London. It was the year that horse with a foreign name won the Derby."

Broke smiled. It was a little grim, but it was a genuine smile.

"What did your father say?"

"Something suitable, I'm sure. He's a professional diplomat. By the way, did you know you were coming to luncheon with us the day after tomorrow? If you're not otherwise engaged, that is."

"Thursday? I'm not sure—"

"Tom Proctor's going to be there."

10

"Tom! Is he in Florence?"

"Not yet. But he's getting in tomorrow night. He's a trustee of yours, or something, isn't he?"

"He's my sister Felicia's trustee and he's my solicitor. Yes, if Tom's there, I suppose I ought to turn up."

"That's not the most enthusiastic acceptance I've ever heard," said Elizabeth. "Most people consider that an invitation to luncheon with the British Consul confers a considerable social cachet."

Broke said, "I'm sure it does," and smiled again.

Twice in one morning, said Elizabeth to herself, as she drove back to the Consulate. If we go on at this rate, we may ultimately let our hair right down, go the whole hog, and *laugh*. She opened the window of the car and said, in excellent Italian, "If the Signore would spend less time sounding his horn, and more time using his eyes, he would observe that my left indicator is out, demonstrating that I intend to turn to the left. Thank you."

The gallery shut for two hours in the middle of the day, and this gave Broke plenty of time to walk home to lunch. It was his custom to cross the Ponte Vecchio, and make his way back along the left bank of the river, thus completing the circuit which his morning walk had started.

As he passed the café on the corner of the Lungarno Acciaioli he noticed the two strangers, sitting at a table under the awning. They were clearly not tourists. He judged that they might be from Naples. Even, perhaps, from Sicily. Both were dressed in charcoal-gray suits, cut in the latest fashion.

Broke had an artist's interest in faces, and these were a couple for the sketchbook. The one on the left, the longer and thinner of the two, had a bent nose that ran up to a skull-like forehead, the sides of which were hollowed out in a way that suggested skin stretched over vacancy. The

11

side of the face that Broke could see was seamed with creases, which might have been natural, but had the look of scars.

His companion was short and stout. With his rounded olive cheeks, soft brown eyes, and sulky mouth he had the look of a bad-tempered girl.

A couple of thoroughly ugly customers, thought Broke; and then forgot all about them.

2

Dindoni
TUESDAY AFTERNOON

Tina had long ago given up her attempts to make Broke eat a proper lunch. He ate far too little. Also, he neglected his siesta, returning too soon to his business in the shop.

Tina had considered the matter very carefully, and had come to the conclusion that this behavior was connected with his private tragedy. She knew about it, because he had told her, in very simple words, almost as soon as she came to work for him. Not as one seeking sympathy, not even as a personal thing, but dispassionately, as a man might recount the history of a distant acquaintance.

The night after she had heard it, she had dreamed it all over again, and had waked up in tears. She wondered if Signor Roberto had ever cried. She thought it unlikely.

She finished washing up, put away the plates and glasses, and cleaned the flat. Then she went out to do the shopping, spending some time gossiping with the stout Signora Colli at the gate of her garden next door. She purchased the materials for a cold *colazione,* which she prepared and left ready in the icebox. Then, in the cool of the early evening, she walked home, down the Viale, across the bridge, and through the honeycomb of streets that lay behind it.

The Zecchi house was in the Sdrucciolo Benedetto, a steep street of old-fashioned houses with blind fronts and enclosed courtyards. It was a part of the city that for centuries had been given over to workers in wood and stone and precious metals. The front door of the house opened directly into the kitchen, where her mother sat, enthroned beside the spotless hearth.

Annunziata Zecchi was a queen among women. At fifty she was still broad in the hips and full in the bust, and her gray hair was piled, pompadour fashion, above a face beginning to wrinkle, but full of life and authority. She said, "How was Signor Roberto today?"

"He seemed more cheerful. Something had pleased him. Or perhaps, with each day, he becomes a little more reconciled."

"A great sorrow is like a deep wound," said her mother. "At first you imagine it will never heal. Then, very gradually, it closes. So slowly you can hardly notice it. But at last it is only a scar. It gives you a twinge sometimes, when the wind is in a certain quarter. Otherwise you forget about it."

"I hope you are right. I do not like to see him suffer."

"He is a perfect gentleman. If you have to work for anyone, it is good fortune that you should work for such a man." She added, "Not that it is right that you should have to work at all."

"Am I a princess, then, that I should sit in idleness all day?"

"You are the daughter of one of the finest craftsmen in Florence. By rights you should have been to the finest schools. By now you should be—"

Her mother paused, to pass in review the highest prizes for girls, and Tina grinned, and said, "Well, what should I be?"

"You should be a secretary."

"Phooh. To squat all day in a rabbit hutch of an office, hammering at a typewriter."

"Then a model."

"Taking my clothes off, to amuse old gentlemen."

"It is a very respectable calling."

"And a very dull one. Sitting all day in a draft, getting pins and needles in your bottom."

"Your language might be more delicate," said her mother.

There was a scuffling of feet across the paved backyard as the crippled Dindoni hobbled in, dragging behind him one leg encumbered with a built-up boot. He said, ignoring Tina, and addressing his remark pointedly to Annunziata, "Perhaps you will be good enough to tell your husband that I have finished the pair of alabaster boxes he was making for the Marchese Semprini. They had to be ready by tomorrow morning."

"That was thoughtful of you," said Annunziata, without enthusiasm. "Had you not done so, I have no doubt Milo would have finished them himself when he returned."

"No doubt," said the cripple. "And no doubt he would have made a remarkable hash of them."

"What does that mean?"

"Nothing, nothing. Except that when I saw him at the Café del Centro at twelve o'clock he had already poured several libations to Bacchus. Judging by the number of friends and hangers-on that he had attracted, he must have been spending his money with his customary liberality."

Annunziata said, "You obtain great enjoyment from relating bad news to me. I find that curious."

Dindoni had the grace to look uncomfortable. He said, "Is it bad news, then, that he should enjoy himself, with his friends? At his time of life, a man is surely entitled to enjoy whatever years the good God may grant him. It seems to me that in his life there is a time for work and a time for play."

"You are suggesting?"

"I am suggesting that he should retire from the practice of his craft, before that craft retires from him."

"Why can't you say plainly what you mean, you little creature?" said Tina, a dangerous red spot showing in each cheek.

Dindoni did not even deign to look at her. He said, "This is a matter of business. Might it be better not to discuss it in front of the child?"

"Tina can hear anything you have to say."

"Very well. For some years now most of your husband's work has come to him from one man. From Professor Bruno Bronzini."

"The Professor has been very kind."

"Certainly. But there is a limit. In the last few months your husband's hand has not been as steady, or as accurate, as—as the hand of a good craftsman ought to be. Valuable objects have been broken. Costly material has been wasted. It would be a pity to turn good will into bad will."

"And *if* Milo agreed to retire, then his business would go to you. Yes?"

"That is logical. I have worked with him for some years now."

"Would you pay him for it?"

"I have no great wealth. But, yes, I could pay him something, by installments, from what I earn."

Annunziata drew herself up to her full queenly height. She said, "I will think about it. Good night." Dindoni accepted his dismissal with surprising meekness.

When he had gone Tina said, "How *could* you? Do you wish us to live on the charity of that—that thing? On the crumbs which fall from his table? On his leavings? I would rather starve."

"People speak lightly of starving who have never tried it," said Annunziata. "If you had been alive during the war you would know the feel of an empty stomach."

"It is true," said Tina, abashed. "I have always had enough

to eat. And a father and mother who were good to me."

"And in any event, *cara mia,* there is no need for such thoughts. We are not destitute. In the old days, when your father was one of the finest craftsmen in the city, when he could pick and choose his patrons, he made money, and, being a sensible man, he handed some of it over to me. Possible he has forgotten all about it. But it is safely invested, never fear."

"You are a mother in a thousand."

"Dindo is a clever little creature. He has not got your father's touch with metals. But at woodwork and stonework he has picked up most of the more obvious tricks of the trade. If anything were to happen to Milo, the business would fall into his hands. There would be no question of him paying for it. *But* if he wishes to step into Milo's shoes before Milo is ready to step out of them, then that is another thing altogether. For that he must pay. We will have a bond properly drawn up by lawyers."

"You are a mother in a million," said Tina.

When Dindoni left the house he hobbled briskly up the Sdrucciolo and into the street beyond. It was not a very agreeable quarter. Even now, the debris of the great flood had not been cleared away. When, on that never-to-be-forgotten evening in November, a roaring avalanche of gray and froth-flecked water had swept down on Florence, this was the part of the town that had been first and hardest hit. And this was the part that the authorities had troubled least to repair, since no tourist would be likely to penetrate its dark mazes. The gratings at pavement level were still choked with a mixture of mud, twigs, and furnace oil, set hard as cement. Many of the doorways and windows were boarded. Broken lamp standards had not been replaced.

Dindoni cared for none of these things. He had seen them

so often that he had stopped thinking about them. His mind was on the café at the end of the Via Torta, and on the attraction within.

He did not observe the tall man, with a bent nose, who had been loitering on the pavement opposite; nor the stout man, with a petulant face, who had been taking great interest in the contents of a shop window farther along the street. He went into the café, passing straight through the outer room, which was empty, and through the beaded curtain at the back, into an inner room, where a girl was busy unpacking a cardboard carton of canned beer.

As she straightened up, Dindoni slid one arm around her waist, and pulled her down onto the seat beside him.

She said, "Take your hands off me, you little monster. I have work to do. There will be customers to serve. I must get these cans out. There!" It was a ring on the shop bell as the street door opened.

"Come back when you have got rid of them," said Dindoni. He settled himself comfortably. Two men had come into the outer room of the café. He judged from their voices that they were southerners. He could see the bottoms of two pairs of charcoal-gray trousers over expensive patent leather shoes. City types.

He heard the order being given for two *grappe,* and hoped that the men would drink up quickly, so that Maria might come back to him.

An argument seemed to be developing. He heard Maria saying, "I am afraid that is a private room. You cannot go in there."

Then a voice in reply: "But there is a friend of ours in there. We saw him go in. We wished only to say hello to him. Surely that is permitted."

"The room is not open to the public. If you wish to speak to the gentleman, I will ask him to come out—"

Before she could finish, the beaded curtain had swung

open and the men were coming through it. Dindoni stared at them. Their appearance confirmed what their manner of speech had suggested. They were from the south, from Sicily perhaps. Dindoni was quite certain that he knew neither of them. He started to say so, and then, obeying an instinct which he found it hard to identify, changed his mind.

The tall man set his drink down on the table. As he did so, a little slopped onto the surface. With the tip of one finger the tall man idly traced something in the moisture. It seemed to be in the shape of the numeral 5, but lacking the bar at the top.

"Are you deaf?" said Maria. She was really angry now. "Must I say it again, or would you have me send for the *patron?*"

A further sweep of the finger put a circle around the cedilla on the tabletop. The pattern seemed to be hypnotizing Dindoni. He wrenched his eyes away from it, and said to the girl, "These are old friends of mine, Maria. I should be happy if they could share the hospitality of your room."

"Friends," said Maria scornfully. And saw, suddenly, that he was frightened.

"Come now," said the stout man, edging his way forward. "A drink for my friend Dindoni. You will take *grappa*, too? No? A glass of wine. And for you, Maria?"

The girl muttered, "For me, nothing," and went out through the curtain. As she poured out Dindoni's drink she noticed, angrily, that her own hand was shaking.

3

Professor Bruno Bronzini
TUESDAY EVENING

"An instructive treatise," said Commander Comber, "could be written—I may even write it myself— on the difference between English and European drivers. As a nation we are law-abiding, intolerant, and insistent on priorities. One of the results of this is our morbid passion for queuing. We become bad-tempered if another driver interferes with those priorities by, say, cutting in or jumping the lights, or pulling out into the wrong lane, even if— *Get out of my way, you cross-eyed cow.* Europeans, on the other hand, and more particularly Italians, regard driving as a sport. Provided the referee isn't looking, you can cheat and bluff to the limit. *See that taxi? He thinks I'm going to give way, but I'm not.* But you must be cheerful about it, and good-tempered when your bluff's called. *Mille grazie, signore.*"

"If I was running Florence," said Broke, "I'd put in a few more traffic lights."

"Of course you would. And 'Stop' signs and 'Yield' signs and carefully marked traffic lanes; and it'd take everyone three times as long to get through. We'll be clear of the worst in a moment."

They crossed the railway, and turned up the tree-lined Viale Alessandro Volta, out of the heat and turmoil of the city and up into the coolness of the foothills.

It had been a blazing day. With the coming of evening a light mist, the thinnest of bridal veils, was rising from the valley of the Arno. The color of the sky deepened, from pale blue into indigo, and from indigo into steel. A few lights began to show.

"Lovely, isn't it," said Comber.

"Most cities are more attractive," said Broke, "when you're far enough away not to be able to hear them; or smell them," he added.

"Don't be such a bloody realist."

"Who's going to be there tonight?"

"Apart from the Professor? I expect Mercurio will be there. He's an adopted son. A remarkable specimen. Danilo Ferri will be somewhere in the background, running things in his usual quiet and competent way. He's Bruno's steward. Oh, and a lot of top brass from the Uffizi and the Pitti Palace, and of course the Museo Archeologico. They're the Etruscan experts—but I imagine you know that."

"I know Solferini and Bartolozzi, and I've met two or three of the others. What's the form—will it just be drinks?"

The Commander laughed so heartily that the car nearly mounted the pavement.

"I can see that you don't know Bruno. This is an Etruscan orgy. There'll be eats, drinks, music, dancing, if you like. The last guests leaving at daylight."

"I hope," said Broke, "that not everything one associates with an Etruscan orgy will be taking place tonight."

"Not in public, anyway. Here we are."

The car had turned off the road, through high gateposts of squared stone, and passed down a tunnel of driveway between a double row of cypresses, which emerged, with theatrical suddenness, into a paved courtyard blazing with lights.

A boy in dark overalls, belted at the waist and clipped at the wrists and ankles, ran up almost before they had stopped, and opened the door. A second boy, similarly dressed, appeared at the other side, and said, "Leave the keys, signori; I will take the car."

"The devil you will. What are you going to do with it?"

"Over there." The boy pointed to a row of cars on the far side. "She will be quite safe."

The Commander said, "I'm not worried about it being safe. I want it parked where I can get it out quickly if I have to."

The boy grinned, and said, "I put her at the end. You want to get her out, take a young lady for a ride perhaps, you can get her out quick."

"You flatter me," said the Commander, but handed the keys over. They walked under a semicircular arch into an inner courtyard, set around with orange trees in terra-cotta urns, and up a shallow flight of steps. The front door was opened for them by a burly character, dressed in the loose-fitting overall that seemed to be the uniform of the place. He ushered them into an inner hall, where a dark-haired, pale-faced man of medium height, unremarkable appearance, and entirely conventional dress was awaiting them.

"Danilo Ferri," whispered the Commander. And, as they reached him, "Allow me, Signor Ferri—Robert Broke."

"Good evening, Commander Comber, good evening, Mr. Broke." Ferri handled the tricky pronunciations with remarkable efficiency. "Let me take you in. The Professor will be so pleased that you could come."

The Villa Rasenna had originally been built around a central courtyard. A later owner had enlarged it, roofing over the courtyard in the process, and the result was a complex of rooms of different sizes and at different levels. From somewhere ahead came music.

"Watch the steps," said Ferri. "They're tricky, even when you're sober."

The music was unlike anything Broke had ever heard before. Predominantly it was pipe music, with a background of strings and castanets.

"Etruscan style," said Ferri. "A little monotonous at first,

22

but you'll find that you'll get used to it." They had turned a corner and were now in the main hall of the villa, a long, low room, with a beamed ceiling, hung with tapestries. Broke could see the musicians, and confirmed what he had suspected. The instruments they were performing on were the double flute and the zither. Considering the limitations of their instruments they were performing very well.

A small round figure detached itself from the group in the far corner, and came bouncing across to meet them. It did not need Comber's whispered warning to tell Broke that this was his host.

Professor Bronzini was dressed in pointed slippers and a robe, similar to that worn by his servants, but of richer and more elaborate stuff, with a short tunic, or chlamys, on top. His body was circled at the waist by an elaborate leather belt, hung with small gold ornaments. A cherubic silenus countenance, crimson cheeks, flat nose, thick lips, and gray hair astart seemed to be balanced on the high collar that topped this remarkable outfit.

"Commander! I am so pleased. And you have brought Mr. . . ?"

"Broke."

"Mr. Broke. Delighted. I saw you looking at the orchestra. The instruments they are playing are exact reproductions of the double flute, or subulo, and the ancient lyre. You have studied the Etruscans, Mr. Broke?"

Comber started to say, "As a matter of fact, he's rather—" but got no further. The Professor had turned away to clap his hands, and a boy came across with a tray. The glasses on it were heavy green beakers. The drink inside seemed to be an aromatic wine.

The Professor bounded away to greet some new arrivals and Broke had time to study his surroundings. Apart from the tapestries the only ornamentation consisted of two circular bronze mirrors on the stone shelf over the fireplace, and a remarkable bronze strigil, the handle formed in the shape of a goat on its hind legs. He was examining these, when he found Ferri beside him again.

"Interesting work," said Broke. "Fine copies."

"Copies?" said Ferri.

"Well," said Broke mildly, "they could hardly be the originals, could they? Both the mirrors are in the Archaeological Museum in Dresden, and the goat comes from the Villa Giulia in Rome."

"I know very little about these things," said Ferri. "I expect you're right. Let me get you another drink."

The room was filling up. Broke spotted Dr. Solferini, curator of the Museo Archeologico, talking to a severe-looking lady in black, and made his way across to join them. The Doctor greeted him warmly, introduced him to the lady, who turned out to be his wife, and said, "Is this the first Rasenna party you've been to?"

"It's the first party I've been to since I've come out here."

"A severe baptism of fire," said the Doctor.

"What actually happens?"

"We drink, and eat. In a modified version of the Etruscan style."

"Modified?"

"We could hardly go the whole way. Wine served by naked slaves! Orgies under the table!"

"I'm afraid," said Broke, "that I never really believed any of that. I think their paintings show the slaves waiting on them as naked in order to demonstrate that they were *slaves*. It was a convention. Like always showing women dressed in a chiton and himation, or men in a chlamys and tebennas. And as for the orgies—"

"Orgies," said Professor Bronzini, popping up behind them like a porpoise out of the waves. "Lies. Lies invented by that Greek gossip Theopompus, and p███████ated by the Romans, in a deliberate attempt to vilify the Etruscans. Your

24

glasses are empty, gentlemen. More to drink." He clapped his hands again and a boy slid through the crowd toward them. The Professor disappeared as suddenly as he had arrived.

"Where on earth does he get all these servants from?" asked Broke.

"He breeds them," said Dr. Solferini.

"My dear!" said his wife.

"I don't mean literally. I mean that he has two or three large properties in the neighborhood of Volterra, and the young men from the farms come up and help him at the villa. I expect they enjoy it."

"I see," said Broke, trying to keep the disapproval out of his voice.

One of the difficulties he foresaw was going to be the disposal of drinks. He had no idea how long the preliminaries were going to last, and the idea of consuming half a dozen beakers of wine before dinner was not one that appealed to him at all. At a civilized cocktail party there would have been a number of useful little tables on which you could have deposited one nearly full glass before accepting another. The furnishing of this room inhibited such tactics.

He edged his way toward the entrance at the far end. This gave onto a small and much darker room. It seemed to be some sort of conservatory. There were plants growing in pots, arranged on slatted shelves, and other plants trained on trelliswork. Broke tipped the contents of his glass into a pot that contained a very large and very prickly cactus, and was on the point of retiring when he heard a low chuckle behind him.

He swung around and saw a young man watching him. Seen even in the half-light of that anteroom it was a remarkable face. It was the blond, straight-featured, Anglo-Saxon face that came over with the Crusaders and has never died out in northern Italy; a remarkable contrast to the coarser,

25

black-haired, thick-featured farm boys. The features had more than regularity. They had a sort of prettiness that was startling. This was a young divinity descended, for a whim, from Olympus, to consort with hinds and satyrs. The fashionable Florentine drawl dispelled the illusion.

"I don't blame you," said the youth. "Personally I'd prefer a martini every time, but unfortunately martinis weren't invented in the fifth century B.C. My name's Mercurio, by the way. I'm the son of the house. The adopted, not the natural, son."

"My name's Broke—I'm running the Galleria delle Arti for Welford Hussey."

"Oh, yes. I heard he'd gone off chasing Aztecs. While you're here, would you like to look at the holy of holies? The old man will take a conducted tour later, I expect."

Broke said, "Thank you. If you think your father wouldn't object."

The young man led the way across the conservatory and down three steps to a low door. "Have to mind your head here," he said. "The whole thing's constructed to look like a tomb. Ghoulish sort of idea. Typical of the old man, though." He took out a key and unlocked the heavy wooden door, which swung back with a soundless ease that betokened good workmanship. Mercurio clicked on the electric light.

The room was in two parts, divided by an arch. It was paved with stone and walled in naked brick. A low stone bench ran the length of one wall, continuing through into the far part of the cellar, and along the short wall at the far end.

"That's for the corpses," said Mercurio.

The other long wall was covered with shelves of varying depth. On them were set an astonishing collection of objects: terra-cotta vases, hydriae and kraters; figures human and animal, kouroi and kriophoroi; candelabra, stampiglia, small

26

oil lamps, locks and keys, pots and pans, mirrors of polished bronze, and a bewildering array of personal ornaments, fibulae, diadems, bracelets, earrings, and finger rings in worked and knurled gold and set with precious stones. Hidden lighting from behind the shelves showed up these treasures in artful relief.

"Sort of mixture between a funeral parlor and a museum," said Mercurio. "Do you know anything about these things?"

"A certain amount," said Broke. He was particularly interested in the terra-cotta figures. It was impossible, without a closer examination than he could make as they stood on their shelves, to be certain whether they were genuine Etruscan relics or very fine copies.

"I always feel a bit embarrassed about this one," said Mercurio, with a giggle. He indicated an incense burner. It was in sculptured bronze, and the stem was in the form of a dancing boy, naked except for the leather shoes that came halfway up the calf. "That's me."

"I see," said Broke. "Are the others all modern copies, too?"

"Some are, some aren't. I believe most of the pottery things are real. There wouldn't be much point in faking them, would there? I mean, they're so ugly."

Broke made no comment on this. He was wishing that he could have a few hours alone in the place, with direct instead of indirect lighting, and a strong glass.

"I take it the rule is don't touch?" he said.

"As long as you don't drop anything," said Mercurio. "The old man thinks rather highly of these bits and pieces. They're the ones he means to take with him into the next world."

"Do you mean to say he intends to be buried here?"

"That's the big idea. Embalmed, and laid out on that shelf."

"But would the authorities allow it?"

"I've no idea," said Mercurio. "But since the old coot'll be dead, it'll be no skin off his nose if he does end up in the cemetery, like other people."

Broke had nothing to say to this. Presumably Mercurio owed anything he had to the Professor. He thought that he might have spoken a bit more kindly about him.

Mercurio was looking at him with a curious glint in his almond-shaped eyes. It reminded Broke of something, a fleeting likeness, which he could not pin down.

"You don't like me, do you?" Mercurio said. "Very few people do. If you want to look at anything, you'd better hurry. You may not get another chance."

Broke was examining a black-figure amphora. He was fairly certain that he had seen one like it, either in the Antikensammlungen in Munich, or in the Metropolitan Museum in New York. It had a scene, painted continuously around the base, of lions pulling down a deer. It was full of the brutal detail that the Etruscans loved. The claw of one of the lions was sunk into the eye of the deer. Another lion had his fangs deep in one haunch, which it seemed to be detaching from the living animal.

Broke had his hand out to pick it up when a deep voice behind him said, "I am sent to call you to dinner."

It was the burly janitor who had opened the front door to them. He had a beefy but placid face, and moved like an athlete.

"All right, Arturo. We'll come when we're ready."

"Your father particularly told me to find you. The other guests are already seated."

For a moment it seemed as though the boy would refuse. Then he said, "I suppose we'd better go. The old man gets terribly touchy about his meals."

He stumped out. Arturo held the door open for them to leave, turned out the lights, and pulled the door shut. It closed with a click against its spring lock.

Broke had half expected that they would be required to eat their dinner reclining on couches, but he found a conventional table laid in the garden room at the back of the house. The seats were solid, and well cushioned. The guests, most of whom had been standing about for a couple of hours, seemed glad to be sitting down. One Etruscan custom, at least, was faithfully observed. There was no hurry about bringing on the food. Dishes of nuts and olives were circulated, and the wine goblets were kept topped up.

There were twenty-four people at table. Broke found himself near his host, separated from him only by Dr. Solferini's wife, with the Doctor next to him. Opposite sat a swarthy young man whose face seemed vaguely familiar. Broke was not left long in doubt. The young man said, "Antonio Lucco, from Rome."

"Robert Broke, from England."

A whisper from Signora Solferini said, "The celebrated association football player."

Broke remembered him then. He also remembered an account of a very ugly incident in the European Cup semi-finals the year before, in which an English player had broken his ankle.

Lucco said, "I had thought you might be English. You speak Italian well, but by no means perfectly."

"I will hope to improve during the year I am here," said Broke. And to Dr. Solferini: "I imagine you have seen the remarkable treasures which our host keeps in his"—it seemed indelicate to say "tomb"—"in his strong room?"

"I have indeed. But I have had no real chance—"

"The English," announced Lucco, "invented the game of football. But they have forgotten how to play it."

Since this remark appeared to be directed to him, Broke turned away, reluctantly, from the Doctor, and said, "Oh?"

"They make the mistake of treating it as a science. We recognize it as an art."

"We seemed to do all right in the World Cup."

"On English pitches. With selected referees."

The insult was too childish to upset Broke. He laughed. "I don't think we could afford to bribe *all* the referees. We're a very poor country, you know. You were saying, Doctor..."

"I was saying," said Dr. Solferini, "that although I have been permitted to walk through the strong room on more than one occasion, I have never yet had an opportunity of examining the contents in detail. If they are as fine as I suspect they are, one would wish that they could be on public exhibition in one of our museums, for part of the year at least."

"Where do they come from?"

"All of them, I imagine, from the complex of tombs near Volterra which are being gradually explored. The tombs are, of course, on the Professor's own property, and are being opened under his control."

"Are the public allowed to watch the process?"

"They are not available to the public, but you could certainly get permission."

"Direct and virile play," said Lucco to his neighbor, a wide-eyed girl, "is confined now to Continental and South American teams. We play football. The English play at it."

"That's right," said the girl. She knew nothing about football, but she thought Lucco was terrific.

"Now, Signor Broke," said the Professor from his throne at the top of the table, "you shall tell us what you think of the Etruscan way of life."

It was on the tip of Broke's tongue to make a complimentary and entirely noncommittal reply; but he was hungry, was conscious that he would have been much wiser not to have come, and had been provoked by Lucco. He said, "I find it extremely interesting, Professor. It corresponds so exactly, in my opinion, to the stage we have reached in our own modern Western civilization."

The Professor cracked a nut with his teeth, and said; "And what do you mean by that?"

"The Etruscan civilization was, at the start, an aristocracy founded on prowess in war, but it degenerated into an aristocracy of wealth. As soon as an aristocracy loses its martial character, it loses its true spirit and its will to lead. It is like a football team which buys its stars from abroad, instead of breeding them for itself."

"Because we have a Brazilian center-half—" said Lucco, angrily.

"Quiet, Antonio," said the Professor. "We are talking about something more important than football. Can you justify your generalization, Mr. Broke?"

"It *was* only a generalization, I agree. We know too little about the Etruscans to be certain of anything. But I would say, on the evidence available, that they were a nation who preferred to pay other people to do things for them, rather than doing them for themselves. A Greek gentleman could compose a set of verses, play a musical instrument, or run a mile in the games. We've lost the Etruscan language, so we'll never know about those verses. But we do know that the Etruscan had his music played for him, by slaves, and his sports performed by professional gladiators. Wouldn't you agree, Professor Bartolozzi?"

Professor Bartolozzi, a mild old man with a goatlike beard and a sad face, said, "I think that comparisons between Greeks and Etruscans have been overstressed. The Etruscans are sometimes held to be mere copyists. Now, that is a view I will never accede to."

"I agree," said Broke. "Rather talented youngsters learning from a revered elder, and then producing minor masterpieces of their own."

"Minor?" said Bronzini. "If you call Vulca of Veii a minor master you must have very odd ideas of what constitutes a major art, Mr. Broke."

"There are exceptions, of course."

"I perceive that you are at heart a Roman. The Romans"—the Professor was now addressing the company at large—"were the traditional enemies of the Etruscans. The enmity was based on envy. The Etruscans had made the Romans what they were. They had transformed Rome from a second-class village, on a swamp, into a city with temples, places of entertainment, paved roadways, municipal government—"

"And drains," said Broke.

"You laugh at their achievements?"

"Far from it. The drains were their most important achievement. The Colosseum may be in ruins, but the Cloaca Maxima is still working."

"I find your attitude, Mr. Broke, a typical Roman compound of ignorance and arrogance."

"Don't let's quarrel over it," said Broke. "The Etruscans were a fine people. They enjoyed life more than any of their contemporaries. More than most people do today, I should say. Wherever they've gone to from those lovely tombs of theirs, I wish them nothing but well."

Dr. Solferini said, "Hear, hear," in a loud voice, and conversation was resumed all around the table. Boys appeared carrying tureens of soup, and the dinner got underway at last. Professor Bronzini still looked ruffled, but he confined his comments to his immediate neighbors. Fish stuffed with almonds followed the soup. Duck stuffed with chestnuts and sage followed the fish. A rich but unanalyzable Florentine confection followed the duck. The lengthy intervals between the courses were occupied by talking, listening to the musicians, and drinking.

As the evening went on, Broke found it more and more

32

difficult to keep awake. If he had been doing anything more than sip at his constantly refilled goblet of wine he might have managed to keep his end up better. He felt that he had exhausted every possible conversational gambit with the Doctor and his wife. He was so tired that he found himself thinking, and framing his sentences, in English and then translating them belatedly into Italian.

Opposite him, Commander Comber was enjoying himself with a vivacious Italian brunette. He seemed to be reciting to her Macaulay's Lay of *Horatius*, translating it into Italian as he went along. When he reached the verse about the grapes in the vats of Luna being trampled under the feet of laughing girls whose sires had marched to Rome, his rendering of it reduced his neighbor to such extremes of mirth that she leaned her head on the Commander's chest and was quietly and elegantly sick down the front of his shirt. At this point Broke felt a thud on his own shoulder and found that Signora Solferini had fallen asleep. He shifted her head around until it was comfortable, and closed his own eyes.

At an immeasurable time after this there was a general stir among the guests, and Broke realized that dinner was over. He propped the Doctor's wife in a vertical position, and rose stiffly from his seat. A glance at his wrist told him that it was a quarter to four.

He strolled out onto the terrace to smoke a cigarette. It was the darkest moment of the night. In less than an hour, as the earth completed one more of its uncounted circuits, the stars would be going out, the mountain peaks in the east would be hardening as the sky paled behind them, and another day would be born.

"'See how the dawn, in russet mantle clad,'" said Commander Comber, from behind him, "'walks on the brow of yon high eastern hill.' Wonderful chap, Shakespeare. *He* didn't need stage lighting. He gave it all to you in the script. Do you think we could find our host, and be slipping quietly away?"

"What have you done with that brunette?"

"I surrendered her, without too much of a struggle, to one of her compatriots. He has taken her down into the olive grove, to listen to the cicadas."

"Then let's go."

As they turned back into the house Comber said, "I did warn you it wouldn't be an ordinary cocktail party, didn't I?"

"You did," said Broke. "And next time I'll pay some attention to your warnings."

They found Professor Bronzini with the hard core of the party in the reception room. He was demonstrating his prowess on the double pipes and had just finished a rendering of what sounded like "The Flowers of the Forest."

"Go?" he said. "Of course you mustn't go, my dear fellow. The night is still young. You have work to do tomorrow? No true Etruscan every thinks about tomorrow. But I had forgotten. You are not an Etruscan. You are a Roman. The *disciplina Romana!* A code which starts with self-control, but always ends by imposing control on others. The ax and the rods, eh?"

Broke was too tired to argue.

He said, "It's been an unforgettable experience, Professor. I envy you your lovely house, and all those beautiful things you have downstairs."

"You have seen them?"

"Mercurio was kind enough to show me round."

"You found them interesting?" said Bronzini. There was a curious look in his silenus eyes.

"Extremely interesting."

"You must come and inspect them more at leisure. They are worth looking at."

"I'm sure they are."

Out in the hall there was trouble. A voice, which Broke recognized, was shouting. It was Antonio Lucco, the great

34

footballer. His face looked as if it had been clawed. The front of his shirt was hanging out and there was a long red stain down the front of his jacket which Broke thought, at first, was blood, and then saw was only wine.

Lucco was screaming insults at the little knot of men who were shepherding him slowly along the passage, like bees dancing a struggling intruder out of the hive.

The gentle Arturo appeared at the end of the passage and the crowd opened. As Lucco started to shout, Arturo grasped the collar of his coat and shirt in one large hand and picked him up, holding him suspended. The pressure on his windpipe silenced Lucco, and Arturo turned, still holding him, and carried him to the door. It was an extraordinary feat of strength, for Lucco was by no means a small man.

At the door Arturo paused for a moment to say, "Will one of you find this gentleman's hat and coat?"

Broke said to Comber, "What was up? Was he just tight, or what?"

"He was tight, all right," said Comber. "But that's no crime round here. I gather he made a pass at one of the boys."

They found their car at the end of the line of parked vehicles. As they were backing it out, Arturo loomed through the dark.

"I must apologize for the disturbance," he said. He was entirely unruffled. Broke noticed that he was not even breathing hard. "The gentleman will be all right. He is in the back of his own car, asleep."

"As long as he doesn't try to drive home," said Comber.

"I have taken the precaution of removing the keys."

"He sounds just like Jeeves, doesn't he?" said Comber. They turned into the main road and drove slowly down toward Florence, asleep and cradled in the mist at their feet.

4

A Busy Day
WEDNESDAY

Despite the fact that he had had less than three hours of sleep, Broke was at the gallery at the usual time next morning.

He went to the section of the bookshop that dealt with Etruria, took down half a dozen books, told Francesca to attend to any customers who came in, and retired to the office. This was so full of filing cabinets and clutter that there was barely room for a small table and a chair, but it was private.

He started his search in the big book edited by Poulsen, recording the work done by the Swedish Institute in Rome at the San Giovenale excavations; dipped into a work by P. J. Riis of Denmark; and then switched to *Die menschliche Gestalt in der Rundplastik bis zum Ausgang die orientalischierenden Kunst* by the German Hanfmann.

It was a vagrant memory, a fleeting likeness that he was trying to track down; a bronze statue, not more than twelve or fifteen inches high, and forming, he thought, the upright of an incense burner or a candelabrum.

His search had traversed five centuries of Etruscan civilization before he found what he was looking for, and found it where he might well have looked in the first place, in the illustrated catalogue of the collection at the Museo Nazionale of the Villa Giulia in Rome.

The likeness to the statue he had seen the night before was unmistakable. But it was a likeness in style and conception. The one was not a carbon copy of the other. On the other hand, any disinterested expert, looking at the statuette in the Bronzini treasure house, would have pledged his reputation that it was genuine Etruscan work.

But since Mercurio had said, with that embarrassed giggle of his, "That's me," the implication clearly was that he had posed for it. Which made the statuette a modern reproduction; or Mercurio a liar. Curious either way.

As he was turning the pages another picture jumped out at him. It was the head of the young man from Veii, which was known from its petulant expression as "Malvolta," and bore such a curious resemblance to Donatello's youthful Saint George. There was a good deal of Mercurio in the pouting mouth and the eyes that were young and old at the same time.

"Signor Broke. *Scusi.*"

A pair of pebble-brown eyes in a yellow and wrinkled face were peering at him around the door.

"Come in, Milo."

"I have brought the frames."

"Good."

"I regret that I could not finish them earlier. I have had trouble with my stomach." He patted the part of his body that a lot of people wrongly suppose to be the organ in question. "Much trouble."

"Tina told me."

"Tina is a good girl. It commences after meals, with a burning pain, which travels slowly, first across and then downward. There." He placed his hand on the bottom of his shabby waistcoat. "There it rests. Sometimes it passes away. Sometimes not."

Broke, who was fairly certain he knew what was wrong with old Milo Zecchi, had nothing to say. He grunted, in what he hoped was a sympathetic manner, and opened the parcel that had been laid on the table.

Inside were three small wooden frames, carved and gilded.

He held the first one up to the light, and said, "This is very good, Milo. Your hand has not lost its cunning."

The old man opened his almost toothless mouth in a smile. "You are right there," he said. "Milo Zecchi is still the finest carver in Florence. Wood, bronze, marble—although there is small demand for marble now—"

Francesca looked into the room and said, "There is a gentleman who wishes to see you."

"You told him I was busy?"

"I told him. He says he will not keep you for many minutes."

Broke came out of the office and found Professor Bronzini occupying the center of the shop. He was wearing a cloak of dark-blue cloth, embroidered with gold thread, and a small blue felt cap. A boy was in attendance on him.

Francesca was fluttering anxiously in the background. Two tourists who had just come into the shop were observing the Professor and making notes for their next letter home.

Broke did not know whether to be annoyed or amused at this visitation. The Professor made a short, but definite, inclination toward him. Broke said, "Good morning."

"I have come," said the Professor, "to make a profound apology."

"On the contrary," said Broke. "It is I who should be thanking you for a most interesting party."

"It was an agreeable gathering. But in the course of it, I discovered that I had—unwittingly—insulted you. I assumed that your knowledge of the Etruscans was superficial only. It was not until this morning that I realized that I had been entertaining a celebrity unawares. That you were *the* Robert Broke, author of the standard work on Etruscan terracotta, proprietor of the Tarquin Gallery, and adviser on Etruscology to the Department of Antiquities in the British Museum."

The tourists had not understood a word of this speech, but had rather assumed, from the manner in which it was delivered, that the small round man in a cloak was challenging the thin serious Englishman to a duel.

"I'm afraid," said Broke, "that you greatly exaggerate my standing."

"On the contrary, through ignorance I have probably understated it. Did you not act as technical adviser to the excavations at Caere two years ago?"

"I was at Caere," agreed Broke. "I'm not sure that anyone asked for my advice, or would have taken it if I had proffered it."

"You are too modest. But I did not interrupt you solely in order to flatter you. My object was to make some slight reparation. Should you care, at any time, to visit the few, the not very exciting excavations which are currently taking place on my property near Volterra, I should be more than pleased—I should be flattered."

"Kind of you," said Broke. Feeling that this was perhaps a bit brusque, he added, "Very kind of you."

At this moment Milo Zecchi, who had sidled out of the office and crept down the far side of the book counter, reached the door. The movement caught the Professor's eye. He swung around, and said, "Milo! What are you doing here? I didn't know you were interested in art books."

Milo grinned. His embarrassment was plain; but to Broke inexplicable. He said, "Milo makes frames for my pictures. He is a fine craftsman. Do you know him?"

"Yes," said the Professor. He seemed to lose interest in Milo, who had escaped from the shop and was shuffling off down the pavement as fast as his arthritic legs would carry him. The Professor took out a card and scribbled something on the back.

"If you should have any trouble at Volterra show that to

my factor," he said. "We have to be careful. We have had trouble in the past. Tomb-robbing is by no means an extinct pursuit in Etruria."

He gathered his cloak around him, gestured to the boy, and swept out into the street.

As Broke walked home to lunch, he was thinking about the events of the morning. It seemed improbable that a busy man like Bronzini should have come all the way down from Fiesole, in person, to apologize. The invitation to the diggings could have been dealt with by letter. Could he really have imagined that Broke had taken offense at the dinner-table discussions the night before? That, too, seemed un-likely. The Professor, with his enthusiasm and his didactic manner, must have upset plenty of his guests before now, and not bothered to make a parade of apologizing to them.

He said to Tina, when she was bringing in the pasta that, in one shape or another, invariably formed his first course at lunch, "Does your father know Professor Bronzini?"

"Certainly he knows him. He has done much work for him in the past. He has done restoration work."

"What sort of restoration?"

"I know nothing about these things. It would be pottery, I think."

This seemed probable enough. Terra-cotta figures were often discovered in pieces and needed careful restoration.

"Why do you ask?" said Tina. "Did the Professor say something about it last night?"

"No. They happened to meet in my shop. I gathered they knew one another."

"Oh, I see. Will you take some wine?"

When she had poured it, she recorked the bottle and put it back on the sideboard. She did this so slowly that Broke knew she was summoning up the courage to say something. He continued placidly with his meal. When it came, it was a surprise. She said, "Would you be able to speak to my father?"

"To Milo? I spoke to him today at the shop."

"Not in public. In private, at our house."

Broke finished his mouthful while he thought about this. Then he said, "If he wishes it, yes. Can you tell me what it is about?"

"Lately he has been very unhappy. Partly it is his stomach. But mostly it is something different."

"Money?"

"Always money. But something else, too, I think."

"When would you like me to come?"

"It must be tonight. It is Dindo's night out."

"Dindo?"

"Dindoni. He helps my father in his workshop, and he spies on him. He is not a nice person. He would like to take over the business from my father."

"Very well. I'll come round after supper. About ten o'-clock."

Tina smiled at him. "You are a good man," she said.

"Save your halo," said Broke, "until I've seen whether I can do anything for him."

At half past two he telephoned the shop. Francesca was there. He said, "I shall be going out this afternoon. Can you look after things? Good. Then I will see you tomorrow."

The idea had come to him as he finished his lunch. It was a perfect afternoon. The wind had swung to the north-east, bringing a dappling of cloud off the mountains and taking the edge off the heat. It was the sort of afternoon when one would like to be out in a boat. The thought of spending it in a shop was intolerable.

From the closet in his bedroom he extracted the satchel that held the field kit of an archaeologist, the hammer and calipers, the watchmaker's optic and the big flashlight. He had not touched them for more than a year. The battery in the flashlight needed renewing. What else? A small-scale map of Tuscany, and a large-scale map of Volterra. A pair of leather gloves. He went down to the car. The house, of which he rented the top floor, was one of four in a cul-de-sac off the Viale Michelangiolo. The garage was detached from the house and stood at the far end, up against the wire netting that bounded the tennis courts of the Campo Sportivo.

The car should have gone when Joan went. Broke realized that. It had been such an integral part of their marriage. She had so often sat beside him in it, during those long, slow journeys through France and down into Spain, or Italy, and on occasions farther afield, into Greece and Turkey. The worn bucket seat had become almost the husk of her body, the cocoon when the chrysalis is out. It was one of the last of those beautifully made Sunbeam Talbot drop-head coupés, looked after with anxious care, fitted with every extra from the reversing light at the back to the special fog lamp slung low on the front bumper.

Broke fitted himself into the driver's seat, backed out of the garage, and turned up the Viale. That way he could avoid going through the town altogether. There was a secondary road to Empoli, quiet and pleasant to drive on, now that the autostrada had channeled off the fast drivers. At Empoli he would head southwest, for Cecina and the coast.

It was four o'clock, and the sun was toppling over toward the west, when he came to the turning that led toward the Bronzini farms. A bristle of notices warned against unauthorized entry, hunting, and the picking of flowers. They mentioned also the presence of fierce dogs. Broke drove carefully up the flinty path and parked the car in front of a group of outbuildings. There seemed to be no one about.

The stillness of midafternoon blanketed everything. Even the chickens were asleep.

Broke locked the steering wheel, got out, and started up the footpath. The grass was knee-high and full of flowers. There were grape hyacinths and sea-blue vervain, and a sort of wild reseda, which a gardener would call mignonette, anemones of all colors, and bushes of heath and broom. Above him, larks were singing. It was not unlike one of those forgotten corners on the top of Salisbury Plain, which the military have taken over and then abandoned.

How wise had the Etruscans been to bury their dead in free, happy places. Not to put them in solemn churchyards, under black yew trees, or in hygienic metropolitan cemeteries, marble-slabbed, like butchers' shops; but tucked away in little rock caves, in the open hillside, with all the small requirements for their journey, all the luggage for an afterlife stacked neatly beside them.

But had they really believed it? Could a people who were practical enough to invent dentistry, drainage, and town planning; sophisticated enough to enjoy concerts and spectator sports; meticulous enough to divide the liver of a beast into sixteen sections and attribute a different significance to each—could they *really* have believed in a future life in which pots and pans, axes and ropes would be useful? Or were they whistling in the dark?

Broke was a rational agnostic. He had no wish for a second inning in a fourth dimension. He believed that "this be truth, though all the rest be lies. The rose that once is blown forever dies." What happened to that tiny, personal, inner consciousness that men called self was a mystery. He was inclined to hope that it, too, went out like a snuffed candle.

When the first shot came he stood staring. When a second followed, instincts dormant for twenty-five years reasserted

43

themselves and he went down flat on his face. At the third, he raised his head cautiously. It seemed to be aimed well above him, where a white bird was fluttering. As he watched, the bird tumbled awkwardly to the ground.

Broke got up, brushed the grass from his knees, and ran up the path. Once over the crest he saw the marksmen, three boys, carrying light rifles. They were looking at a pigeon on the ground. It was dragging itself around in a circle, but making no attempt to fly. As Broke came up, one of them prodded the bird with his foot and said, "Perhaps if we set fire to its tail, it might fly once more."

Broke saw a cage on the ground, with two other birds in it. He said angrily, "What are you doing?"

The boys swung around, and he recognized the two boys who had taken charge of the Commander's car the night before. The third, he thought, had been one of the waiters.

The tall boy said, "We are practicing our shooting. We are sorry if we frightened you. But this is private property."

"What are you doing to those birds?"

"We pluck their wing and tail feathers so they can fly a little, but not too far, and we shoot at them. We are using rifles, as you see, so they are not easy to hit. Sometimes they fly five or six times. This one, I think, is tired."

Broke stooped down, caught the bird, and wrung its neck. The boys shouted in anger, and Broke realized that if they attacked him he would be in trouble. The leader of the boys was as tall as he was, and probably stronger, the other two nearly as strong.

Out of the concrete hut beside the tumulus shambled the untidy figure of a man. He looked as if he had been wakened by the noise from the siesta that should follow a heavy lunch. His red face was moist and fringed with a stubble of gray beard.

He said, "What the hell's going on? What are you shouting about, Lorenzo?" And as his bleary eyes took in Broke,

44

"Who is this man?"

The tall boy said, sulkily, "He killed our bird. No one asked him to interfere."

"What are you doing here?"

Broke took Professor Bronzini's card out of his wallet, and said, "I am here by invitation of the owner. He invited me to inspect the digging."

"I know nothing of that," said the man. He seemed to be working himself up into a rage. "You must leave, now. At once." When Broke held out the card he pushed it away, repeating, "Now, at once."

"I've come quite a long way to see these tombs," said Broke. "The owner has invited me. Until he withdraws his invitation, I have no intention of going away."

His coldness added to their fire. The man said, the edge of venom showing plainly in his voice, "If you do not go quickly, perhaps you will be made to go, and perhaps it will not be so pleasant for you. You understand the frog march. That is not very dignified for the frog."

The boys laughed. Broke said, "If you do anything so stupid, I promise that you will be very sorry for it."

"It is you who are going to be sorry," said the man. He was spitting in his excitement. "Take his arms, two of you."

The smaller boys had been working their way behind him. Now they jumped at him, grabbing an arm each. Broke stood very still. The man came up and thrust his face close to Broke's; so close that he could smell the wine on his breath and see the spittle that dribbled from his open mouth into the hog bristles of his beard. "Now," he said, "you will go, whether it pleases your lordship or not."

Broke twisted to the right and, as the resistance built up, reversed the motion, tearing his right arm free, and hit the man hard in the stomach. The man doubled up, mouthing obscenities, and a cool voice said, "Would someone kindly explain what this entertainment signifies?"

The car must have come very quietly along the rutted track. Danilo Ferri had got out of it and the giant Arturo sat behind the steering wheel. The boys had released Broke and were standing in a sheepish group, reduced suddenly in size to naughty children. Ferri said to the tall boy, "Well, Lorenzo?"

The old man had got his breath back. He said, "Our orders—"

Ferri ignored him. He continued to talk to the tall boy. "Were your orders to assault a friend of your master who comes here, with his permission? You have earned a whipping, all three of you."

The boys said nothing, but stared down at the ground, scuffling the dust with their feet.

"Be off." They went, without looking back. The red-faced man said, sulkily, "How was I to know?" but he sounded frightened, too.

The card had fallen to the ground. Ferri stopped to pick it up.

"It seems that he showed you this card. Are you unable to read?"

The man said nothing. Ferri handed the card to Broke, and said, "I am grieved that you should have had such an uncivil reception. Had I known you were coming, I would have been at pains to accompany you myself." As they walked across to the tumulus he added, "They are primitive people here. They have to be dealt with in a primitive way. But that is no excuse for Labro's behavior. I have long suspected that he was a drunkard. He will have to go."

Broke said, "I was partly to blame. The boys were shooting at crippled birds. I interfered." He pointed to the dead pigeon and the two captive birds.

Ferri said, "I will have the birds destroyed. I see that you have brought a flashlight with you. Good. Allow me to lead the way."

The tumulus rose, gently as a breast, from the body of the earth. It covered an acre of ground. They went down three steps, through a gap in the stone girdle, along a man-made cleft, and into the tumulus itself. There were small chambers, cut in the rock to right and left, all quite empty.

"These, and the two beyond, were ransacked long ago," said Ferri. "Fortunately the vandals got no farther. The passage was a false entrance. We found another on the other side. That, too, led to an apparently blank wall of rock."

"Which you broke down?"

"Certainly. With modern implements it was not difficult."

"What did you find?"

Ferri chuckled. "We found that we were back in the first passage. They were intercommunicating. An Etruscan joke. There were some interesting terra-cotta figures in the tomb which lay off the second passage. Some the Professor has kept. Others he has given to different museums in Italy. Also two caskets of alabaster containing ornamental jewelry."

They made their way down the central passage, which dipped and curved to the right, then started to rise again. In the beam of his flashlight Broke could see the chiseling of recent excavation in the rocks. Daylight showed ahead. Broke was counting his paces. It was sixty-five yards before they emerged at the far side of the tumulus. Ferri led the way around to the left.

"Here we broke in again," he said. "We are working here now. You will find this more interesting, I think."

Broke scrambled through the hole that had been cut in the rock and turned on his flashlight. He was in a tiny room, some eight feet by six, with the usual rock shelf around two sides of it. The walls above were covered by a continuous painting. It was a seascape. A curly border, halfway up the wall, gave a formal representation of the surface. A multitude of fish and strange marine creatures swam below it

47

and from the rocks along the bottom anemones grew, and crabs lurked in stylized fronds of weeds. Higher up, porpoises broke the surface. And on the water there floated, as centerpiece to the picture, a single open-decked ship, with high poops at each end and a line of rowers in the waist.

Broke drew in his breath sharply. He said, "This is very fine. Has it been recorded?"

"The Professor has had color photographs taken of it. He places it as fifth century, I believe."

"Sixth or fifth," agreed Broke. He had out his glass and was examining the ship carefully. "This is a representation of a pirate ship. You can see the iron beak at the prow which was used for ramming. The man at the back is armored, too—the captain, or pirate chief, one presumes, since he is wearing such a splendid helmet." It was an elaborate contraption, like a dowager's Ascot hat, but constructed in metal sections. At the front, in the center, was a small lion's head.

"It is interesting that you should say that. This cluster of tombs is thought to have belonged to a pirate and his family. His name seems to have been Thryns. It is supposed that he ruled over this settlement. He may have owed allegiance to the Lucumo of Volterra, or he may have been independent. His name has been seen on the lintel of a door at Vada, on the coast."

"Fascinating," said Broke. "Winter quarters here; a summer house on the coast, near his ship. If he was really a big shot his burial chamber would be worth finding."

"Of course. That's what we're hoping for."

"What have you got so far?"

"Some interesting mirrors and some small alabaster figures. Come, I'll show you."

With a last look at the pirate chief, erect in the stern of

his galley, peering forward over the bowed backs of his slaves at the oars, Broke followed his guide. Each small chamber led, by a mousehole in its wall, to a further one.

"There would be more logic in it," said Ferri apologetically, "if we could divine the plan of the central passages. As it is, we have had to make our way in ignorance, supplemented by force. This is where we are working now."

The innermost chamber was lit by a single electric light. Two youths were working quietly at the far end, chipping into the soft rock with steel chisels and mauls. The dust had blackened their faces and when they grinned their teeth showed white in the flashlight beam.

"This must have been the tomb of some lesser members of the household. Women, probably."

Set out on one of the low rock benches was a collection of terra-cotta jars, lamps, combs, and brooches, and an incense burner with three goats' feet.

"If we go out this way," said Ferri, "we come back to the linked passageways."

"Yes," said Broke. He was trying to picture in his mind the ground plan of what he had seen. An acre of tumulus offered a lot of hidden space. A team of excavators, working systematically, could probably cover it in a year. Tackled piecemeal in this way it might take ten years. If the linked passages divided the mound roughly into two, all the work so far had been done on the left-hand, or northern, side. Or most of it. He glimpsed one opening to the right and peered in. Ferri, ahead of him, swung around.

"I wouldn't go in there," he said. "There's been a lot of settlement on that side. We've had to shore up as we go."

The beam from Broke's flashlight cut a strong white swath through the room. It rested for a moment on something that stood on the shelf of rock at the far end of the room.

"I don't want to hurry you," said Ferri, "but I myself

have to be back in Florence by eight o'clock. And I think—in view of what happened—I had better see you back to your car, if you don't mind."

"Of course," said Broke. He clicked off his light and followed his guide out into the blinding sunlight of an Italian evening.

"You will want more time to examine it all properly," said Ferri. "Why not have a word with the Professor? He could take you around himself. You would find much to talk about."

"I'd like to do that," said Broke.

He spoke absently, because he was thinking of something else. He was thinking about it as Ferri drove him back to where he had left his own car; and later, as he drove himself back to Florence.

What he had seen, for a few seconds, in the beam of his flashlight, was a helmet, shaped like a dowager's Ascot hat made in metal sections. In that one glance he had, he thought, seen the small reproduction of a lion's head that formed the center piece in front. He wondered how it could have come there, and why Ferri had not commented on it. He wondered very much if it would still be there when the Professor eventually found time to show him around.

Annunziata Zecchi put down the worn coat in the elbow of which she was inserting a patch, and said, "Are you sure he will come?"

Tina said, "Yes, Mother. If he said he will come, he will come."

"You have confidence?"

"Yes. I have confidence."

"Where is your father?"

"He went up to the workshop as soon as he had finished his supper."

"He eats so little," said Signora Zecchi. "Hardly enough

50

to keep a sparrow singing. And he worries. All the time, he worries."

"Perhaps when he has spoken to Signor Roberto it will relieve his mind."

"*If* he speaks. He has become so secretive. He goes to confession, but I know that he tells the priest nothing."

A door banged in the courtyard behind the house and steps approached. The two women looked up hopefully, but it was Dindoni who came into the kitchen, the usual malicious half-smile on his face.

He said, "Not sitting at home tonight, Tina? What are the young men of Florence thinking about? Have they no eyes in their heads?"

Tina said, "Be off, and mind your own business." But Dindoni seemed inclined to linger. He perched on the corner of the kitchen table, and said, "Who was that sweet, that really *very* sweet young man, who stopped his car in the Via Tornabuoni yesterday afternoon to speak to you? And held up all the traffic for two minutes."

"It was the Sheik of Araby. He is in Florence to choose himself two or three more wives. Didn't you know?"

"He looked to me to be very like Mercurio, the son— or, to be accurate, the adopted son—of Professor Bronzini. A pretty boy, isn't he? Really very attractive."

"Which is more than can be said for you," said Tina.

Dindoni hobbled to the door and turned for a parting shot. He said, "But we mustn't make Signor Roberto jealous, must we?" He shut the door, and they heard his feet clattering off down the pavement.

"Oaf," said Tina. But the color had come into her cheeks. "How I hate the little toad."

"You shouldn't allow him to tease you," said her mother. "I don't care for him a great deal myself, but he is a hardworking little man, and it would be difficult for your father to get by without him."

51

"He's vile," said Tina. "Do you know where he has gone now? To drink with that woman Maria. She is no better than a whore."

"Agostina," said her mother, "that is a word no woman should use of another."

"All right," said Tina, "I won't use the word. But it's true, all the same. He's gone to sit in her lap, like a little dog."

But Tina was wrong. Dindoni had not gone to the café to visit his Maria, although this was the impression that his carefully staged exit had been designed to create. He had hobbled off along the road and turned to the left as though he were indeed making for the café. Ten yards down the street he had turned to the left again, and was now in a small, dark passage that paralleled the Sdrucciolo Benedetto, running along the backs of the houses. Dindoni paused at a door in the wall, extracted a key from the side pocket of his coat, and let himself in. He was now immediately behind Milo Zecchi's house and workshop. An external iron staircase ran up the end of the building, and led to the back door of Dindoni's own quarters, which occupied the story above the workshop. The staircase and back door constituted a private means of going out and coming back again, which was much to Dindoni's secretive taste.

He clambered awkwardly, but quietly, up the stairs and let himself into his own flat. But he did not turn on the light.

Broke had left home, on foot, shortly after nine o'clock. The afternoon wind had dropped, and the sky was clear. As dusk fell, the hard blue of the afternoon took on subtle shades of green and gray, as though an Italian primitive painting were being retouched by a French impressionist.

Over the river, Broke turned to his right, and found himself in the streets of the old quarter. He had taken the precaution of working out and memorizing his route. He knew that, sooner or later, he would strike the Via Torta, and had then only to continue along it until he found the Sdrucciolo Benedetto on his left.

He was at the top of the Via Torta when he heard a clatter of excited voices. Two girls, English or Americans, he guessed, were walking along the pavement, trailed by half a dozen youths on motor scooters. They were the *pappagalli*, the "little green parrots," who infested the streets of Florence and considered any girl fair game. Broke's knowledge of colloquial Italian was insufficient for him to understand most of the screeched comments and invitations. He imagined that the girls didn't understand them, either, but they were beginning to look unhappy. Broke wondered whether he ought to interfere. The *pappagalli* were not usually dangerous. Their weapons were mostly verbal. More like geese than parrots really. They made a lot of noise but retreated if you shook a stick at them. But they could turn nasty and there had been one or two incidents lately.

As he was hesitating, the flock took flight. One moment they were there. The next, with a popping of exhausts, they were gone. A black sedan came cruising slowly down the street. In front, a carabiniere sat beside the driver. He was thickset and black-haired and his face was bisected by a thin black mustache. He leaned from the car and said to the girls in tolerable English, "That turning on your left, ladies, will take you straight back to the Lungarno."

The girls awarded him an embarrassed smile and scuttled away.

The carabiniere cast an eye over Broke, hesitated, then signaled to the driver, and the car slid away.

"Campaign to keep Florence safe for tourists," thought Broke.

He found the house without difficulty, and Signora Zecchi, who was waiting for his knock, let him in. Tina was sitting sewing in the corner of the kitchen. As he came in she gave him the urchin grin that made her look several years younger even than she was. There was no sign of Milo.

"He is over in his workshop, behind the yard," said Annunziata. "He would like to speak to you there, I think. But before you go, might I be permitted to say one word?"

"Of course."

"My Milo is not well. He is not well in his mind. Nor is he well in his body. He desires very much to speak to you, but he may find it difficult to do so. I would ask you to be patient with him."

"I'll do what I can," said Broke awkwardly.

"No one can do more. Agostina will show you the way."

Milo's workshop occupied the ground floor of the two-story erection that blocked in the rear of the courtyard behind the house. The windows of the floor above were curtained.

"Dindo lives there," said Tina. "He is out just now, which is a good thing. He is forever spying and prying into things which do not concern him."

She pushed open the door, stood aside for Broke to go in, and shut it behind him. Milo was crouched over a bench under the strong overhead light at the far end of the room, his hands and arms visible, the rest of him in shadow.

He put the object he was working on carefully down on the bench top, and climbed to his feet. Broke was shocked at the apparent change in his face. It might have been some trick of the light, but in a few hours he seemed to have grown years older. The cheeks had shrunk, leaving black cavities under the eyes, and the nose had a pinched and quill-like look that Broke didn't like at all. Only the brown eyes were still bright and shrewd.

"That's a fine bull," said Broke. "Did it come from the old pirate's tomb, at Volterra?"

"It came in sixteen pieces," said Milo. "It was a fine

animal. It will be again when I have finished with it. Two pieces only are missing. The tail and one of the horns."

The restoration had been most skillfully done. The hairline joins were hardly visible. The master of the herd was pawing the ground in Etruscan arrogance. Broke wondered what the unknown artist who had fashioned the animal would have said if he could have seen it coming back to life under the gnarled fingers of Milo Zecchi nearly three thousand years after its creation.

"You will take wine?" said Milo. Without waiting for a reply he filled the two large beakers that stood ready on the bench, and pushed one across to his guest.

"Good health," said Broke.

Milo said, "Good health is indeed a blessing. You appreciate it only when it has gone. I fear that I am not long for this world, Signor Broke."

Broke found no easy reply to this, and took a sip of wine to cover his embarrassment. It was good wine. It must have been brought out in his honor.

"I am in the hands of the doctors and the priests, and I can find little comfort in either. The doctors examine me with their machines. Then they whisper among themselves, and when I ask them what is wrong with me, they tell me I must drink no wine and be patient. That is all. Patient!" Milo gave a laugh, which had little mirth in it. "The priests are worse. They talk of penitence. What have I to be penitent about, tell me that? I have worked hard, all my life. My family has never been in want."

"An honest workman has nothing to fear in this life or the next," said Broke. He had intended it as a platitude and was not prepared for its effect.

Milo looked at him for a long moment without saying anything. Then he jumped to his feet and started to pace up and down. A twinge of pain brought him to a halt. He stood opposite Broke, rocking on his feet, and said at last, in a voice that was little more than a croak, "What do your words signify, Signor Broke?"

"Sit down, Milo, or you'll do yourself harm. I meant only that a man who works hard and does his duty by his family in this life has little to fear in the next."

"You said, 'An honest workman.' Those were your words."

"If I said it, I meant it."

"Yes," said Milo. He sat down abruptly. Then he put a hand out, picked up the bottle without looking at it, refilled both their glasses, and raised his own to his lips.

Broke thought, I wish I knew more about medicine. He's acting as if he's had a mild stroke. I wonder if I ought to stop him from drinking. But when Milo spoke, his voice was unslurred, and the hand that held the glass was surprisingly steady.

He said, "Signor Broke, there is something I must tell you. You are a man who has much knowledge of these things. You will be able to advise me what I am to do."

"Of course," said Broke. "I'll do anything I can."

"Tina says, if I may be forgiven for referring to such matters, that you are of an understanding nature, having suffered yourself."

He's like the man on the high diving board, Broke thought, wondering whether he dare take off, knowing that once he has committed himself he can't stop; looking for any excuse to postpone the moment of decision. The silence was absolute.

The noise that finally broke it was so slight that Broke was uncertain whether he had imagined it. Had there been any wind it might have been the click of a timber as it shifted; or it might have been the sharp claw of a mouse on wood; or the *tock* of the deathwatch beetle at work in the beams. Only Broke knew that it was none of these things, and he knew that, on that night at least, he was not going to hear what Milo was screwing up his courage to say, had brought himself to the very point of saying.

In the room above them Dindoni was cursing his own clumsiness. He was lying in the dark, flat on his stomach, beside a gap in the floor from which two floorboards had been removed. He had been lying in the same position for nearly half an hour, and a sudden spasm of cramp had caused him to twist onto one side. As he did so, his cigarette lighter had slipped from his pocket and fallen onto the rafter below him.

Dindoni could hear the change in Milo's voice. "But I must not bore you with my private troubles, Signor Broke. I did not drag you all the way down here for that. I wished your expert opinion on this bull. A lovely creature, is it not? From the sixth century before Christ, I am told. I know very little of such technicalities. I am only a craftsman. But I have an eye for beauty...."

Dindoni cursed again. He rolled over and climbed to his feet. He was stiff and sore, and angry. To have been so close, and then to have lost it at the last moment. He brushed down his clothes and crept cautiously back the way he had come.

Five minutes later he was hammering on the door of the café down the street. There was some delay before any notice was taken; then a girl's voice said, "Who is it? Go away. We're shut."

"Maria? It's Dindo."

The girl said, "You're late. I thought you weren't coming. What's up?"

"Who's in there?"

"Those two."

"What are they doing?"

"Having a drink. What do you think they're doing? Washing up?"

57

"If the café's shut, they oughtn't to be here."

"I told you, they're just finishing their drinks. Then they'll go."

"If I hadn't turned up, I wonder when they'd have gone."

"Your mind's as twisted as your body," said Maria. "If you think they shouldn't be here, why don't you throw them out?"

"That's right," said the stout man, putting his head through the beaded curtain. "You come and throw us out. The exercise'll do you good."

"I never said anything about throwing anyone out," grumbled Dindo.

"That's all right then, isn't it. Come right in and join us. Give him a drink, Maria. He looks a little down in the mouth; maybe he's had some bad news. Some horse he backed didn't turn up. Is that right, Dindo?"

They went through into the back room. The tall man was seated at the table reading the *Corriere*. He looked up as they came in, then went on with his reading.

There were three glasses on the table, as Dindoni noted. The stout man followed his glance, and said, "That's right. We were all having a drink together. That's what I like about Florence. People aren't standoffish. It's share and share alike here. That's right, isn't it?"

The thin man said, "You talk too much."

"Talking is a useful device," said the stout man. "It facilitates cooperative effort. It enables people to communicate with each other. How did things go tonight?"

"They didn't," said Dindoni sulkily.

"The meeting did not take place?"

"It took place."

"But you could hear nothing?"

"I could hear perfectly."

"Then what went wrong?"

"What went wrong was that the old devil must have

sensed that I was up there. As he was about to speak, he changed the subject. He talked of nothing at all."

"Did he hear you?"

"Of course not. I tell you, it was just natural caution."

"I see," said the stout man. He eyed Dindoni thoughtfully. "Then we must think of something else. If he fears to speak in his own workroom, where *will* he talk?—if he desires to talk in confidence."

"In his own kitchen, no doubt."

"And it would not be possible for you to hear what is said in that room?"

"Of course it wouldn't. The windows are always shut, summer and winter. Or do you suggest I should hide under the table? Or secrete myself behind the stove, like a cricket on the hearth?"

"I suggest," said the stout man, "that we talk sense. And that we summon science to our aid. Surely there is somewhere in the room"—he had opened his briefcase, and brought out a small round black metal object—"that such a thing could be hidden."

Dindoni eyed it curiously.

"You would need less than ten minutes, alone, in the house. The wire is very thin, and painted black, as you see. It can be laid behind a picture rail, or along a wainscoting or crack of the floor, and it will pass through a ventilator, even under a shut window. . . ." He proceeded to instruct Dindoni, who listened with growing interest.

In the substation in the Via de' Bardi, Carabiniere Scipione, a thickset, black-haired Sicilian, his young-looking face bisected by a line of black mustache, sat laboriously filling out a report form. Tenente Lupo came in, a sheaf of papers in his hand. He picked one out and tossed it onto the table.

"There is a note," he said, "from the Stazione Centrale.

On Monday evening two men arrived on the Rapido from Rome at ten to seven. They were thought to be Sicilians. They made a telephone call, and then walked out into the town. They had some luggage, and it seemed they might be intending to stay. The report describes them as 'suspicious.' I wonder why."

Scipione recognized the question as rhetorical, and said nothing.

"Perhaps it is worth checking. At railway stations they have a nose for these things. Tomorrow let me see all new hotel registrations."

Scipione said, "The Lieutenant realizes that there will be several hundred of them. All these tourists—"

"Try to employ the brains that God has given you," said Tenente Lupo kindly. "These two men were certainly Italians, possibly Sicilians. Therefore you may omit all Americans, Englishmen, Frenchmen, Danes, Norwegians, Spaniards— No, on reflection, possibly you may keep in the Spaniards."

5

Luncheon at the Consul's
THURSDAY

If, as has been maintained, the mere possession of a name can influence the character of its holder—the Blacks becoming gradually blacker and the Whites whiter—it was, perhaps, something more than a coincidence that the Weighills (who, of course, pronounce their name "Whale") should have become, in successive generations, increasingly whalelike; their bodies larger and blander, their eyes smaller, and their skins thicker.

Sir Gerald was the finest specimen of all Weighills to date. He turned the scale, in his underpants, at two hundred fifty pounds, moved with the majesty of an aircraft carrier, and needed, unkind persons asserted, almost as much seaway to turn in. While he was still at an early age it had become clear that such talents must lead him into the Foreign Service.

His wife being dead, he was looked after efficiently by his elder daughter, Tessa, every inch a Weighill herself; and, spasmodically, by his younger daughter, Elizabeth, who was so startlingly different, with her light hair, blue eyes, and boyish figure, that she might have come from a different family altogether.

"She's a throwback to the Trowers," explained Sir Gerald. "My wife's family." He added, "They came from Shropshire," as though this explained everything.

Sindaco Trentanuove, the Mayor of Florence, nodded his agreement. He knew nothing about Shropshire, but if Sir Gerald asserted that it was so, that was good enough for him. In his view, Sir Gerald was all that a diplomat should be. The last two or three English consuls had not been up to the mark at all; small, clever, anxious men, hurrying through Florence as though it was a railway junction on the route to some more important terminus. But Sir Gerald was clearly a fixture. Even when his term of office expired he would probably remain, a notable addition to the corps of ex-diplomats in Tuscany.

The party was gathered in the Consul's drawing room. Elizabeth was pouring out the second of the prelunch drinks for her father and the Sindaco. Tessa was seated at one end of the sofa, dividing her attention between Miss Plant, Tom Proctor, the solicitor from England, and the American, Harfield Moss, who was suspected of being very rich, and was known to be interested in Roman and Etruscan relics.

Sir Gerald looked at his watch, and said, "I hope Broke hasn't forgotten us. It'll upset the seating plan for lunch."

"He promised he'd come," said Elizabeth, "and I sent him a card to remind him. He's getting terribly absent-minded, though."

"Give him a ring at his house. We can't keep Miss Plant waiting much longer. She's finished a whole plate of cocktail biscuits. No. Stop. I hear the bell. It's probably him."

Broke came in, full of apologies, with a story of a difficult last-minute customer. It sounded a bit thin to Elizabeth, who guessed, correctly, that he had forgotten all about them and gone home to lunch in the ordinary way, only to be chased out by Tina.

Introductions were effected. Miss Plant gave Broke her hand to kiss. Harfield Moss said that he was certainly pleased and proud to meet the author of *Five Centuries of Etruscan Terra-Cotta*, and the Sindaco, who had been staring at Broke with undisguised interest, suddenly strode across, seized him by the hand, pumped it vigorously up and down, and said, "Captain Roberto."

Broke had been looking at the Sindaco with a faint frown of puzzlement between his eyes. Now he grinned (Yes, positively, he *grinned,* said Elizabeth, thinking about the scene afterward) and said, "Marco! Good heavens! How very nice to see you again. How fat and prosperous you've grown."

"It's true," said the Sindaco. "One's youth departs. One's waistline loses its boyish trim. When last we met I was very poor and very thin. And very happy. Full of the joy of youth. Untouched by the cynicism of advancing years. A ragged adventurer, sword in hand——"

"I take it," said Weighill, "that this was during the war."

"It was in the autumn of nineteen forty-three," said Broke. "Near Vallombrosa. I was on the run from a prison camp in the north. Marco—by the way, *is* your name really Marco?"

"A nom de guerre. But it gives me great pleasure that you should use it again."

"Marco was commanding a troop of very irregular soldiers, and gave me hospitality for some weeks."

"Hospitality," said the Sindaco. "Yes indeed. And we afforded some warm hospitality during that time to certain Germans in the neighborhood—very warm indeed! But I must say no more. We are all friends now, even with the Germans."

"I completely disagree," said Miss Plant. "I have never spoken to a German since a disagreeable experience I had in the winter of nineteen forty-four. I was short of fuel, and it seemed to me that the Germans had plenty, so I went to see their General—I forget his name——"

"What happened?" said Weighill. He had heard the story at least three times, but it would be new to some of his guests.

"You may find it hard to believe, but he refused to see me. I said to the young officer who did see me, 'Your stupid

Reich won't last forever, you know. Someday you'll wish you hadn't been so rude to everybody.' He had to answer to *that*. He just clicked his heels. A pointless habit. I believe they acquire it as students at Heidelberg. Along with the scars."

"That sounds like the luncheon bell," said Sir Gerald. "Let's go through, shall we? Lead the way, Tessa. That's right. Sindaco, will you do us the honor of taking the other end of the table. You shall have my daughters on either side of you."

"High priest guarded by vestal virgins," murmured Elizabeth.

"Miss Plant on *my* right. Tom, come and sit on my left. Broke and Moss in the middle. That's right. I hope, by the way, that you can all eat lobster. I am devoted to it myself."

"As a girl," said Miss Plant, "I was put off lobster by the sinking of the *Lusitania.*"

"In anticipation that it might not be to everyone's taste," said the Consul smoothly, "I have had an alternative dish of ravioli prepared."

Miss Plant looked chagrined. She had disrupted many dinner parties by declaring a last-minute aversion to the principal dish. And ravioli was *not* her favorite form of food. Recovering rapidly, she said, "But I was taught by my mother that personal fads have no place at table. I shall eat lobster with the rest of you."

Broke wondered if Sir Gerald really had ravioli in reserve, or whether he had scored a point, by superior bluff, in this game of gastronomic poker.

"Lobster," said Harfield Moss, "is a favorite dish in the state of Maine. We also eat clams."

"You are straight out from England, Mr. Proctor?" said Miss Plant. "You must find us a strange community in Florence. We must seem Edwardian to you who are a visitor from *swinging* London."

Tom Proctor, who divided his time between a farm in Herefordshire, an office in Bedford Row, and the Athenaeum, looked a little taken aback, but said that he found Florence a refreshing change.

"It can be refreshing in the off season," said Sir Gerald. "But at the moment we seem to have about twenty thousand tourists. A lot of them are British subjects. And at least half of them will lose their passports, and apply to me for help. I sometimes wonder whether it wouldn't be a sensible rule that tourists should have their passport numbers tattooed on their arms."

"They'd lose them, too," said Elizabeth.

In the course of her long reign, Miss Plant had adopted certain queenly habits. She liked to ration her attention equally among her subjects; and she tended to make pronouncements rather than to ask questions.

She now turned on Harfield Moss, and said, "You come from America. You are interested in the collection of antique objects."

"Well, not *all* antique objects," said Moss. "That would constitute rather a wide field of endeavor. I myself am personally interested in Roman and Etruscan antiquities. I am also collecting for the Moss Foundation."

"What a curious coincidence!"

"A coincidence, Miss Plant?"

"That your name should be Moss and that you should be collecting for the Moss Foundation."

The American smiled and said, "Not so much of a coincidence, when you consider that I founded it. It's my private charity."

"I've always envied you that bit of your law," said Tom Proctor. "I understand that if you buy for an artistic or educational foundation, you get almost complete exemption from taxation and death duties. Is that right?"

Harfield Moss dived happily into the complexities of

American tax law, and Miss Plant began to wish she had never raised the subject. She switched her fire across the table, and said, "You must find the Gallery an interesting place, Mr. Broke. All those books. It gives me a headache just to think of them."

"I don't have to read them all," said Broke. "Only sell them." Something Moss had been saying had caught his attention. "Were you telling us that something startling had come up lately in your field? I thought the discoveries at Caere were the last big find . . . ?"

"I wouldn't assert that it has just come up. It would be more accurate to say that it is in the course of coming up. Two or three of our major institutions have been warned—" Here Moss punctuated his sentence by twirling a forkful of pasta around and inserting it in his mouth, leaving his audience in suspense. He consumed the mouthful placidly and concluded, "—have been warned to be on the lookout."

"On the lookout for *what?*" said Elizabeth.

"If I knew that, Miss Weighill, I'd have a piece of information that a lot of collectors would give a good deal to possess. It could be silverware, or jewelry. The last big item to reach the American market was that silver helmet in the Chicago Museum. I happen to know what the Museum authorities paid for that, and it was *plenty.*"

"How do these things get to America?" said Tessa. "I thought the Italians wouldn't let them out of the country."

"That's the sort of question you mustn't ask," said Sir Gerald.

"Actually," said Moss, "I don't know. As a collector, I simply pay my money—my institution's money, I should say—to a reputable shipping agency in Rome. They pull whatever strings may be necessary. I ask no questions."

"But suppose whatever you'd bought didn't arrive?"

"I should be very upset," said Moss gravely.

"I won't have you grilling my guests," said Sir Gerald. He turned to the Sindaco, and said, "What's going to happen at the next election?"

"That is a question which is worrying a lot of people," said Trentanuove. "I myself am, as you know, a Communist." He grinned, and his teeth showed white under his gangster mustache. "That is a statement I should have to apologize for in England. Yes?"

"It's something you'd have to keep pretty quiet about," agreed Sir Gerald.

"In Italy it is possible to be proud of it. People still remember that the Communists were the best fighters. You agree, my old friend?"

"They were very good fighters," said Broke. He said it as though his thoughts were a long way off. "Not the only ones, though. The most bloodthirsty partisan I ever met was a Quaker." It was clear that everyone would have liked to hear about the bloodthirsty Quaker, but Broke had continued quietly with his meal.

"As I was saying," said the Sindaco, "I make no secret of my support for the Communist party. I think we shall do well at the national elections next month. Not well enough to form a government of our own, but well enough to secure some of the key posts for our men."

"I'm a bit confused," said Elizabeth. "What sort of government *have* you got? I mean, it's not straightforward like us, Labour or Tory."

"What we have at the moment is a government of the left center. Basically it is Social Democrat, with ecclesiastical and Liberal support."

"How many parties have you got?"

"At the last complete count, thirty-seven. But only seven of them are important. They range from the Communists, on the left, to the Citizens Union on the right. According to the way the votes go between those parties, you construct a government of a right, center, or left complexion."

"Like mixing face powder," said Elizabeth. "So much red, so much white, and a little natural tan color."

"More like cooking a cake," said the Sindaco, grinning again. "The operative word being 'cooking.'"

Miss Plant had finished her pasta, and had had enough of politics. She said, "Talking of cooking, have you seen the accounts of the Church Committee..." and proceeded to slander the English Chaplain. (He had incurred her displeasure by moving the lectern from the right-hand to the left-hand side of the aisle, and making other popish innovations.)

As the Consul was aware, once Miss Plant had started on a topic there was no way of stopping her. As with a runaway railway truck, all you could do was to switch the points and hope it ended up in a safe siding.

He said, "I see we've got General Anderson back on the Church Committee. He should be a tower of strength. He knows Florence well. He was here during the war."

"He spent precisely two days in Florence during the war," said Miss Plant, "and was intoxicated most of the time. You could describe that as being here, I suppose."

"Do I understand, Miss Plant," said Moss, "that *you* were in residence during the whole of the German occupation of the country?"

"Naturally. I saw no reason to put myself out to suit a parcel of jackbooted bullies...."

The Consul relaxed. They were safe for the next ten minutes. He caught an appreciative gleam in his daughter Elizabeth's eye, and wondered if his tactics had been obvious to anyone else. Apparently not. Tessa was practicing her Italian on the puzzled but patient Sindaco. The rest appeared to be listening to Miss Plant.

The lobsters arrived on the table.

"There was a German officers' prison camp at Vincigliata

during the First World War," said Miss Plant. "One met quite a number of them. They were, at least, gentlemen. The officers of Hitler's army, on the other hand, were not. They were vulgar little upstarts and bullies with no pretensions to manners or breeding. . . ."

"Come si chiama la piccola animalia dei bosci?" said Tessa. The Sindaco looked blank. Tessa imitated a squirrel. The Sindaco beamed. "I know him. *Coniglio.*"

"No, not rabbit. Squirrel."

Broke thought, The Germans might not have been gentlemen, but they were damned efficient fighters. He was remembering the half-section they had trapped in a farmhouse above Lucullo, in the foothills of the Apennines. Thirty partisans had closed in at dawn. There were seven or eight Germans, a foraging party, under a corporal. They had placed a sentry at the corner of the building, and the rest of them were asleep in the barn.

"They had a band," said Miss Plant. "A brass band with trombones and cornets. And a huge instrument that went *oompah-oompah,* can you imagine it? And they marched up and down the Lungarno, completely upsetting the traffic, not that there was much traffic in those days."

"A weasel? A stoat?"

"No. Not a weasel or a stoat. Daddy! What is the Italian for squirrel?"

They had stalked the sentry, and Guido, who had been a horse slaughterer's assistant, and boasted of his prowess with the knife, had stabbed him, but had bungled the butchery and the sentry had screamed. Within five seconds the Germans inside the barn were on their feet, and returning their fire. Five seconds! No chance of rushing them. Get under cover, and pick them off as they showed themselves. The sentry had tried to crawl back to the barn, and the partisans had been such rotten shots that it had taken a dozen rounds to finish him off.

"And if you tried to walk on the pavement," said Miss Plant, "the silly little officers kept pushing you off into the gutter. Or trying to. I had to be very firm."

"Squirrel? I'm afraid I don't know. Broke will tell you."

Who had suggested incendiary bullets? Could it have been Marco, now so stout and so respectable, with his easy politician's manner? Someone had suggested it, and in five minutes the straw in the lower barn had been well alight. When, at last, it was a choice between being burned alive or being shot, the Germans had tried to surrender.

"A squirrel? Broke?"

That had been the worst part. Particularly the smell, in the burning barn—

"A squirrel?"

—when, at his insistence, they had gone in to pull out any of the Germans who might be wounded but unable to move. And had found the youngster with bullets through both his legs, and his clothes and body alight. Like the lobster on his plate, with its red crust, charred black in places from the hot grill—

"Broke. Are you feeling all right?"

"Let me look after him," said Elizabeth. "You get on with your lunches. Don't let the lobster get cold. It's delicious. Have mine put back in the oven for me, Daddy."

Luckily he had died very quickly. He would have died anyway. There were no doctors up in the mountains.

They were in Elizabeth's car, and she was driving it very competently. By the time they reached his house he was himself again. The old gray past had disappeared and he was securely anchored in the present.

"*What* a stupid thing to do. It's weeks since I've had a turn like that. The doctors had some name for it. It's to do with the blood supply to the brain. It's psychosomatic."

"What does that mean?"

She had brought the car to a halt in front of the house

and neither of them seemed anxious to move.

"Medical jargon. It means that it isn't anything physical that brings it on. It's just that some coincidence starts me thinking about the past—a train of thought starts up inside my head, and I find it's running away on its own, and I can't stop it. The train, I mean."

"A train accident." They both laughed. "Which particular coincidence started it this time? Or can't you remember?"

"It was talking about the Germans—and meeting the Sindaco again. Oh, and the lobster."

"Lobster?"

"I can't explain that bit. It's rather horrible."

"Then please, don't," said Elizabeth. "I don't want to be put off lobster for the rest of my life, like Miss Plant. It's one of my favorite foods. Will you be all right now?"

"Absolutely. When this thing's over, it's quite over. I'm as fit as a fiddle." He demonstrated his fitness by jumping out of the car. *"And* rather hungry."

"Then come back and finish your lunch."

"I don't think I could face that. Tina'll knock me up something."

Tina met him at the door of his flat, with an anxious face. "What has happened? Why have you come back so soon? You are not well."

"I had a little turn," said Broke. "It was nothing. I'm all right now."

Tina burst into tears.

"Come on," said Broke. "It's not as bad as that." He patted her awkwardly on the shoulder. "You can't cook my lunch if you're crying into the spaghetti."

"You would like something to eat?" The thought cheered her up at once. "I will cook it for you. It will not take a moment. You can have a piece of melon while I cook the pasta."

Food, thought Broke, a woman's sovereign remedy for

all ills. If you are tired, eat. If you are worried, eat. If you are dying, you can at least die with a full stomach.

Elizabeth did not hurry back to the Consulate. By the time she got there the others had finished their lunch, and were taking coffee in the drawing room.

"Your lobster's in the oven," said Tessa.

"If you don't mind," said Elizabeth with a slight shudder, "I don't think I will. Just a cup of coffee, please."

"How is Broke?"

"He's all right, Daddy. He's been having turns like that, ever since his wife died."

"Sad," the Sindaco said, "to lose a wife, at his age. But he is young enough to marry again. He is the sort of man who needs a wife to look after him."

Sir Gerald said, "What happened to his wife? I heard some story about an accident."

"What happened," said Tom Proctor, "was that she was coming home, in her car, early one evening, and a truck was coming the other way. There doesn't seem to be any doubt at all that the truck was being driven scandalously fast. A farmer, whom it had passed half a mile back, said it was 'blinding.' I think the truth of the matter is that the driver was in a hurry to get home for his tea and his favorite television program. He came round the corner, in the middle of the road—not a very wide road—saw the car, much too late to stop, and hit it head on. Mrs. Broke died in hospital twenty-four hours later. The truck driver was unhurt." Tom Proctor added, in a voice that was deliberately devoid of expression, "She was pregnant at the time."

"I hope they put him in prison for a long, long time," said the Sindaco.

"In England we don't put truck drivers in prison. His union briefed good counsel for him. There were no witnesses of the accident itself; only things like skid marks and the damage to the car, and those can always be interpreted in different ways. He was fined twenty-five pounds for dangerous driving. The union paid it. That was when Broke decided that England was no longer a country he could live in."

Elizabeth said, "What a horrible story," and choked over her coffee. She was very close to tears.

"It must have been a hard decision," said Proctor. "Because Broke is English of the English. In fact, he's a bit of an anachronism. He's the nineteenth-century European's idea of an Englishman. Inarticulate, basically sure that all Englishmen are twenty percent better than all foreigners, tiresomely honest, upright, rigid and un*simpatico*."

"That's not fair," said Elizabeth.

"My dear Miss Weighill," said the lawyer, "you do me an injustice. I didn't say that Broke *was* that sort of man. I said that was what he appeared to be. There is an obverse to the coin. After all, his grandfather was Leopold Scott—"

"I knew him," said Miss Plant, waking up from her after-luncheon snooze. "He painted a picture of my mother's three Dandie Dinmonts. It hung in our nursery."

"He was a very successful artist," said Proctor dryly, "and he bequeathed a large sum of money, and a measure of artistic talent, to his daughter, who was Broke's mother. She encouraged the artistic side of his nature, which is unquestionably there, buried under layers of conventional Englishry. Did you know that he is an accomplished violinist?"

"I confess," said Weighill, who had been following this with all the interest of a connoisseur of human nature, "that Broke had never struck me as a sensitive person. It's true that he runs a bookshop and art gallery, but I had always thought of him as more of a businessman than an artist."

The Sindaco said, "Might that not be because you did not know him before the death of his wife? A thing like that can change a man. Most of us have two sides to our nature. A tragedy like that can bring one side to the top— perhaps permanently, who knows?"

Elizabeth got up and started to collect the empty coffee cups. Her father opened his small, whalelike eyes a little. This was a job that was normally left to Antonio from the kitchen. As the door closed behind her, he said, "There is very little permanency about human nature, you know."

"You are quoting D'Annunzio," said the Sindaco. "Did he not observe, 'There is nothing permanent in life except death'?"

"One of my uncles," said Miss Plant, "turned his face to the wall in eighteen ninety, and never smiled again."

"What made him do that?" asked Tessa.

"I've forgotten the details," said Miss Plant. "It was something to do with cricket."

Tenente Lupo studied the report in his hand. It was a businesslike if negative document.

Reference to the message of last Monday, received in this office at 21:15 hours, relating to the reported arrival of two men at the Central Station. Inquiries have been made at all hotels and *pensiones* and the registration particulars of all indigenous incomers there have been checked.

Even Tenente Lupo, attached as he was to official language, felt that "indigenous incomers" was going rather far. He underlined the phrase lightly in pencil to remind him to talk to Carabiniere Scipione about it.

No one corresponding in any way to the two men concerned has been traced. It is respectfully pointed out that there were a number of trains leaving Florence later that night for Bologna, Milan, Faenza, and Arezzo, in addition to trains returning in the direction of Rome. It is therefore most probable that the two men in question had business to transact in Florence and having transacted it, proceeded to their destination later that evening.

Tenente Lupo studied the report carefully. Scipione was a keen and painstaking policeman. Apart from the "indigenous incomers," it was a good report. On second thought, he crossed out the words "most probable" in the last sentence, and substituted "possible." This seemed to him to commit them less.

The next thing was to decide what to do with it. There was, on the shelf beside his desk, a large box file labeled "Miscellaneous." This seemed to the Tenente to be the appropriate destination, and he placed the report carefully in the file, and restored the file to the shelf.

6

The Zecchis at Home
THURSDAY EVENING

Just as wild animals who have moved to strange hunting grounds will quickly tread out their private paths to the water hole, will fix hours of eating, drinking, and sleeping, establish places of watch and places of retreat, weaving a pattern based partly on instinct and partly on experience, so did the two strangers establish themselves, falling into a routine of fixed times and places.

They rose late, from the rooms they occupied in the Pensione Drusilla, and made a careful toilet, which involved lavish use of hair oil, aftershave lotion, and eau de cologne. When dressed and perfumed, they strolled out to a café near the end of the Ponte Vecchio, where they took their prelunch drinks, and from there to another café, where they ate a large midday meal. In the afternoon they slept. At dusk they rose again, making a second, and equally careful, toilet, the tall man finding it necessary to shave twice a day. Thereafter they visited a *ristorante* for drinks and the evening meal, which they took late. Before eating, the stout man would have bought copies of every paper on sale, and these he spread over the table, marking the day's prices on the Rome stock exchange, and occasionally commenting on them. The tall man read the racing results.

Their movements after supper depended on whether they had a rendezvous, for business purposes, with Maria or Dindoni in the café in the Via Torta, or whether they were free to pursue their own pleasures.

They had taken a woman each, picking her from the wares on sale at a brothel in the Via Santissima Chiara, which they had visited on their second night in Florence. There had been a difference of opinion with the protector of the women over the commission to be offered, and an argument had developed in the hall of the establishment. The stout man, as usual, had done the talking. After a while the tall man seemed to tire of it. He had walked out into the street, where the protector's new Fiat Milleduecento stood by the curb, had jerked open the hood and, with a small blade that had suddenly appeared in his right hand, had severed all six of the plug leads before its outraged owner came charging out to stop him. The tall man had kicked him, dislocating his kneecap, and then, squatting beside him as he lay in agony on the pavement, had said, slowly and clearly, as to a child, "The inside of a car can be mended at a garage. The inside of a man cannot. *Capite?* Understand?" After which there had been no trouble.

As dawn was beginning to pale the sky, the two men would come padding back separately to the *pensione*, for which they had been provided with a side-door key, and would fall asleep as Florence was waking around them.

That Thursday evening it was nearly eleven o'clock when they reached the café in the Via Torta. They found that Dindoni had not yet arrived. They settled down to wait.

Approximately half an hour earlier Tina had walked down the Via Torta. She had been spending the evening with her uncle and his family, who lived near the Porta Romana, and the young people had escorted her home, saying good night to her at the corner of the street, within sight of her own turning.

At the corner was a sports car, with the top down. As she passed it the door swung open and a voice said, "Hello there, Tina."

77

"Hello," said Tina, "and good night."

"Come," said Mercurio, "that's no way to speak to an old friend, who has been waiting nearly an hour to see you."

"You must have little to do with your time if you waste it like that."

"Maybe. Maybe not. But there is something I thought you would like to know."

"I doubt it."

"It does not concern you. It concerns your father."

"Oh? Perhaps you may tell it to me then, only be quick."

"I shall tell you nothing if you stand five yards away. Jump in beside me, into the car. It's all right. I shall not drive off with you."

"If you tried to drive off with me," said Tina. "I would pull the steering wheel around and smash your pretty car into the wall."

"I don't doubt it. So since you have nothing to fear, get in and let us at least be comfortable."

He held open the door of the car, and Tina, after a moment of hesitation, got in. Mercurio sat down beside her. She said, "Well, your scene is set. Begin."

Mercurio was fidgeting with the steering wheel. He seemed to be more nervous than she was. He said, at last, "Your father has done much work, in the last few years, for my father. Both carving and restoration—"

"The Professor has been very good to him," agreed Tina. "And to you, too, from what I have heard."

"Oh, he's a goodhearted man," said Mercurio. "But there is a limit to the best of good natures. A week ago, when your father was handling a fine Etruscan krater, which was to be repaired, he dropped it, and it was broken beyond repair this time. Again, when he was carving a fine piece of alabaster, the chisel slipped and split it. It could not be used for the purpose intended. It is not your father's fault.

78

That is well understood. But his hand is no longer as steady as it was, nor his eye as true."

"Why are you telling me this? And what has it to do with you?"

"The Professor is very fond of me. He listens to me. He respects my judgment. If I were to say to him, 'Milo Zecchi has done good work for you for many years. He is now near the end of his working life. A suitable thing would be to pay him a generous pension, equivalent to what he can earn by working,' then I think he would see that it is just, and would agree."

Tina thought about this. She seemed, in some curious way, to be in command of the situation. She said, "Was this suggested to you, perhaps, by the creature Dindoni?"

"No. It is my idea entirely."

"And you could procure it?"

"I could almost certainly procure it."

"And what would the charge be?"

Mercurio turned his head, but made no move toward her. When he spoke, there was an odd note of appeal in his voice. He said, "I would ask that you come out with me, sometimes, in the evening."

"To come out? Where to?"

"To the cinema. To the restaurant. To dances. Wherever you wished to go."

"And when the cinema or the eating or the dancing was finished?" There was a note, now, of mockery in her voice.

"I would take you back."

"Take me where?"

"To your home, of course."

"Would it be part of the bargain that I should make love to you?"

"Only if you wished," said Mercurio humbly.

Tina burst out laughing. "Only if *I* wished," she said at

last. "That is a very curious proposition. I have never found before that the girl was given much option in these matters. It is a delicate proposition." She was still laughing as she got out of the car. "I will think about it, Master Mercurio."

Behind her she heard the car start up, and she laughed, gently, again.

When she got home, she found a family quarrel going on. Her mother was in front of the kitchen stove, arms akimbo. Her father was sitting in his chair, his face set. Tina recognized the symptoms, and prepared to retire, but her mother summoned her in with an imperious gesture.

"See if you can talk some sense into your father's thick head."

"If he won't listen to you, he will certainly not listen to me."

"Try all the same. Together we may prevail. He has two ideas in his head. First, he desires very much to have the advice and the assistance of Signor Broke."

Tina looked puzzled. "Was is not for that," she said, "that he came down here the other night?"

"Just so. The Signore came all the way down here. He agreed to talk to your father. Which was kind of him, for one can see that he is a gentleman, and a busy gentleman, too, much occupied with his own affairs. To come down here was very accommodating."

"Then . . . ?"

"Wait. The Signore went across—as you will recollect— to speak to your father in the workshop. The two men were together. They had the evening in front of them. And what did they discuss?" Annunziata paused for effect, raised one hand solemnly in the air, and spat out the word: *"Nothing."*

Milo opened his mouth as if to speak, and then shut it again.

"They were together for an hour, and they talked of nothing, or nothing to the point. They discussed tombs, and bulls, and the art of carving in bronze, and wine, and the weather, and the price of cabbages."

Tina said to her father, "But why?"

Her mother said, "Why? Because there is another idea in his stupid old head. He concluded that it was not safe to talk, *because Dindoni might be listening, from the floor above.*"

Tina thought back. Then she said, "That is impossible. For we ourselves saw him go out."

"He could have come in, by the back way, and up the stairs to his room."

"They would have seen the light."

"Not if he had crept back in the dark."

"Yes," said Tina. "And he'd do it, the miserable little rat. Had you any reason to think he was there?" she said to her father.

"I heard him," said Milo. "It was a small noise, but I have good hearing. He was there, all right, with his ear to the floor."

"Then, if you must speak to Signor Broke, why not bring him here, to this room?"

"How could I presume to bring him all this way again?"

"No," said Tina. "That is true. It would be an act of presumption. If you are to see him, *you* must go to him."

"You will ask him?"

"Certainly. Tomorrow morning."

"He will agree?"

"How can I tell? I can only ask him. You will have to come up to his apartment after dinner."

"Not to his apartment."

Annunziata said, in tones of exasperation, "That is yet another idea that he has. That he is being followed."

"Followed?"

"By men. He sees them everywhere."

"Little green men in pointed hats?" said Tina with a laugh.

"It is not a joke," said Milo angrily. "They are there. I have seen them. They watch me, all the time. If I try to go near Signor Broke's house, they will find some way of stopping me, I know it."

The two women looked at each other. Annunziata said, with a touch of helplessness in her voice, "You see how it is."

"But there is, perhaps, a way," said Milo. "That is, if the Signore would agree. It is asking much of him. Tomorrow I go to the doctor's house, in the Via Marcellina. I am one of the last patients of the evening. By the time I come away, it will be dusk. He has a back door to his office, which leads out, through the garden, into the smaller street at the back. Sometimes his patients do not wish all the world to know they are visiting a doctor. Even if the front of the house is watched, the back will not be."

"Can you not understand," said Annunziata, and now she was angry, "that these men exist only in your imagination?"

"I have eyes in my head."

"It is an affliction of old people. They imagine that everyone is watching them, following them, listening to them."

"It is *not* my imagination." The old man was shaking, with rage and frustration. "A dozen times now I have seen them."

Tina laid a hand on his arm, stroking it gently, as she might have stroked an old dog. "Go on with your plan," she said, and the look that she gave silenced her mother. "Tell us about that. You had left Doctor Goldoni's house by the back gate. What next?"

"I will walk along to the top of the Via Canina, above the cemetery, where there is a little turning space. Cars stop there, by day, to admire the view. But at ten o'clock at night it will be empty. If Signor Broke would drive there—it would hardly take him five minutes, from his house in the Viale Michelangiolo—we could sit in the car and talk without fear."

Tina said, "Very well, I will ask him."

7

A Meeting Is Arranged
FRIDAY AFTERNOON

Harfield Moss sat in his hotel room, writing a letter to his associate, Leopold Cranfield, codirector with him of the Moss Artistic Foundation in Pittsburgh.

. . . I'm as certain as I can be that something big is breaking. Something really big. Every contact I have in this town and in Rome says the same thing. It could be a Regolini-Galassi all over again. When I say that it *is* breaking, I could, of course, be wrong. It may have broken already. There's a recently developed technique that allows the investigator to get an idea of what is inside a tomb long before he actually reaches it. Exploratory drillings are made from the surface of the tumulus. It's not unlike looking for oil. When the drill breaks through the solid rock, or tufa, or packed earth, into an open space, it is taken out and an implement is lowered into the bore hole which can illuminate and take photographs. That way, a very good idea can be got in advance of what will be discovered *when* the tomb is opened. In the case of a really big find, there would most likely be two openings, not one. The first, as you can appreciate, would be highly unofficial! The choicest objects would be extracted, particularly the gold and silver, and the jewelry. The opening would then be carefully resealed, and a second, official break-in take place, with all the hoopla of press publicity. Experts from all countries flock to the place. Photographs are taken, and learned papers are written, and the contents of the tomb are deposited in one or another of the museums in this country, with considerable *réclame*. The really valuable things extracted at the first opening will meanwhile have been sold to the dealers and spirited out of the country, ending up in private collections. This time, I am determined that the best of them shall end up in the Moss Foundation, so don't be surprised if I requisition a very considerable credit, in the near future, at the Banca Toscana. It's not going to be easy. I suspect the Rossis and the Bernasconis both know what's cooking and their agents are already in Florence. So keep your fingers crossed....

When Broke came home for lunch that day he knew, as soon as he saw her, that Tina had something she wanted to say to him. He knew, also, that her sense of propriety would prevent her from saying it until lunch had been served.

It came as he was finishing the pasta.

"Would I *what?*" said Broke.

"It is a great piece of presumption on my father's part," said Tina.

"It's such a curious way of doing things. Why doesn't he just come up here? That was an excellent wine he gave me. I'd like to return his hospitality."

"He cannot come here."

"Why not?"

Tina sighed. "He says he is being followed. If he tried to see you here, the men who are following him would prevent him."

Broke laid down his knife and fork and stared at her. "If he is being followed or interfered with, tell the police."

"The police could not arrest the men who are following him."

"Why on earth not?"

"Because they exist only in his imagination."

During this, Broke had kept his eyes fixed on Tina. In fact, he was not thinking about her at all. He was glimpsing the terrifying bogies of loneliness and old age. But she shifted awkwardly under the stare of his gray eyes. She said, "It was an impertinence. Take no notice of it. He is getting old, and very shaky. He drinks too much. That is no secret. But he is a craftsman. And when a craftsman loses his cunning, and his occupation is gone, it throws him back upon himself, and he begins to imagine things. As his hand becomes less steady, his brain becomes less steady, too."

"*Is* he losing his skill? The last work he did for me was some of his best."

"He can still work well, but he breaks things. Mercurio said—" She stopped suddenly as she remembered what Mercurio *had* said, and the blood rushed into her cheeks.

"Well," Broke teased her, "what did Mercurio say to you?"

She told him. Broke did not laugh with her, when she had finished her account of the very halfhearted effort at seduction. He said, "I have met the young man. Speaking for myself, I neither like him nor trust him."

"*È finocchio,*" said Tina, as if this concluded the matter once and for all, and she stalked out of the room with the dirty plates.

Broke had never heard the word before. Clearly Tina could not be asked about it. It was plain from her demeanor, when she came back with the next course, that she had reverted to her role of housekeeper and regarded the topic as closed. He put the point to Commander Comber, who blew into the shop that afternoon to borrow a book on type faces. The Commander roared with laughter.

He said, "*Finocchio* means fennel. It's a sort of herb. I trust no one's been using the term about you."

"What's so funny about it?"

"It also means pansy. Don't ask me why. Come to think of it, why do *we* call pansies pansies?"

"Tina used it when she was describing Mercurio."

"A very perceptive description, I should say. What's he been up to?"

"As far as I could understand it, he proposed a platonic arrangement. If she would decorate his evenings out, he would put in a good word for her father."

"She's a damned attractive girl," said the Commander. "I wonder her mother allows her alone in the house with you."

Broke said, "Don't talk nonsense. Are you going to buy that book?"

"Certainly not. It's much too expensive. I just wanted to look up a word in it."

Some evenings a cold *colazione* was left for Broke at home; on other evenings, such as this, he ate out, at one of the many little family restaurants in or around the Piazza della Signoria.

He had finished his meal, and was crossing the square, when a man on the pavement ahead of him stopped so suddenly that he ran into him.

Broke apologized, the man swung around, and he saw that it was Labro, the overseer from the Bronzini farm, and that he was drunk. He was not too drunk, however, to recognize Broke.

"Well met, signore," he said. "I had been hoping that I should encounter your lordship before long."

Broke sidestepped, and walked on.

"So now you turn tail and run, my brave Englishman."

Broke continued on his way. Labro broke into a shuffling run, caught up with him, and grabbed him by the arm. Broke swung around, breaking his hold, and said, "Go away."

"We are not in the army now. You do not give orders to me. If I wish to speak, I will speak."

Broke sighed. The street was empty for some way in either direction. He could run, and probably outdistance Labro. But that would be undignified. He could knock him down, but Labro was undoubtedly drunk, and it went against the grain. Or he could listen to him.

He said, "If you have something to say, I will listen. But don't take all night about it."

"Fine," said Labro. "Excellent. You will listen."

"But stop grabbing my coat. I'm not going to run away."

"First, let me tell you that I have been dismissed from my job, by Signor Ferri. I care nothing for Signor Ferri; or for his master, Professor Bronzini. . . ." Labro proceeded to describe Danilo Ferri and the Professor. Broke hardly understood one word in five of the gutter Italian, but was left in no doubt of Labro's opinion of his employers. "To cease to serve such people is a blessing. But there is another side to it. For a man must live."

I thought money was going to come into it somewhere, thought Broke. He could see a distant figure patrolling toward them.

"Money is always difficult," Labro said. "I am not a beggar, I am not asking for money for charity. But I have something to sell. Something of great value, to the right person."

"Yes?" Twenty yards to go.

"To someone interested in the affairs of antiquity."

"If you have something you wish to sell me, come to my house in the morning. You will find me in the directory. Meanwhile, good night."

Labro started to say something, realized that he was being observed by a sardonic carabiniere, thumbs hooked in his black leather belt, and shuffled off down the pavement. Broke proceeded on his way. The carabiniere watched both men, turning his head slowly from one to the other, as though memorizing their faces.

He was a big young man. He had smooth black hair and his face was bisected by a line of black mustache.

* * *

At a quarter to ten Broke backed his car out of the garage, and drove up the Viale, using dimmed headlights. The rush of traffic had thinned out, and the last of the stall holders on the Viale Michelangiolo had sold the last copy of the statue of David, closed up his stall, and gone home to count his profits. Broke turned into the Viale Galileo, still climbing, and brought the car to rest in the parking area at the head of the Via Canina.

He got out and sat on the parapet. Below him, to left and right, as far as the eyes could see, the lights of Florence filled the valley. A shaving of new moon hung in the sky.

"On such a night as this, when the sweet wind did softly kiss the trees, and they did make no noise..." But you could still hear the unsleeping traffic of Florence's narrow streets, muffled by the distance, like a bee in a bottle.

What had Labro wanted to sell him? Information or some Etruscan relic, filched from the digging? Or nothing at all, like the beggar in the street who offered you a box of matches and was hurt if you took it.

The clocks of Florence started to say ten o'clock.

A car passed the end of the street, slowed as if to pull into the parking area, changed its mind, and drove on. Broke smiled to himself. A courting couple, he guessed, cursing him and now looking for somewhere else to park.

His own courting had been swift and, on the face of it, unromantic. He had met Joanie when he was spending a duty weekend with his older sister, Felicia, at Ware. They had gone for a walk after tea, and had discovered a sheep with its head stuck in a wire fence. It was while they were releasing the wildly kicking animal that he had decided he liked her. Liking her had gone on for a month. Then he had discovered he wanted her. They were married two months later. And, by God, it had been a right thing, from the very start. Better not to think too much about it. Bury it. Try to forget about it.

When Broke looked at his watch it was nearly half past ten. He had no sensation of time having gone past. It was evident that Milo was not coming that night. He climbed back into the car, feeling stiff and cold, and drove off slowly down the Via Canina, passing the cemetery on one side and the row of shuttered houses on the other.

The road was badly lit, with long patches of darkness between the lamps. The surface was bumpy, too, and at one point the near-side tire caught in a break in the flagstones and nearly wrenched the steering wheel out of his hand. He pulled the car back onto the crown of the road and drove carefully until he was back in the Viale.

He backed his car into the garage, turned the engine off and the lights out, and sat in it for a few minutes, as if unwilling to get out. This was the hardest part of all, coming back to an empty house. He had a feeling that it was not going to be a good night.

His first sleep was broken by his neighbors' dog, Benito, a temperamental Alsatian, who lived in a kennel and had the run of the garden behind the garage. Benito seemed to be having a bad night, too.

After that it was a long, dim sequence of turning from one side to the other, seeking comfort where no comfort was to be found. It was the sort of night in which half-dreams mingle with dreams, running together into an endless cinema show of fact and fantasy, as the mind ticks over, hovering between consciousness and oblivion.

The gray light was creeping back into the sky before he fell into a proper sleep.

8

In the Via Canina
SATURDAY, EARLY MORNING

The sun climbed slowly from behind the mountains. The sky was of that clear and innocent blue which carries with it a threat of rain to come. The first rays struck the gilded summit of Brunelleschi's Duomo, then, as the sun climbed higher, they tilted slowly downward, lighting up the high buildings, penetrating into the courts and back streets, edging their way into cracks and corners.

The Via Canina is one of the oldest streets in Florence. Age has sunk it below the surrounding surface. The eastern side is bounded by the low brick wall and iron railing of the Cimitero di San Antonio, a forest of white crosses and crooked cherubim; the left-hand side is a continuous row of very old houses, some of them condemned, shuttered, and empty, a few of them still occupied.

The sun cleared the eastern edge of the street, lighting up the space between the cemetery wall and the street itself, a narrow strip of pavement and a deep gutter.

In the gutter lay a bundle of old clothes. The sun inspected it carefully before passing on. First, a pair of boots, toes twisted inward, heels outward. Then a pair of trousers and an old jacket. The far end of the bundle lay in the gutter, and was not easy to make out. It looked like a child's pink and white woolly ball, but it was barred with stripes of a darker color.

The door of one of the occupied houses opened and a woman came out, yawning. She crossed the street, started to walk up the pavement, and stopped when she saw the bundle.

Her mouth opened slowly, as if she were going to yawn again, but what came out was a scream.

PART TWO

The Net Closes

1

Arrest

Life in the Royal Navy had taught Commander Comber the advantages of order and method. In his tiny flat, which occupied the top floor of a decaying palazzo in the Borgo San Jacopo, everything was as neat and as deftly arranged as it had been in the cabin of the Lock-class frigate that had been his last seagoing command.

One wall was totally made up of closets with sliding doors, and another was covered by shelves of books, predominantly gazetteers and standard works of reference. Two of the shelves were taken up with the blue volumes of the *Dictionary of National Biography* and another with the last English edition of the *Encyclopaedia Britannica*. There was a model of the *Lock Gair* on the mantelpiece, with a Toby jug, two silver cups for archery, and a traveling clock subscribed for by the lower deck on his retirement.

By ten o'clock that Sunday morning the Commander had finished his breakfast and his after-breakfast pipe, had washed up, dried up, and stacked away the breakfast things, tidied the bunk that occupied one end of his tiny bedroom, and was settling down to work at the desk in the window.

An observer might have found his work odd. It seemed to consist of search through books of reference, the marking of selected points in them with a pencil, and the final production of a meaningless jumble of words on the sheet of paper in front of him.

Tiring of this, the Commander took down an old brown

book with a well-used look about it, and opened it almost at random.

> Now, from the rock Tarpeian,
> Could the wan burghers spy
> The line of blazing villages
> Red in the midnight sky.
> The fathers of the City
> They sat all night and day—

He paused in his reading to jot down: "First example of an all-night sitting of Parliament?" The thought seemed to cause him some amusement.

> And every hour some horseman came
> With tidings of dismay—

Footsteps outside. Someone was coming up the final flight of steps, and coming fast. He slid the piece of paper on which he had been working into the drawer of the desk, locked the drawer, and had crossed to the door and opened it before the knock came.

It was Tina.

"Well," said the Commander. "Come right in. It's Tina Zecchi, isn't it? You aren't, by any chance, bringing tidings of dismay."

"I—" said Tina, and could get no further.

"Sit down. Those stairs aren't meant to be run up."

"I—"

"Can I fetch you a glass of water? Take a deep breath. Take several deep breaths."

Tina had got herself under control. She said, "It is Signor Roberto. They have taken him away."

"Who has taken him away?"

"The police. They came last night. I heard it this morning from Signora Colli next door. They took his car."

"Let's have this in some sort of order," said the Commander, in exactly the tones he would have employed if a midshipman had come bursting into his cabin to tell him that the enemy was in sight on the starboard bow. "Do I gather that when you went to Broke's house this morning, one of his neighbors told you that he'd been arrested?"

"Signora Colli told me. She had a great affection for Signor Broke. She was in tears."

"We'll take the tears for granted. Let's have the facts. What time was he arrested?"

"Late. Very late last night."

"Does anybody know what for?"

"It was something to do with his car. They took that away, too."

"They took him away in his car?"

"No. Signora Colli said that the car was taken separately. It was taken on a big truck."

"Had it broken down, then?"

"No. The Signora says it was in good order. Signor Broke had used it the day before."

The Commander thought about this. It didn't seem to make a lot of sense. He said, "We must go and see the Consul."

Sir Gerald was in his garden, snipping off dead roses with a pair of secateurs. Elizabeth brought the Commander and Tina out to him, and he listened to what they had to say, occasionally clicking the secateurs like an angry stag beetle. He, too, seemed puzzled about the car.

"If it was in running order, why didn't they drive it away? Why put it on a truck?"

"It wasn't a truck," said the Commander. "It was one of those transporters. They used them a lot after the flood, you remember. To cart off derelict cars."

"It looks as though whatever he's been arrested for has got something to do with the car."

"Wouldn't they tell you, if you asked them?"

"I'll get on to Colonel Nobile at once," said Sir Gerald.

Colonel Nobile, head of the Florence City Police, was a tall, thin, serious man. He had been captured by the British, during Wavell's first offensive, and had spent four years in a senior officers' prison camp in Kenya. The commandant of that camp had been the Earl of Plaistow, a Major in the Grenadier Guards, and Colonel Nobile had found him sympathetic. Both were chess enthusiasts, and they had played and talked long into the African nights. By the time the war ended the Colonel had acquired a fluent and idiomatic grasp of English as spoken in Knightsbridge and the Shires. He had acquired most of the camp commandant's prejudices, too. One of these was a mistrust of British officials.

"Box wallahs." He could hear the Major saying it as he fingered his black bishop thoughtfully. "Of course, they're clever. You've got to hand it to them. They're trained to it." He had tickled his long blond mustache with the bishop's miter. "The first year I was here we had one of those Intelligence johnnies round. Do you know what? He wanted to disguise himself as a camp orderly and see if he could worm his way into the confidence of the prisoners. *My* prisoners. Extract military information from them. Of course, I said no. There was a bit of a row about it, actually. They tried to Stellenbosch me. I got straight on to our Colonel Commandant in London an he pulled a few strings at the Palace and quashed it. Thank God we've still got *some* discipline in the Brigade."

Deciding it was too dangerous to promote the bishop, the Major had pushed forward a pawn instead. "Stellenbosch? It means dismiss. Sack. Place in South Africa they sent military failures to." Colonel Nobile had added the expression to his growing vocabulary, and had added, with it, a fixed idea about the British. Their official classes were clever. More than clever. They were masters of duplicity and deceit. The only way of dealing with them was to be noncommittal and wary. Otherwise, one might find oneself being Stellenbosched.

Therefore, when Sir Gerald, having ascertained that the Colonel was not in his office, drove out to visit him at his house on the Bellosguardo, he was received with great cordiality, and achieved nothing.

"My dear fellow," said the Colonel, "I'm dashed sorry that this should have happened. I haven't been told all the details, but I expect that a few inquiries will clear it all up. Don't worry. He'll be quite comfortable. We don't keep our prisoners chained to the wall in damp dungeons, you know, ha ha!"

"Can I see him?"

"There's some sort of tiresome regulation about that. The police have to complete their interrogation first. Stupid, no doubt. But rules are rules."

"How long's it going to take?"

"Not more than a day or two, at the outside. I'll send you a chit as soon as you can get in to see him. I promise you. What about a spot of something before lunch?"

Sir Gerald refused and drove back in a bad temper. He found Elizabeth, the Commander, and Tom Proctor waiting for him.

"Stupid old coot," said Sir Gerald. "Talks like a comedy guardsman and is as obstructive as an octopus. My predecessor warned me about him."

"Surely," said Proctor, "there's nothing to get alarmed about. The police can't hold Broke without making a charge, and *when* they make a charge, we shall know what it's all in aid of. There's certainly been a mistake. We know Robert. He wouldn't do anything bad."

"This is Italy, not England," said the Commander. "In Italy, you're guilty until you can prove yourself innocent."

"There's an element of truth in that," said Sir Gerald. "We've got a state prosecuting machine here. The Procuratore della Repubblica runs it—Benzoni. Quite a decent old boy, incidentally, but he wouldn't have much to do personally with minor cases. Under him there's a whole gaggle of *giudici istruttori*, assistant *procuratori*, minor court officials, prosecuting counsel, and policemen."

"And all of them," said the Commander, "devoted to one object—getting a conviction."

"You're exaggerating," said Elizabeth.

"I'm not, you know. It's a fact of life out here. If the police bring a charge—it doesn't matter what it is: anything from parking in the wrong slot to assassinating the President—they've *got* to make it stick. If they don't, it's a crack in the fabric of the republic. And a nail in the coffin of the officials concerned. In all the time I've been out here I've never known anyone actually acquitted. If you're clearly innocent they find you guilty and give you a suspended sentence. That way, everybody's face is saved."

"You're talking nonsense," said Elizabeth, and stalked off into the house. She sounded quite upset. The three men stood looking after her in silence for a few moments. Then Sir Gerald said, "Well, there doesn't seem to be anything we can do until Monday, does there? Perhaps I will have that drink after all."

Monday morning brought an unexpected visitor to the Consulate offices on the Lungarno. Professor Bruno Bronzini came to the point without any of his customary flourishes.

He said, "I was desolated to learn from my son Mercurio—he had the news from Tina Zecchi—it is correct? Yes, I feared as much. It seemed clear to me, from my short acquaintance with Mr. Broke, that some stupid mistake must have been made. What is he charged with?"

"If I knew that, I should be a lot happier," said Sir Gerald.

"So far, I haven't been allowed to see him."

"That is ridiculous, and shall be remedied."

"Can you do it?"

"Certainly I can do it. Was he arrested by the police or by the carabinieri?"

"By the police, I understand."

"Then it will be Colonel Nobile who has the responsibility."

"I've spoken to the Colonel. He wasn't very cooperative."

"He will cooperate with *me,*" said the Professor. "You will receive a telephone call shortly."

The call came at midday. It was Colonel Nobile himself. He said, "My dear fellow, I'm glad to tell you that I have been able to sever the red tape. You can visit your compatriot as soon as you like. He is still in the Questura. Ask for me when you come, and I will see that all is arranged."

"Well, that's very civil of you," said Sir Gerald. "I'll come straight round."

He found Robert Broke, in the charge of a youthful-looking *agente di polizia,* in one of the interior rooms on the ground floor of the Questura.

"Can I speak to Mr. Broke alone?" asked Sir Gerald.

The *agente* smiled, and shook his head.

"It's all right," said Broke. "I don't think he understands much English. Nice of you to come and see me so quickly." He sounded quite cheerful.

"What's it all about?"

"The idea seems to be that I knocked down old Milo Zecchi with my car, and failed to stop."

"Milo? The father of the girl who works for you?"

"That's right."

"When's this supposed to have happened?"

"On Friday night."

"And it's not true."

"As a matter of fact," said Broke, "it isn't. But it's an

101

odd coincidence, all the same. I *was* out in the car that night. And I *was* meeting Milo."

"You met Milo?"

"I didn't meet him, because he didn't turn up. Look here, I'd better tell you this from the beginning."

He did so. Sir Gerald was a practiced listener. He was listening to the tone of voice as much as to the facts themselves. At the end of it he said, "So you did actually drive down the Via Canina?"

"Yes, I did."

"And you didn't see him?"

"I didn't see anyone."

"Tell me what happened yesterday."

"Two policemen called. The first time was just before lunch. They asked me a lot of questions. I told them what I've just told you. They asked to look at my car, and seemed very excited when they spotted that the fog lamp was broken."

"When did that happen?"

"That's the odd thing," said Broke. "I hadn't noticed it before."

"When do you suppose it happened?"

"I've no idea. When I took the car out that night, I hadn't used it for two days. I suppose it could have been broken without me noticing it. Children throwing stones. Something like that."

Sir Gerald didn't like this much, but decided to leave it. He said, "If this accident happened on Friday night, and the police were round questioning you by lunchtime on Saturday, they must have had a pretty hot tip. It almost looks as if someone must have given them the number of your car."

"I don't follow you."

"What I meant was, if someone had seen the accident, and said that the car involved was a large dark sedan, or

102

an open tourer, or something vague like that, it would have taken them months to narrow down the field. But they got to you in a matter of hours."

"I see." Broke didn't sound very interested. "And where does that take us?"

"Going on the assumption that you didn't do this thing"— he paused for a second—"on that assumption, it means that someone reported that a car with your number was involved. Either by mistake, or out of spite. Can you think of anyone who dislikes you enough to want to get you into trouble?"

"I've trodden on a few toes since I've been out here," said Broke grimly. "But they've been mostly in the upper echelons of the art world. Not the sort of people to pull a trick like that, I shouldn't have thought. The only person—"

"Yes?"

"It's so stupid. I was going to say that the only person who had that sort of grudge against me was a man called Labro. He was overseer at Professor Bronzini's digging at Volterra. He thinks I got him sacked."

He told the Consul about Labro.

"And you met him again, in Florence?"

"On my way home on Friday night. He said he had something he wanted to tell me. I think it was just an excuse to cadge money."

"Would he have known the number of your car?"

"He didn't see it when I was out at the digging, if that's what you mean. I'd left it down the track. He could have found it out, I suppose."

"How?"

"I'm in the telephone book. It's an open garage. He'd only have to come and look."

"I suppose so," said Sir Gerald. The idea sounded wholly improbable to him. He said, "How far have they questioned you yet?"

"I've hardly been asked anything. Just general questions. Was I out that night? Where did I go? That sort of thing. They wanted me to make a statement, but I refused. They didn't like that. I understand that the real questioning starts tomorrow, when the man from the Procuratore's office gets his teeth into me."

"Don't say anything unless your lawyer's there. I'll see about one right away."

"No need," said Broke. "Professor Bronzini has got me his own lawyer. Avvocato Toscafundi. He's said to be hot stuff."

2

The Triple Alliance

Sostituto Procuratore Antonio Risso was thirty years old, baby-faced, and brown-haired. He affected tinted glasses, modeled himself on Henry Fonda, and was nakedly ambitious.

At ten o'clock on Monday morning he called by arrangement on Benzoni, who was the Procuratore della Repubblica and his departmental chief. Benzoni said, "I understand that you wish to take on the case of the Englishman, Broke. By strict rotation it would have been the turn of Cavalliero, and after him, Mazzo. Is there any good reason why I should disturb the roster?"

"Two good reasons," said Risso. "First, from what I have read in the police report, much in this case will depend on scientific evidence, and I have, as you know, scientific training. Secondly, the accused is an Englishman, and I speak much better English than either Cavalliero or Mazzo."

"And thirdly," said Benzoni, "you are a candidate in the forthcoming municipal elections, are you not? And a success in the courts, in a case involving a foreigner as the accused and an honest old Italian citizen as the victim, should redound to your credit and secure you a substantial number of votes."

"The thought had not even crossed my mind," said Risso. He managed to look so genuinely pained that Benzoni wondered for a moment if he had misjudged him. He said, "Very well. Let us accept the first two reasons as valid. But you must not prejudge the case."

"Of course not."

"And I should like to be kept regularly informed of its progress."

"The usual reports—"

"The routine reports will not be adequate. This is not a routine case."

Risso said, cautiously, "I have done no more than read the preliminary report, but it appears to be a normal case of hit and run."

"Appearances can be deceptive," said Benzoni. "I have an instinct in these matters, and I do not think that this is an ordinary case. You will exercise the greatest possible care."

Elizabeth, arriving at Commander Comber's flat, found Tina already there.

"Come in," said the Commander. His beard was jutting out at an aggressive angle and the light of battle was in his eye. "We're glad to see you. I take it you've come to talk about Broke."

"I certainly have. And to help if I can."

"That makes it a triple alliance. And it seems to me that if the forces of truth and light are going to prevail they'll need all the allies they can enlist. I've been getting some extraordinary stuff from Tina here. She seems to think that the villain of the whole piece is a man called Dindoni."

"Dino is a rat. A cockroach. A crawling snake. A creeping beetle," said Tina.

"A one-man zoo," said the Commander. "I think I'd better do the explaining. What Tina tells me is this. Milo made *two* attempts to see Broke. The first meeting was to be at their house, but it was abandoned because Milo got the idea that Dindoni was listening in on them."

"Explain about Dindoni."

The Commander explained about Dindoni.

"Then Milo had a second shot. This had to be arranged rather elaborately. He wouldn't go to Broke's house because he had got it into his head that he was being followed."

Elizabeth said sharply, "Was this true?"

"Alas," said Tina, "we disbelieved him. We said that it was the imagining of an old man. Had we but listened to him . . ." She dissolved into a flood of tears. In a few minutes she stopped crying and said, quite resolutely, "This is no time for tears. We must find the men who killed my father, and see that they are punished."

"What do we know about these men?"

"All her father would say was that there were two of them. They were strangers to Florence, coming, he thought, from the south. And he once saw one of them talking to Dindoni."

"They're going to be a bit difficult to trace, aren't they?"

"If it's the only line we've got, we must hunt it for what it's worth."

"It isn't the only line," said Elizabeth. "My father saw Broke this morning. He mentioned a man called Labro. An overseer at the Bronzini farm. There was some trouble when Broke went out there, and Labro got sacked. He seemed to think Broke was responsible and that he ought to do something about it. They happened to run into each other—this was actually on the Friday night when the accident happened."

The Commander wrote "Labro" on the piece of paper in front of him and drew a circle around it.

Elizabeth said to Tina, "Have you got any idea *why* your father was so keen to see Broke? That might give us a line."

"He would not tell us. But it had to do with his work. That I am sure of."

"What work?"

"Why, for Professor Bronzini. He had done much work

for him. Some new carving and some repairs."

The Commander was still doodling on the paper. He now drew a circle around the name "Bruno Bronzini" and joined it by a line to "Milo." Then he joined the circle around "Labro" to that around "Bruno Bronzini." The pattern seemed to interest him.

"And it was this work that was worrying him?"

"I think so. Yes. But he was very secretive about his affairs. Particularly toward the end."

"Look here," said the Commander. He pointed to his diagram. What had emerged was a sort of star. The five points of the star were "Labro," "Milo," "First Unknown," "Second Unknown," and "Harfield Moss." The center of the star, connected by a line to each of the points, was "Bruno Bronzini."

"What's it all about?" said Elizabeth. "And how does Harfield Moss come into it? All I know about him is that he's mad about Etruscan relics."

"So is the Professor."

"I still don't see it."

"I wouldn't pretend," said the Commander, "that I'm crystal clear about it myself. But a sort of pattern seems to be emerging, and the significant thing about it is that every lead comes back to Professor Bronzini. So let's suppose, just for a moment, that he *is* the key to the whole thing. Suppose he has made a big discovery at that digging of his. Something really sensational. That would account for Harfield Moss being in Florence, wouldn't it?"

"All right," said Elizabeth. "Things like that do happen. But what's the connection with Robert?"

"Step at a time. The Professor is in something of a fix. If he announces his find honestly, none of it will be allowed outside Italy. He'll get something, but only a tenth of what he'd collect if he could sell it to private collectors in Europe and America."

"All right, but—"

"Wait. Milo Zecchi knows about this. The Professor has employed him to restore some of the treasures. Milo is a sick man. The thing is on his conscience. He's aching to confide in someone. Dindoni, who is spying on him, reports all this to the Professor, who has him watched. The watchers are your two unknown men. Then suddenly the situation becomes dangerous. Why?" The Commander lifted his pencil and jabbed it down with dramatic suddenness on the name "Labro." "Because Broke pays a visit to the digging. That would not, in itself, have presented any danger. Any evidence at the digging would be carefully concealed. *But* he becomes involved with Labro. Labro is dismissed. He, too, becomes a possible source of danger. He drinks too much. He is a babbler. *And he is observed making contact with Broke.*"

The Commander paused, his pencil poised over the characters he had assembled. Anyone who had watched him at work, earlier that morning, would have noted a curious similarity. On both occasions he had collected a number of arbitrary symbols on paper. On both occasions he seemed to be striving to arrange them in a related order and thread them on a chain of causation.

"*If* we are right," he said, "it is clear that at this point it was Broke who became the focus of danger. He was the expert. Give him a clue, a hint, and he might unravel the whole conspiracy. If Milo was allowed to have a heart-to-heart talk with him, the fat *would* be in the fire and no mistake. So, at one neat stroke, both dangers are removed. Milo is killed. False testimony throws the blame on Broke. And there is the man who is responsible. Professor Bronzini. The advocate of the Etruscan way of life. And, by God, it's just the sort of plot that would have appealed to an Etruscan."

He placed the pencil gently down on top of the paper. It

was the gesture of a conductor replacing his baton after interpreting a tricky passage.

Tina clapped her hands together. The Commander had spoken in English and she had only a shadowy idea of what he was talking about, but one thing was clear to her. The blame was being lifted from Signor Roberto and placed on the shoulders of the Professor.

"*Sì, sì,*" she said. "It is that vile Professor who killed him. He shall be punished."

"It's ingenious," said Elizabeth. "But how on earth are we going to prove it?"

"I will ask Mercurio," said Tina. "The old man is infatuated with him. If he has secrets, Mercurio can wheedle them from him."

"Even if he is in the Professor's confidence," said the Commander, "which I doubt, how can you be sure that Mercurio will confide in you?"

Tina held out her right hand, bending thumb and forefinger and crooking the three middle fingers. "Mercurio is like that to me," she said. "He is a little dog. If I whistle, he will come running."

"We wouldn't want you to go getting into trouble."

"Trouble," said Tina. "The only person who will get into trouble will be Mercurio." She opened her mouth, showed her sharp little teeth, and clicked it shut.

Elizabeth said, "Poor Mercurio."

After Tina had left, Elizabeth said, "Was that an act, put on to cheer the child up? Or were you serious?"

"I'm completely serious," said the Commander. "I believe that Broke's been made the victim of an elaborate frame-up. I think, to employ a well-worn metaphor, that all we can see at the moment is the tip of the iceberg, and that there is depth beyond depth below it. Whether we shall be able to plumb it is of course another question. But if you

110

and Tina will help me I'm going to have a damned good try."

"Of course I'll help. But—"

"This is no time for ifs and buts," said the Commander. "We've burned our boats.

> "Hew down the bridge, Sir Consul,
> With all the speed ye may.
> I, with two more to help me,
> Will hold the foe in play.
> In yon strait path a thousand
> May well be stopped by three.
> Now who will stand on either hand
> And keep the bridge with me?"

"If you put it like that," said Elizabeth, quite carried away by the Commander's enthusiasm, "the answer is, Of course we will. But there's something you'd better know first. When Robert was having lunch with us the other day he had a sort of—I don't know the name for it—a temporary blackout. He wasn't unconscious, but he wasn't with it, either. Suppose Milo was delayed, and was hurrying up the Via Canina to meet him. I know the place. It's badly lit, and there's hardly any pavement. Isn't it possible that Robert *did* hit him and didn't notice anything because he was having one of these attacks? It's possible, isn't it?"

"It's possible," said the Commander, "but it isn't true. I'm prepared to wager any sum you like to name that there's more to it than that. I can't give you any logical reasons for it. Call it instinct, if you like."

Those interested in coincidences should note that at the precise moment he said this, Procuratore della Repubblica Benzoni was saying the same thing, in almost the same words, to Antonio Risso.

3

Interrogation

"Then the last time you had your car out prior to Friday night was on the afternoon of Wednesday?"

"Yes."

"I believe you went out to lunch with your Consul on Thursday. Did you not take the car out then?"

"No. I walked there. And I was given a lift back."

"Who by?"

"By the Consul's daughter, Miss Weighill."

"It is not far from your flat to the Consul's house?"

"No. It's quite a short distance."

"You walked there. Why did you not walk back again?"

"I wasn't feeling very well."

"And that was why you were taken home by car?"

"Yes."

"I see." Antonio Risso considered the matter, playing with the silver pencil in his hand, holding it up to catch the light, twirling it between his strong brown fingers. "What exactly was wrong with you?"

Avvocato Toscafundi, who had so far kept silent, stirred in his seat, and said, "Surely this line of questioning is irregular. It can have no bearing on the matter being investigated."

"If the accused refuses to answer, his refusal will be noted. The information can probably be obtained elsewhere."

"I've no objection to telling you," said Broke crossly. "I felt faint. That's all."

"And was this faintness something that had happened before? Or on this one occasion only?"

"It had happened before."

Risso paused, to make sure that the shorthand writer was keeping up, and then said, "Let us revert to Wednesday afternoon. Where did you go?"

"To Volterra. To a farm between Volterra and Montescudaio."

"That would be one of Professor Bronzini's farms?"

"Yes."

"And you went at his invitation?"

"Certainly."

"Was it dark when you got back to Florence?"

"No. Getting toward dusk, but not dark."

'When you return your car to the garage, do you normally drive it in forward, or do you back it in?"

"I make a practice of backing it in."

"And that was what you did on this occasion?"

"Certainly."

"You will appreciate why I ask the question, Mr. Broke. If you had driven the car in forward in the dusk, it is just possible that you might have broken the fog lamp without noticing it."

"Possible, but most unlikely."

"I agree. But since you backed the car in, the lamp could not have become damaged then."

"No."

"Then when did it become broken, do you think?"

"I've no idea."

"Did you look at it on Thursday?"

"I didn't actually look at it."

"But since it stands in an open garage, between your house and the house of Signora Colli, it is possible that one of you may have seen it?"

"I didn't. She may have."

"Oh, she did, Mr. Broke. When she took her dog out for a walk at about six o'clock on Friday evening."

He paused invitingly, but Broke said nothing.

"She has often remarked in what good condition you keep your car. Had the lamp been broken—not just cracked, but as badly dented and broken as it is—she says she would almost certainly have noticed it."

"Well, that settles it."

Risso looked a little baffled, and said, "Settles what, Mr. Broke?"

"The lamp must have been broken after six o'clock. The Colli children are always playing about in the road. I've complained to their mother before about it, but of course she can't keep them indoors all the time."

"On Friday evening the Colli children were at the cinema."

"I didn't say it *was* them. A lot of children play round there."

Risso said, "It is odd, though, that none of your neighbors seems to have seen or heard anything of the sort that evening. May I turn to another point. You say that you went out in your car that evening to meet someone. But he did not arrive. So, after waiting for a little, you turned round and drove home."

"Yes."

"Are you prepared to tell us who it was you were going to meet?"

Broke said slowly, "I can't see that it's got anything to do with it really."

"Then you withhold the information?"

Broke thought about it. Then he said, "No. If you put it like that. I don't actually want to withhold it. I think it's irrelevant, that's all."

"It is for us to judge the relevance of any information, Mr. Broke."

Avvocato Toscafundi said, "I think the Sostituto Procuratore is within his rights in pressing the question."

"All right," said Broke, "It was Milo Zecchi I was going to meet."

If he had expected some reaction, he was disappointed. Risso said, "Milo Zecchi. Yes." It might almost have seemed that the information had come as no surprise to him.

4

Funeral

Black satin sashes around their headlights and bumpers, black ribbons on their handles, black rosettes at their windshields, the cars crawled in a long line up the Via Arte della Lana and headed for the Church of Orsanmichele.

Commander Comber had arrived early and was standing by the church door. He had counted fifteen cars in the cortege. Let no man say how many relatives he possesses until he comes to die. When you were young, funerals were a bore. In your prime, they were a joke. As you grew older, every funeral became a rehearsal for your own. Here came another half-dozen cars! He had thought of the Zecchi family as an isolated unit of three people. He had overlooked the fact that they came of country stock on both sides. The Italian family was a complex and cohesive unit, a long-lived matriarchy spreading its roots sideways and downward into the soil of the *campagna*.

The women were predominant; erect, self-possessed, portentous, dressed in suits of weeds that had graced half a hundred such solemn occasions, attended by uncomfortable brown-faced husbands and retinues of scrubbed children. It was a woman's day.

In the leading carriage Annunziata and Tina sat alone. Annunziata had hardly stopped talking from the moment they had left the house. This flow of words was so unlike her that Tina was worried. She mistrusted the febrile mood. Something was bound to give way soon. She would have preferred silence, or even tears.

"If we crawl like this," said her mother, "we shall be late at the church, and the arrangements afterward will be upset."

"We started late. It was because you insisted on locking everything up. Not only the house. The workshop, too. Did you imagine that thieves would break in while we were at the funeral?"

"Ordinary thieves, no." Annunziata's mouth was set in a firm, hard line. Onlookers who noticed this approved. Tears on such occasions, they considered, were for young widows and weaklings.

"Who then?"

"Who other than Dindoni? Three times already he has tried to make his way into the house. *Our* house. Does he think, perhaps, now that Milo has gone, that he owns it?"

"He has little sensibility," agreed Tina. "Did he say what he wanted?"

"On the first occasion it was to offer condolences. Did I need *his* condolences? On the next, some story of accounts that had to be paid. I told him it was no time to think of money. The third time, he came sneaking into the house through the kitchen, when he thought I had gone out. Fortunately I had changed my mind, and came back, and found him. Otherwise who knows what his thieving fingers might not have lighted on. Since then I have kept *all* doors locked, *all* the time."

"At least he can be up to no mischief now. He will be at the church."

"Certainly he will be at the church. I allotted him a place in the last carriage but one. Are all arrangements made for after the interment?"

"For the tenth time, yes," said Tina. "The Professor himself has seen to everything. We go from the cemetery to the hotel. A room has been reserved, and a meal arranged."

"He was good to Milo during his life," said Annunziata, "and his kindness continues after his death."

The church was already crowded. the Guild of Carpenters and Picture Framemakers and the allied guilds of Carvers in Metal and Stone had sent full delegations. The townspeople seemed to have turned out in force. The Commander sensed something behind this, and it made him uncomfortable.

He could not put out of his mind a phrase he had read in the *Giornale* the day before: "... being knocked down by an English motorist and left to die." That was, of course, a flagrant prejudging of the case, and it would have got an English editor committed for contempt of court on the spot; but Italian newspapers seemed to enjoy more freedom. There was an air of demonstration about the assembly in the church, quiet but menacing.

The coffin had been placed on a black-draped erection of benches at the back of the church. After the requiem mass it would be followed, in procession, to the cemetery and interred.

Here came the family. Heads were turning as they walked to their seats in the front row. Tina saw the Commander and gave him the ghost of a smile.

"L'eterno riposo dona loro, Signore, e splenda ad essi la luce perpetua...."

The church was hot and stuffy. The candles guttered on their sconces like souls about to take flight.

"In Sion, Signore, ti si addice la lode...."

Why did the Christian Church make such a somber matter out of exchanging this life into what, according to their teaching, was a better and a happier one? The Etruscans had a sounder notion of it. They celebrated the departure with feasting and dancing, and sent the traveler on his way with food and drink, and his luggage packed for the journey.

"Ascolta la preghiera del tuo servo, poichè giunge a te ogni vivente...."

Hello! Someone was going. It was Milo's widow.

There was a disturbance in the front row, as Annunziata groped her way to her feet. With Tina's strong right arm around her, she stumbled toward the small door in the transept. Heads turned in the congregation, but the priest continued, unfalteringly, with the office. His business was with the soul of the departed. The feelings of the living, the weaknesses of their flesh, were irrelevances.

Commander Comber pushed his way out of the west door, circled the church, and found Tina and Annunziata sitting on a tombstone. Annunziata was still white, but she had herself in hand again.

"She wishes to go back into the church," said Tina. "I have told her no. If she does, in five minutes she will be as bad again."

"It's pretty stuffy," said the Commander. "I shouldn't risk it if I were you."

"I must go back," said Annunziata. But when she tried to get to her feet her legs gave way under her and she sat down again suddenly.

The Commander said to Tina, "You get back and show the flag. I can deal with this. My car's just round the corner. As soon as your mother can move, I'll get her home and make her lie down."

"Are you sure you can manage?"

"Trust the Royal Navy."

"Then I will go. I will come away as quickly as I can. You will do what he tells you, and be sensible."

"Sensible," said Annunziata crossly. "How can I be sensible when my legs feel as though they belong to someone else?"

"All right if we take it slowly," said the Commander. "Put one arm round my shoulder, and put all your weight on me. That's it."

The car ride seemed to revive Annunziata. By the time they had reached her house, she was almost herself again.

She was a lot more worried about the funeral ceremonies she had abandoned than she was about herself.

"You go in and sit down quietly," said the Commander. "No one's going to think any the worse of you for missing it. I'll bring Tina back as soon as it's all over."

"You are kind," said Annunziata. She unlocked the front door and went in. The house was very quiet. It was so quiet that when she heard the sound there was no mistaking it. There was someone in her kitchen.

Dindoni? Of course! He must have slipped from the church and made his way back to the house. But how had he got in? She would soon find out.

She strode across the room and jerked the kitchen door open. There were two men there. The stout man was standing close to the door. He kicked it shut as Annunziata came through. The tall man with the broken face was standing on a chair, doing something over the fireplace. He had a small metal box in his hand and was detaching a length of black wire from behind the wainscoting, coiling it up neatly as it came away from the wall.

"What . . . ?" said Annunziata.

The stout man picked a kitchen chair up in one pudgy hand, pushed it behind her legs, and said, "Sit down and keep quiet."

Annunziata said, "I will not sit down, and I will not keep quiet. You will leave at once."

"We'll leave when we've finished."

Annunziata glared at him, her faintness quite banished by the shock. She looked at the door. It was clear that she could not get back through it in time. Shouting was useless. The walls were too thick. She needed a weapon. There was a knife on the table, a heavy sharp paring knife. She grabbed it.

"Now," she said, "get away from that door."

"You're being silly," said the stout man. The thin man

had not even turned around. He was quietly finishing his job.

"Stand away, or take the consequences," said Annunziata. She was a big, heavy woman and she held the knife resolutely.

The stout man allowed her to come within a pace of him. Then, instead of retreating, he leaned forward. The knife went up, but with no great resolution. The man's hand followed it. He did not try to grab her wrist. He executed a chopping blow and the knife fell from Annunziata's suddenly nerveless hand.

"Enough of these heroics," said the man. "I told you to sit down and keep quiet. Do I have to tear your dress off your back to make you do as I ask? Well?"

Annunziata sat down. Even now she was more angry than frightened. She said, "I will do as you say, because there are two of you and you are stronger than I am. But you cannot stay here forever, and when you go, I will send for the police. Then we shall see."

"What shall we see?"

"You are criminals. You have broken in here. To— to—"

"Well? What will you say to the police? We have broken in. Prove it. To steal. To steal what?"

"That black box. I know what it is. I have heard of such things. It is a listening machine."

"A listening machine! They will laugh at you. Why should anyone trouble to put such a thing in *your* kitchen? Are you a politician? An ambassador? A general?"

"I am a householder," said Annunziata with dignity. "This is my house. And you have broken into it. The police will draw their own conclusions."

The tall man had finished his work. He had removed each of the tiny black staples that had held the wire in position, and had drawn in the loose end of the wire through the ventilator above the kitchen window. There was no sign that anything had been disturbed. Both men, she noticed, were wearing gloves.

"I think it would be better for you if you said nothing at all to the police."

"I'm not afraid of you," said Annunziata. "As soon as you have gone, I shall go straight to the police. They have pictures of criminals such as you. I will point you out to them. You will not escape easily."

The stout man examined Annunziata carefully. What she had said was true. This middle-aged, gray-haired queenly woman was not afraid of him. He was something of a specialist in the inspiring of fear, and was unlikely to be mistaken about it.

He considered the problem, rubbing his round chin with his stubby fingers. Then he said, "I don't think you have any idea of what you are doing. That we are in your house is unimportant. You have not been hurt. Nothing of yours has been damaged. But if you do what you say and go to the police, then it will be different. Then you will be interfering with people more important than you. And you will suffer for it."

"You tell me," said Annunziata, her voice choked with anger and outrage, "that nothing of mine has been damaged. *What of Milo? What of my husband, Milo?*"

The two men looked at each other. The thin man, speaking for the first time, said, "He was knocked down by the Englishman, in his car. It had nothing to do with us."

"It had something to do with you. You *knew* that he was going out that night. You knew it because you had heard it, with that box of yours."

"This box is one thing you are going to forget about," said the thin man. It had disappeared into his pocket, with the coil of black wire and the little envelope full of black staples.

"I shall *not* forget about it, and I shall see that the police do not forget about it."

The thin man slid a hand inside his jacket and pulled out a leather wallet. From it he took a newspaper clipping, creased and faded with much fingering, and unfolded it.

"Read it," he said.

"Why should I read it?" Annunziata took it suspiciously. "What has it to do with me? What is it about?"

"It is about a young girl who was found by the police in a street in Palermo." The thin man's finger pointed to a paragraph. "There, you see. It describes how she had been injured. It does not tell you the whole truth. I saw the girl myself, afterward. The left breast had to be removed entirely."

Annunziata was staring at the newspaper clipping. Her eyes flickered between the print and the man who was holding it. She said, in a whisper, "Why do you show me this?"

"It was not the girl's fault. It was her family. They had been stupid. They did not heed a warning—two warnings. Then this happened. It was sad for them because she was their only daughter." The thin man's mouth opened, showing discolored teeth. "You have a daughter yourself. Bear in mind that what happened in Palermo could happen, just as easily, in Florence."

He folded the newspaper, put it back in the wallet, and put the wallet away. All his movements were neat and economical.

After the men had gone Annunziata sat for a long time, only her lips moving. Two hours later Tina found her, still sitting there. She saw the look in her eye and ran to her, saying, "Mother, what is it? What is wrong?"

The woman put an arm around her waist and said, "Nothing is wrong, *carissima*, and nothing shall be wrong."

5

The Commander Gets Up Steam

It would appear [wrote Harfield Moss to his colleague in Pittsburgh] that some sort of hitch has developed. I got the red light about it yesterday. It came through third-hand, because none of the principals here can afford to be seen talking to each other. The opposition is very much in evidence and everyone is watching everyone else like cats around the cream bowl. It did occur to me that the delay might be a ploy to jack up the price, but I don't believe it. They're as anxious to close the deal as we are. Anyway, I'll stay on for a week or so to see how things turn out. Nothing much else to report from this end. There seems to be some sort of election coming up. All the walls are covered with posters, and loudspeaker cars and helicopters are all over the place. The Communists are making most of the noise. They seem to think they may swing a few more seats this time. A man I had lunch with the other day—an Englishman, called Broke—has been arrested for hit and run. I'm told you can get seven years for it. . . .

"I've had a letter," said the Commander. It had become a daily routine for Tina and Elizabeth to meet in his flat. "I can't make all of it out. The spelling's phonetic and the handwriting doesn't win any prizes. It's from a man who signs himself Labro Radicelli."

"Labro!" said Elizabeth. "Isn't that the man Robert was talking about?"

"Let me see it," said Tina.

The Commander handed the letter to her. It was a double

page of green deckle-edge paper, and the laborious writing was in purple ink.

"Did you keep the envelope?" said Elizabeth.

"Naturally. But if you're pinning your hopes on the postmark, you can unpin them. Like all Italian postmarks, it is illegible. It might end in *o*."

"And conceivably begins with an *A* or an *E*."

"Equally likely," agreed the Commander. "What do you make of the letter, Tina?"

"It is clear this man has information to sell. It relates to Signor Broke. He asks for a hundred thousand lire, to be sent to him at the Poste Restante in Arezzo. Then you will get the information."

"In other words," said the Commander, "if we're prepared to send off sixty or seventy pounds into the blue, we might, or might not, get something back for it. I'm not playing games like that."

"Oughtn't we to hand the letter over to the police?" said Elizabeth. "If he's got information about the accident, he ought to be *made* to tell it. He can't try to sell it. It's a criminal offense."

"Trouble is, he doesn't say information about the accident. He just says information. It might be anything."

"All the same, it sounds shady. If he'd been honest, surely he'd have given us his address, so that we could have gone along and talked to him about it."

"Agreed," said the Commander.

Tina said, "Do you wish to speak to this man? If so, I can probably find out where he is living."

"You can?"

"It would not be too difficult. The Radicellis are a large family, many hundreds of them. They come mostly from Arezzo. My mother's nephew, the son of her elder brother, married a Radicelli. They would know what part of the family Labro came from, you see. If he is frightened to stay in Florence, it is most probable that he has gone out into the country to stay with them for a time."

"Sounds hopeful," said the Commander. "See what your mother can tell us."

A cloud passed over Tina's face. "I will ask her," she said.

The other two stared at her.

"What's up, Tina?" said Elizabeth. "Is your mother in some sort of trouble?"

"It's nothing," said Tina. "Since the funeral she has been a little upset. I will see what I can do."

After she had gone, Elizabeth said, "Whatever we find out, we ought to keep Robert's lawyer, Toscafundi, informed. After all, he's the man who's going to fight the case for us."

"True," said the Commander. He said it reluctantly. It was foreign to his nature to fight battles by proxy. "I suppose he'll have to be kept in the picture. I ought to go along and make my number with him."

The Toscafundi office was in an old building in the Corso Borgo degli Albizi. The entrance, fronting the street, was a thirty-foot archway embossed with the arms of the Cardinal Prince who had originally owned the building. A notice pinned to the lintel of the door said: "It is strictly and absolutely forbidden to bring bicycles or perambulators into the interior." The hallway itself was entirely occupied by a low-slung open Maserati coupé, with olive-green coachwork and old-fashioned brass headlights. The Commander squeezed past it and located the lift, which lurched up with him to the third floor. Avvocato Toscafundi, whom he had warned by telephone, kept him waiting just long enough to suggest what an important and busy lawyer he was.

"Please be seated," he said. "This is indeed a sad case.

You are a friend of Mr. Broke's. Will you please have a cigarette?"

"Don't smoke myself,'" said the Commander. "Can't afford it."

Toscafundi smiled faintly, and inserted a cigarette into a long holder. He said, "I have just received a copy of the *verbale* from the Procura."

"Verbale?"

"It is the statement Broke made to Sostituto Procuratore Risso. An ambitious young man, that one. But reasonably capable."

The Commander turned rapidly through the half-dozen pages of typescript. "There doesn't seem to be much here. Nothing new, that is."

"I agree. It confirms the facts as we knew them. Broke was out in his car that night. He drove down the Via Canina. He has no recollection of striking Milo Zecchi."

There was something in the lawyer's tone that the Commander found disturbing. He said, "When you put it like that it sounds as though you think he *may* have hit him."

"It is a possibility which has to be borne in mind."

"I should have thought our job was to put it right out of our minds."

"That, if I may say so, Commander, is because you are not a lawyer. My task, as I see it, is to visualize all possibilities, and to advise my client as to his best course in the light of these possibilities."

"I'm not sure that I follow you."

"There are two points in Broke's statement that I find disturbing, and if I find them disturbing, be sure that the court will, too. First, that he suffers from periodical fits of amnesia. Secondly, that he can offer no real explanation of how his fog lamp came to be broken. Not just cracked, you see. The glass shattered and the metal rim dented. He speaks of children playing. But no one saw them. No one heard them."

"Are you suggesting—better get this straight—that Broke ought to plead guilty?"

"It would not be a light responsibility to advise him to take such a course, but I might have to do so." The lawyer shifted in his chair, leaning forward slightly, as though to underline his words. "If this case was mishandled it could have very serious consequences." He pulled another paper out of the pile on his desk. "I have seen the report of the autopsy. Milo Zecchi was alive *for at least two hours* after the main blow on his head, which probably paralyzed him but did not kill him. Can you visualize the reactions of a court to this evidence, the picture which they will form of old Milo, lying in the gutter for two whole hours, helpless, dying, but not dead? So that had the motorist stopped and summoned help, *he might still have been saved.*"

"It raises the stakes," said the Commander uncomfortably, "but why do you suggest that it alters our course?"

"It offers us, if I may pursue your own metaphor, Commander, a choice of courses. On the one hand—and I appreciate that this is what you wish to do—we could fight the case, as you would put it, tooth and nail. We could say that he did *not* hit Milo. That the identification of the car by this witness, Calzaletta, was either a mistake or a downright lie. That the damage to the fog lamp was unconnected with the accident. We could say all that. But . . . if the prisoner is disbelieved, if he is thought to be covering up, it will follow that his failure to stop and render assistance will also be thought to be deliberate. And the consequences of that would be very serious indeed."

"All right. What's the alternative?"

"The alternative is for Broke to plead guilty—to the lesser offense. To admit, on the evidence, that he may have struck Milo. But to say that he had no recollection of doing so. In that case the evidence of his amnesia could be used for him, not against him. You follow me?"

"Yes," said the Commander grimly. "I follow you."

"Excellent. Now, if there is nothing else just at this moment—"

"There is one thing I came round to tell you. It may not fit in with the rather definite view of the case which you seem to have formed, but you may as well have it. It's about this man Labro Radicelli...."

"Ah, Labro, yes."

Toscafundi listened politely. At the end he said, "I fear it is a wild goose, but there is no reason why you should not chase it."

"Then you don't think Labro has anything to do with the case."

"I am perfectly sure he has not, and I advise you to forget all about him. Thank you, my dear." This was to a girl, wearing her hair over one eye, and a skirt so short that it hardly started. She had come in carrying hat and briefcase. "Will you telephone the Commendatore and tell him I shall be a few minutes late."

"I am sorry to have made you late for your appointment."

"Think no more of it."

The two men traveled down in the jerky lift together. When they reached the hall the porter was already holding open the door of the Maserati. Toscafundi said, "Perhaps I can give you a lift somewhere?"

"Thank you," said the Commander, "but I enjoy walking." The olive-green coupé slid confidently out into the traffic, which seemed to open up and make way for it.

The Commander stood for a moment looking after it. His beard was at a dangerous angle. Then he swung around on his heel and stumped off in the opposite direction.

* * *

"I understand, Commander," said the Sindaco, "that you are working in the interest of Robert Broke. In such a case, you may undoubtedly count on my assistance. Signor Roberto, as you know, was a companion in arms during the war, and such experiences forge bonds which are not lightly broken."

"That's right."

"Nevertheless, at this precise moment it is hard to see exactly what I can do."

"For a start I'd like to know what you think of a lawyer called Toscafundi."

The Sindaco smiled faintly.

"I know him, of course," he said. "In fact, I was qualified as a lawyer myself, and we passed our examinations at the same time. Then our ways parted. I branched off into politics. He adhered to the law. He has undoubtedly made a lot more money than I have." The Sindaco glanced around his homely-looking parlor. "Whether he has had such a satisfying career is another matter."

"But do you think he's a good lawyer?"

"He is a very successful one. Probably the most successful in Florence."

"Is he honest?"

"Really, Commander, that is not a question you should ask one lawyer about another. I think he will fight very hard, and very skillfully, for the man who pays his fees."

"Quite so," said the Commander. *"But it isn't Broke who's paying his fees."*

The Sindaco opened his heavily lidded eyes and stared at Comber. "Indeed," he said. "Then who is?"

"Professor Bruno Bronzini."

"That is very generous of him. Is he also a friend of Robert Broke?"

"As far as I know, they have met once. At a party, at

130

the Professor's villa. In the course of which they had a heated argument, which nearly developed into an open quarrel."

"I can imagine that they would not have found each other sympathetic. Robert Broke is a stoic. The Professor is an epicurean."

"Then why should he help him?"

"I imagine you will find the answer to that in the forthcoming elections. The case against Broke is being handled by Antonio Risso. He is a political animal. This year he is standing for a seat on the Municipal Council. If he is successful, next time it will be for the National Assembly. Who knows—maybe he will end up as Minister of Grace and Justice. The Professor is of the opposite party to Risso. He would think it well worth paying Toscafundi's fees to put him down. This case has already aroused feelings out of all proportion to its merits."

"I noticed the crowds at the church," said the Commander grimly. "I realized then that we might be up against it. And that was before people knew that Milo was alive for two hours after he was hit."

"Who told you that?"

"Toscafundi."

"And how did he know?"

"He said he had seen something he called the *verbale*. I imagined that the autopsy report was part of it. I didn't look at it closely."

"It is nothing of the sort. The *verbale* is a record of the two interrogations. The first one at the police station, and the subsequent one at the Procura. Neither of them would mention the medical evidence, or any other part of the prosecution's case. This is a matter that wants thinking about. It needs most careful consideration. Thus." The Sindaco held out a thick left hand, to tick off the points, "First, there was no need to bring forward this medical evidence

131

at all. In a legal sense, it does not affect the issue of guilt. Although it might affect the feelings of the court. But to bring it forward demonstrates to us the danger of a heavy sentence. Therefore, it could have been the first move toward a bargain with the defense. *If* they will plead guilty to the lesser offense, they will not press the graver charge of hitting him, and running away and leaving him." The Sindaco, who had started with his thumb, had now reached his little finger. The Commander noticed that the top joint was missing. "So we can deduce a final point? That their case is *not* as strong or as conclusive as they would wish us to believe. Yes. I think, perhaps, we can."

"I've got a very simple mind," said the Commander. "I think Bronzini was up to something crooked. He wanted Broke out of the way. Very likely Milo's being knocked down was an accident. It's a dangerous stretch of road. Somebody identified the body, was afraid to tell the police, but told the Professor, who saw his chance and took it. All he had to do was to bribe someone to tell the police they'd seen a car driving away and noticed the number. And send someone round with a hammer to smash Broke's fog lamp."

The Sindaco listened to this in silence. Then he said, with a smile, "You realize that there is a third, and even simpler, explanation. That Broke did it."

When Commander Comber got home he picked up two letters that had arrived in his absence. One was from an old naval friend who had gone to New Zealand, and was so enthusiastic about it that the Commander suspected he was getting bored. The other contained a sizable check with a compliment slip from a London newspaper. It was while he was putting this away that he realized that something was wrong.

The contents of his desk were as methodically arranged as all his other possessions. Someone had been through them, replacing them carefully, but not quite carefully enough. Also, the drawer of the desk had been opened with a key that did not belong to it, and the person who had opened it had only succeeded in partially relocking it. Its contents, too, were out of order.

The Commander sat for a long time, stroking his beard and considering the evidence. The look on his face was one of deep satisfaction. There had been moments that afternoon when he had been worried. He had distrusted Avvocato Toscafundi, and had accordingly discounted much of what he said. But the Sindaco he had liked, and his views on the case had had a disturbing ring of common sense about them. Now, however, all doubts were dispelled. The enemy was there, all right. A smudge of smoke on the horizon, a blip on the radar screen, invisible to the naked eye but undeniably and satisfactorily *there*.

6

Wild Geese

On the morning of the third day after his arrest, Broke was moved, handcuffed, from the Questura to the town prison.

The Murate prison, standing at it does at the east end of the Via Ghibellina, had suffered the full impact of the flood. Now, refurbished with a new set of wrought-iron grills on its windows, and with its woodwork freshly painted, it looked, Broke thought, a good deal more agreeable than the grim police headquarters in the town center.

Here, on the afternoon of the third day, the Consul came to visit him.

He found Broke reading a battered copy of *Paradise Lost*.

"It belonged to an Englishman," he said. "They had him here for six months, while they were trying to get up a case for false pretenses. He translated three of the cantos into Italian hexameters. Some of it's not bad at all."

"I trust they won't keep *you* here for six months," said the Consul. "How are things going?"

Broke marked his place in the book with an old bus ticket, shut it carefully, and put it down on the bed. Then he said, "Toscafundi was here again this morning. He seems very anxious for me to plead guilty."

"On a lesser charge?"

"The charge would be involuntary manslaughter. In view of the state of the lighting, and the bad reputation that road has got for accidents, the court might accept the view that I'd hit Milo without realizing it. I'd still be legally responsible, but I'd get off a good deal more lightly than if they thought I'd hit him, realized what I'd done, and left him to die."

"And that's the course that Toscafundi advises?"

"Yes."

"It's reasonable. All the same, there'll be three disappointed people if you do. Your friend Commander Comber, your housekeeper, Tina Zecchi—and my daughter Elizabeth."

"A formidable trio," said Broke politely. "What is *their* idea of what happened?"

"It's a bit complicated. But as far as I can gather it goes something like this. Professor Bronzini is up to something. Possibly criminal, at least shady. He thinks you may be a danger to his plans. Therefore he has—I think the correct Americanism is—'framed' you. If you are tucked away in jail awaiting trial you won't be in any position to interfere with his schemes."

"I see," said Broke. "And why has he sent me his own lawyer? A fit of conscience, do you think? Or to disarm my suspicions? Or is the idea that if he can get me to plead guilty, he will be certain that I shall get some sort of sentence?"

"The latter, I fancy."

"And how do they suggest that the frame-up was operated?"

"They think that someone saw Milo lying in the gutter, recognized him, knew that the Professor was his patron, and telephoned him. Someone was then suborned to say they had seen your car at the scene of the accident. And to add a little color to the charge, your fog lamp was broken during the night."

"Ingenious. It makes the Professor a positive Moriarty of crime. I don't see him in that role somehow. Do you?"

135

"To be honest, I don't believe a word of it."

"And what particular shady work do they suggest he's up to?"

"I don't think they've quite worked that out yet. But it would be something to do with the sale of Etruscan relics."

Broke thought about this, riffling through the pages of *Paradise Lost* as he did so. It seemed as though he was anxious to get away from reality back to the Garden of Eden, to the mighty opposites of Good and Evil at warfare in the starry void. Sir Gerald had talked to many men in prisons in different parts of the world, but never to one so apparently disinterested in his own fate.

"Though I don't suppose there's anything in that idea, either," he added.

"I'm not sure," said Broke. "There *was* one rather odd thing. When I drove out to the digging that afternoon, the Professor's steward, Ferri, showed me round. He seemed quite knowledgeable about it. He said it was the clan tomb of a well-known Etruscan pirate, thought to be called Thryns. There was a picture of him, on his warship. He was wearing a very elaborate and distinctive helmet. Later on, when we were going out of the tomb, I wanted to look into one of the lesser chambers, on the other side of the central passage. Ferri didn't seem keen on the idea. He hurried me past it. But I had my torch with me, and I did happen to see something in it. It was the same helmet that I'd seen in the picture."

"The helmet itself?"

"That's right."

Sir Gerald thought this out. He said, "I don't quite see—"

"If Thryns was the man who owned the helmet, and he was head of the whole family or clan, the helmet would have been in *his* tomb. Easily the most important tomb in the whole complex. The treasure house. The thing they are meant to be still looking for."

"I see," said Sir Gerald. "You're suggesting that they may already have found the important treasure, and are keeping quiet about it."

"Well, it's one explanation."

"I *told* you so," said Elizabeth. "I *knew* there was something going on. We've *got* to do something about it."

"But, my dear old girl, even if Broke is right about the helmet there's no reason to suppose it had anything to do with his accident."

"There was a connection and we shall find it."

The Consul sighed. He was very fond of his second daughter. He had watched her grow up from an amiable dumpling to a leggy equestrienne of twelve; from an intellectual snob of seventeen to a reasonably balanced young lady of twenty-four. She was no longer his daughter. He realized that. She was an independent person in her own right. The umbilical cord had been finally severed. But the habit of years was hard to break and he still worried about her sometimes. He had got over his earlier apprehensions that she would marry someone disastrous. He was now beginning to fear that she might not marry at all.

"Don't do it," said Elizabeth.

"Do what?"

"Sigh like that. I won't involve you in anything undiplomatic, I promise you."

"I wasn't thinking of myself," said Sir Gerald. "And to tell you the truth, I wasn't thinking of you. I was thinking of Broke."

"You mean, if we thrash round we may make matters worse for him."

"That's exactly what I mean."

"That's because in your heart of hearts you think he did it. You think he hit Milo when he was having one of those fits, and knew nothing about it. Admit it."

"I—"

"Confession is good for the soul."

"I will not have opinions thrust upon me. I am too old to be bullied. I admit nothing."

"It's what you think all the same, and that's why you want to get him off as lightly as possible. I think he *didn't* do it, and I want to prove it, and get him off altogether."

The Consul sighed again.

Sostituto Procuratore Antonio Risso laid down the folder, already pregnant with documents, upon the table of his official superior, the Procuratore della Repubblica, and said, "The scientific evidence now available from our laboratories in Rome appears to me to be of a conclusive nature—the microphotographs particularly. You have studied the microphotographs?"

"I have seen the microphotographs."

"I think we might almost regard the evidence as complete."

"I don't agree," said the Procuratore. "The scientific evidence is convincing. It demonstrates beyond any question that Broke's car struck Milo Zecchi. And there can be no reason, I agree, to suppose that anyone but Broke was driving it at the time."

"Then—"

"But you are pressing a much more serious charge. The charge that he struck him knowingly, and drove away afterward. What evidence have we of that?"

"The evidence of the woman Calzaletta. She states that she was walking along on the other side of the road, farther down, and that she heard a car coming fast. Then the squeal of its brakes—which made her turn around. She saw that

138

the car had skidded, and come to a stop. Then, *after a pause*, it started up again and came toward her. She was interested enough by now to take note of its number. And when the body was found next morning, she very properly gave information to the police."

"Very properly," agreed the Procuratore.

"The skid marks and braking marks were still visible next morning, and entirely support her story."

"And she said that this happened at half past ten. How does she fix the time?"

"She had been to visit her sister. She left the house at twenty past ten and she knows that it takes her exactly ten minutes to reach the Via Canina."

"It is curious," said the Procuratore, "that people who are usually entirely vague as to what time it is have only to become involved in criminal proceedings, when their memories become wonderfully exact."

"Have we any reason to doubt her story?"

"None at all. But then, have we reason, either, to doubt the story of the keeper of the cemetery? What is his name?" The Procuratore was leafing through the pile of documents on the table in front of him. "Carlo Frutelli."

"Frutelli is, in my view, an unreliable witness."

"Oh! Why?"

"He is old, and stupid. And, I suspect, more than a little deaf."

"He says, quite definitely, that *he* heard a car driving down the road. *He* heard the squealing of brakes, and the sound of a car skidding. And he is quite certain that this happened at half past *eleven*. How do you explain that?"

"Quite simple. He was right about what he heard, but wrong about the time."

"And yet," said the Procuratore maliciously, "he, too, seems able to fix it with commendable accuracy. Curiously enough, he, too, had been visiting his sister. He says that he left her house at eleven o'clock and that it takes him exactly thirty minutes to walk from there to his lodge inside the cemetery gate."

"Then he is mistaken as to the time he left his sister's house."

"Have you confirmed that by questioning his sister?"

"I had not thought it necessary."

"Then do so. It is a mistake, in cases of this sort, to pursue only the evidence that tells in favor of the case one is pursuing."

"I hope I know my duty."

"My dear Antonio, I am certain you know your duty. And I am certain you are doing it admirably. But we must have *all* the facts."

The Commander studied the small-scale map, and looked at his watch. It was five o'clock. He had about four hours of daylight left and he reckoned he was going to need them all.

The list that Tina had made out for him contained the names of twenty-six families in the Arezzo area allied by ties of blood to the Radicellis. The map was based on a prewar survey. Most of the roads, and many of the houses, had been built since the war. A less resolute man would have despaired. The Commander ran his fingers through his beard, ticked off one more name (a deaf farmer with a paralyzed wife and four suspicious dogs), and got on with it.

It was shortly after six when he turned into the muddy track which, according to a board nailed to a tree, led to a farm called San Giovanni. The surface of the track was so unpromising that he hesitated. Then he saw that one other car at least had been that way. There were the marks of a set of new Michelin all-weather tires on the road.

"If he can do it, I can," said the Commander. Five bumping and skidding minutes later he had corkscrewed around the last corner and arrived at the farmhouse. He rang the bell, rehearsing the story he had already used fourteen times that afternoon. The door was opened by a very old lady in black.

The Commander explained that he had been sent by the Ministry of National Insurance to speak to Labro Radicelli about certain irregularities in his employment record.

Most of this went clear over the old lady's head, but she got the part that mattered.

She said, "You wish to speak to Labro?"

The Commander's heart leaped up. He said, "Yes, yes. That is correct. To speak to Labro."

"I will see. You are an Englishman?"

"Yes."

"In the war we had an English soldier here. He came from Australia."

"Did he though," said the Commander.

"He had been a prisoner of war, you understand. He promised to marry my granddaughter." The old lady laughed disconcertingly.

"And did he?"

"He went back to Australia. I think he was married already. I will see if Labro is finished talking to the other gentleman."

She scuttled off. Twenty minutes passed. The other gentleman had not finished. The Commander examined the photographs on the wall. There were twelve of them, and they were all weddings. He hoped that the Radicelli granddaughter had found an acceptable substitute for her unfaithful Australian. There were footsteps in the passage, the door opened, and a middle-aged, red-faced man came in, kicking the door shut behind him.

"Are you Labro Radicelli?"

"I have that impression."

141

When he got near enough, the Commander could smell the drink on him. He said, "Then I have a proposition to make to you."

"On the subject of National Insurance," said Labro, with a smile that showed his brown and broken teeth.

"That was a subterfuge."

"It was unnecessary. I know precisely why you are here."

"That will save trouble."

"Your name is Comber." Labro made quite a creditable effort at the name. "I wrote a letter to you. You are a Captain in the British Navy."

The Commander accepted the promotion without comment. There was something in Labro's manner that disturbed him and he wanted to get to the bottom of it.

"I wrote to you because you are a friend of the other Englishman, the one who is in prison for killing Milo Zecchi. For knocking him down and leaving him lying in the gutter. Correct?"

The Commander's beard came forward a few inches, but still he said nothing.

"Now you want my help. Before, I offered him my help. If he had taken it, who knows? None of this trouble might have happened. But he would have none of it. He turned up his English nose. Now I fear you are too late. The offer is withdrawn." He slapped his hand down on the table. The Commander's silence was disconcerting him. He wanted to fight, and could find no opponent except himself.

"The goods I had to offer are no longer for sale."

"What were the goods?"

"I have no doubt that you would like to know that. You would pay handsomely now for the information. You have come out here with your pockets bulging with money. Then let me tell you, Captain, exactly what you and your friend can do. . . . " He articulated the street-boy obscenity carefully.

"I see," said the Commander. He walked to the door. "Then it would seem that I've had my journey for nothing." His calmness infuriated Labro. For a moment it looked as though he was going to hit him. But there was a warning in the Commander's eye that restrained him.

"If you should change your mind, you know where you can get in touch with me. I'll wish you good evening."

The Commander walked out into the farmyard. There was a suspicion that had to be confirmed. The tracks of the Michelin tires were visible in the film of mud over the cobblestones. They led around toward the back of the building. The Commander followed them carefully.

7

Statics and Dynamics

"It is *my* house," said Annunziata. "All of it. The front part and the back part. Every room. And I say that Dindoni shall not stay in it for another day."

"We can't turn him out into the street," said Tina.

"Then he shall be given a week to find other accommodation."

"What of the business?"

"Why should I care about the business? As I told you, I have money. Sufficient for our needs."

"If you're sure of that," said Tina doubtfully. "Perhaps we could rent the room at the back to an artist. There are many who require accommodation. I saw an advertisement in the papers only yesterday— God in heaven!"

She had been turning the pages of the *Corriere di Firenze* as she spoke. A photograph in the news section had suddenly caught her eye.

"What is it?" said her mother.

"Look! Look! That woman."

"What does it say, *cara?* Read it to me."

"It says: 'An important witness in the case of the Englishman Broke, accused of running down and killing a citizen of Florence, Milo Zecchi, is Maria Calzaletta...'"

"Well?"

"There is a photograph of her. See?" She pushed the newspaper across. Her mother had found her glasses. She said, "It is a face that has a certain familiarity."

"It's Maria. Dindoni's woman. She works at the café on the corner. I have seen her a hundred times."

"Are you sure?"

"It is not a good photograph," agreed Tina. "But yes, I am certain of it."

"What does it mean?"

"It means that what we had thought is true. There *was* a conspiracy. Dindoni arranged it all. He desired this business. He could not wait."

"Dindoni?" said Annuniziata doubtfully.

"Not on his own. He had help, of course. Do you remember what Milo told us? He was being followed by two men. We laughed at him at the time. But it was true. Dindoni must have told them that Milo was going out that night. And yet—" Tina's enthusiasm suffered a setback. "How *could* he have known? He was so careful to talk about it only in this room. What is wrong, Mother?"

"Nothing."

"You do not look well."

"It's nothing. It was speaking of Milo. You brought it all back to me. What will you do now?"

"I shall question this woman."

"That's good," said Annunziata. "You question her." She seemed anxious to get her daughter out of the room.

Mercurio was sitting in his car at the corner of the street and he climbed out as she came up. Tina's first thought was to ignore him. Then it occurred to her that she could do with some support. She said, "I have business in this café. You can come with me if you wish."

The front room, as was usual at that early hour in the evening, was empty, but they could hear someone moving about inside the alcove behind the beaded curtains. They went through. Maria was dusting one of the shelves. She suspended operations when she saw them, looked indifferently at Tina, more agreeably at Mercurio.

"What can I do for you?"

"We would like some information," said Tina. She slammed the newspaper down on the table. "Is that your photograph?"

"I expect so," said Maria, without looking at it.

"Then it *is* you who are giving evidence to the police."

"I told them what I saw—and heard."

Tina laughed. It was not a pleasant sound.

"You told them what your fancy man, Dindo, ordered you to tell them."

"I told them the truth."

"Strange that you should have chanced to be in the Via Canina at half past ten."

"Is there any law against it?"

"Why were you not here? That is the busy time here, isn't it? As much as a dump like this ever can be busy."

Maria ignored this insult. She said, "If you want to know, we shut at nine o'clock that evening. Old Tortoni agreed to it. I told him I had to visit my sister. She lives near the Porta Romana. I was on my way back from her house when this thing happened."

Mercurio said, "That sounds to me like a story. It is something you have learned to recite to the police. Now tell us what really happened."

"It happened as I have said."

"Odd," said Tina, "that you should have decided, suddenly, to visit your sister when it is well known that you have not spoken to her for two years—since she married your boyfriend."

"That's a lie," said Maria, a spot of color appearing in each cheek.

"And since when has anyone coming from the Porta Romana needed to go down the Via Canina?"

"I refuse to answer your questions."

"Who was here that night, at nine o'clock when you shut the café?"

"Who . . . ?"

"Those two men were here, weren't they? The fat one and the thin one."

Maria said, "I don't know what you're talking about." She said it without confidence.

"Oh, come now," said Tina. "You can't be as stupid as that. They've been here every night for the last ten days, putting their feet up and having drinks on the house."

Mercurio suddenly said, in a loud and authoritative voice, "I smell blood."

The woman stared at him. Maria had turned pale.

"I have certain divine attributes. I can look forward into the future, and back into the past. And I can tell you this." He transfixed Maria with a look of somber power. "On the night you are speaking of, something horrible happened, *in this room.*"

Maria said, "Don't look at me like that. Nothing happened here. Or if it did, it had nothing to do with me. I wasn't here—"

The words were coming faster and faster, and ended with a noise that was half a gasp and half a scream, but this was unrelated to Mercurio. It was caused by the stout man's coming through the beaded curtains. He said, "Are these people annoying you, *carissima?*"

Tina said, "Oh!" Mercurio, who still seemed to be in the grip of some external force, swung slowly around, looked at the stout man, and said, "The blood is on your hands."

"I think you had better go, both of you," said the stout man. "You are upsetting the management."

Tina said, "We've got as much right to be here as you have, fatty."

The man ignored her. He stepped quickly up to Mercurio

and grabbed him by the collar of his coat. He might as well have tried to hold an eel. Mercurio's curiously mobile body twisted under his grasp, and the man was left holding the coat.

Tina looked about her for a weapon. The nearest was a cue from the bar's billiard table. She screamed out, "Take your hands off him, you beast," and swung, butt end foremost, at his head.

The man sidestepped the blow easily. Maria, who was standing behind him, was not so lucky. The heavy butt hit her on the side of the head with a noise like that of an old and well-oiled bat meeting a leather cricket ball, and she dropped.

The stout man ignored them both. He had eyes only for Mercurio. He said, "If you want to turn this into a striptease act, let us play it that way." He darted forward, shot out his hands, grabbed Mercurio's silk shirt, and pulled. It came away with a ripping sound, exposing a blue silk undershirt.

Mercurio said, "Beast," and threw himself at the man, who hit him in the stomach. This, at least, was his intention. But Mercurio, who was as agile as his opponent, half turned at the last moment, took the blow on his hip, and flung his arms around the stout man, clasping him to him. Then, as the man jerked his head away, he buried his teeth in his ear.

Most people when bitten in the ear would scream. The stout man did not. He disengaged his right arm quite calmly, put his hand up, and felt for Mercurio's eyes. Mercurio let go of his ear and twisted his face away.

The hand followed it.

The stout man said, hardly raising his voice, "I am going to blind you."

It was Mercurio who screamed.

This brought Tina back into the fight. Up to that point she had been trying to assure herself that Maria was not dead. Now she picked up the fallen cue, swung it carefully, like a golfer addressing a drive, and hit the stout man very hard on the back of the head, just above the point where his neck joined his skull.

The man folded up. His knees buckled and he fell, without losing his grip on Mercurio, who fell with him. Mercurio seemed to have fainted.

Tina seized the nearest bottle, jerked out the cork, and poured the contents over Mercurio's face.

The boy spluttered, sat up, and said, "Stop that. What on earth are you doing with that stuff? It's gin."

Maria, on the floor, gave a groan and rolled over onto her face.

"Thank God!" said Tina. "I thought I'd killed her."

"What about that one?"

"Him! I don't care if I have killed him."

Mercurio looked at the bodies on the floor, looked at Maria, still holding the billiard cue, looked down at himself, and started to giggle.

"Do you know," he said, "I think we'd better get away from here. Right away. I'll drive you out to my house."

Tina said, doubtfully, "All right. But I hope we aren't stopped. You look terrible. And smell terrible, too."

They reached the Villa Rasenna unchallenged. Mercurio parked the car and led the way to a side door.

"We can go straight up to my bedroom."

"To your . . . ?"

"Oh, that's all right. Come *on.*"

In the bedroom he drew up a chair for Tina, poured her out a drink, and disappeared into the bathroom with an armful of clean clothes. The events in the café seemed to have given him a certain confidence.

When he reappeared twenty minutes later, he was his dapper self again.

"That's much better," said Tina. "You can hardly smell the gin at all. I'm sorry I poured it all over you. I thought it was water."

"You were splendid," said Mercurio.

"You were pretty good yourself," said Tina. "You nearly bit his ear off."

"I wasn't too bad, was I?"

They admired themselves, in silence, for a few moments.

"Did you know," said Mercurio, "that I have certain quite remarkable attributes?"

"One can detect that."

"That is the reason that Bruno adopted me. He was looking for Tages."

"For who?"

"It's part of the Etruscan religion. They believed that every so often a baby called Tages was born, who had divinity."

"How would they know?" said Tina cautiously.

"They would know because he would be perfect in every particular. Physical and mental. His proportions would be exact. He would excel at all natural sports, like running and jumping and riding and swimming."

"How could you tell—babies don't ride or swim, do they?"

"If your proportions are correct, and you suffer from no defect, these things follow."

"I suppose they must."

"But it is not only physical things. The mental side is even more important. It became clear at a very early age that I had exceptional mental powers. Particularly in the field of mathematics. At an early age I could perform astonishing feats of mental arithmetic. When I was seven I gave a demonstration at the University of Perugia—that is Bruno's university. In front of the professors of the mathematical faculty. I multiplied seven-figure numbers in my head, and cubed other numbers of up to five figures."

"Goodness," said Tina. The events of the evening were combining with the drink to produce an overpowering desire for sleep. Mercurio seemed to have got his second wind.

"It did not stop at that. Infant prodigies of this sort are not uncommon. They burn themselves out. I progressed to more sophisticated fields. At nine I was interested in permutations and combinations. At eleven, statics and dynamics. At twelve, the calculus."

"Did it do any good? I mean, knowing all these things— was it any use to you?"

Mercurio grinned, losing some of his divinity in the process. "I'll show you how useful it was," he said. "Come along."

He led the way out of the room and down the back stairs, into the basement. They went along a corridor and came to a stout oak door, set in the thickness of the wall, which Mercurio unlocked with a key from his chain.

"Goodness," said Tina. "What on earth is it?"

"Oh, this is Bruno's tomb."

"He's going to be buried here?"

"That's what he thinks."

"With all these pots and statues and things? Aren't they terribly valuable?"

"They're all right," said Mercurio indifferently. "But they're not the things that really matter. Look at the wall over there. No, a bit lower down. That's right. Tap it with your knuckles."

"It's not stone at all. It's iron."

"It's the door of a safe. Iron painted to look like stone. Clever, isn't it?"

"How does it open?"

"Like this."

Mercurio had taken out a penknife. He pushed the blade into a crack, and a square panel hinged outward, revealing a dial.

"It's a combination lock. If you set the right eight numbers in the right order on the dial, the door opens."

"Do you know the answer?"

"Nobody knows the answer, except Bruno. Or that's what he thought."

Tina was examining the numbers on the lock. She felt excited and wide awake again. She slid the smooth steel dial around with her finger, hearing it click as it moved. She set one or two complete numbers. "Goodness," she said. "You'd have to try for a long time to hit on the right ones—that is, if you didn't know it—wouldn't you?"

"Eight sets of numerals, from one to nine, but excluding zero, will give you forty-three million, forty-six thousand, seven hundred and twenty-one possibilities."

"It would take some time to try all those, wouldn't it?"

"If you took six seconds to set the dial and try the door, and kept it up without stopping, you could do it in eight years, sixty-eight days, and nine hours approximately."

"Approximately?"

"That makes no allowance for leap years."

"I don't think I'll try it, thank you."

"There's no need. As it happens, quite recently I have managed to work out the correct number, but this is the first chance I've had to try it."

"But how . . . ?"

"Few people could have done it," admitted Mercurio modestly. "My father allowed me into this room. As you see, I have a key. On three occasions he has opened the safe when I have been in the room. On each occasion he made sure that I was too far away to see the number he set. But—this he did not know—in each case I had noted the number *at which the dial already stood*. And I was able to memorize which times he turned the dial clockwise, and which times he turned it counterclockwise. This presented me with a reasonably limited number of permutations, and from these I was able to calculate a single number which checked against all the data. . . ."

As he spoke, Mercurio's nimble fingers were twisting the dial. Bright-eyed, Tina hung over his shoulder. Both were too engrossed to see the shadow that had fallen across the doorway, or to hear the soft footfall on the stone floor behind them.

Three things happened in quick succession.

Mercurio clicked the final number into place, grasped the center of the dial, and pulled. The door swung open for six tantalizing inches. Then a hand came over their shoulders and pushed the door shut again.

Danilo Ferri said, "I don't think your father will be very pleased about this."

A call came through to the carabinieri headquarters in the Via de' Bardi at ten minutes to eleven that evening. It was taken by Tenente Lupo. He listened patiently, said, "I will look into it," and made a note on the pad in front of him. To Carabiniere Scipione he said, "The call was from Signora Zecchi. She is worried that her daughter left the house nearly five hours ago and has not returned."

"Zecchi? The name is familiar."

"She is the wife—the widow, I should say—of Milo Zecchi."

"Who was knocked down by the Englishman."

"Who is alleged to have been knocked down by the Englishman," said the Lieutenant gently. "We must not anticipate the verdict of the court."

"Of course not."

"Will you go around now and see what you can do for her? There is probably nothing in it. The girl is young and,

I seem to remember, quite attractive. She is probably out with some man."

So it came about that the magnificent Bronzini Daimler, driven by Arturo, impeccably uniformed, turned into the bottom end of the Sdrucciolo Benedetto at the same moment that the sleek black police car turned into the top. They arrived outside the Zecchi front door simultaneously, and stood, headlight to headlight, like two formidable animals meeting unexpectedly on a narrow jungle track.

Annunziata, who had opened the door, stood staring for a moment, then, as Tina stepped out of the Daimler, rushed forward and clasped her to her bosom.

"But *why?*" said Tina for the third time. "I have often been later before. Much later. It is not yet midnight."

"I know, *carissima.*"

"And you have to telephone the *police,* as if some disaster had occurred."

"I know, I know."

"It is so *unlike* you, *mamma mia.*"

Upon which Annunziata burst into tears. When these had subsided she said, between sniffles, "I was afraid for you. It was what those men said."

"What men?"

"On the afternoon of the funeral."

"Tell me."

"They said that if I told anything, they would hurt you terribly."

"And you believed them."

"I had to believe them. They were from Sicily."

"And because they were from Sicily, does that make them supermen? Does that mean that the police have ceased to exist? Does it mean that there is no more law and order? And besides, see what happens. You obey them. You tell me nothing. And still you are frightened out of your wits

154

when I am not home by eleven o'clock. So what have you gained by your silence?"

"That's logical, you know," said Mercurio. He had been sitting quietly in the corner, seemingly ignoring these family tantrums. "If you're going to be scared either way, you might just as well tell us about it."

Annunziata said, "Very well. . . ."

When she had finished, Mercurio said, "I was quite right, you see."

"Right about what?"

"I felt it when I was in the back room of that café. My instincts are never at fault in such a matter. Something horrible happened there."

8

The Consul Is Troubled

Commander Comber had telephoned the office of Avvocato Toscafundi at ten o'clock in the morning, when he was told that the lawyer had not yet arrived; at eleven o'clock, to learn that he was in conference; and at twelve o'clock, to find that he had departed for an early lunch. At two o'clock and three o'clock he had not come back from lunch. At four o'clock he was engaged again.

At five o'clock the Commander left a message. He said that he quite appreciated that the lawyer was a busy man, and might not be able to fit him in during business hours. This being so, he had ascertained his private address from the telephone directory, and would call on him, at his home, that evening after dinner.

The secretary who took the message sounded doubtful. She said she would call back. The Commander smiled grimly and said that it was very good of her. Ten minutes later the telephone in his flat rang again. The secretary said that if he could manage to come around right away, Avvocato Toscafundi would see him.

The Commander said that he would be with him in ten minutes. He carefully fastened the new mortise lock that he had had put on his door, and ran down the steps.

(It was at about this time that Mercurio and Tina were having a little trouble in the café.)

The Commander came straight to the point. He said, "When we last spoke together, I said that we had suspicions of a man called Labro Radicelli. He had quarreled with

Broke just before the accident, and offered to sell him important information. This offer he repeated to me, in writing, although unfortunately omitting to put his address on the letter. When I told you this, you advised me to forget about it. Labro, you said, had nothing to do with the case."

"That is so. A cigarette? I forgot. You don't smoke, do you?"

"You said that Labro was a wild goose and it would be a waste of time tracing him or chasing him."

"Exactly."

"Then why did you trace him? And not only trace him, but visit him yourself yesterday afternoon."

"I? You must be imagining things."

"Quit stalling," said the Commander. "Your Maserati coupé was tucked away behind the farm when I got there. I saw it with my own eyes."

The lawyer had extracted a cigarette from the silver box on the table, and was now fitting it, with great deliberation, into a holder. He said, with an edge to his voice, "I am afraid I cannot agree that I am answerable to you for my actions."

"Quite so," said the Commander. "That's what's bothering me. *Exactly who are you answerable to?* Your prime object so far seems to have been to persuade your client to plead guilty. When his friends unearth a witness who might be helpful, you hurry off to him yourself and shut his mouth— Don't interrupt, please. It stuck out a mile that Labro had got more money out of you than he hoped to get out of us. He as good as told me so."

"If he said anything of the sort, it was a lie."

"So you admit, now, that you did go to see him."

"I neither admit it nor deny it. And you have no right to question me."

"I've every right to do it. You may be the bigget name in law in this city, but to me you're just a double-crossing little shyster, who's sold out his client because his real backer has paid him to do it."

"I won't listen to this."

"You'll listen and like it. Because I'm going to report you to your professional organization."

Toscafundi smiled. "Do you think," he said, "that they will believe such a wild story?"

"Maybe not. But I'll tell you one man who may believe it, and that's the Sindaco, who has a certain amount of influence in this town and may have more if the elections swing in a certain directions. He happens to be a friend of Broke's."

Toscafundi had got to his feet. There was a red flush across his cheekbones, and the rest of his face was white. He said, "You realize that unless this wild and unfounded accusation is withdrawn, I cannot possibly continue with the case."

"That's the best news I've heard so far."

"You talk of reporting me to the head of the legal faculty. You are mistaken. It is I who will do the reporting. And I should surmise that when I have repeated to him some of the slanderous statements you have made to me, no other lawyer—no other respectable lawyer—will agree to handle the case."

"Better no lawyer than a crook lawyer," said the Commander. "I'll show myself out."

At nine o'clock next morning, in answer to an urgent telephone call, the Commander drove up to the Consul's house. Turning in at the gateway, he had to brake sharply to avoid another car coming out. He thought that he recognized the young man who was driving it. A lawyer, he thought, and one of the candidates in the municipal elections. He had seen his photograph on a poster, but could not remember the name.

The Consul was in his study. He had with him a long,

serious-looking man with a brown face and a gray mustache, who reminded the Commander of Mr. Badger, in *The Wind in the Willows,* but who turned out to be an English solicitor called Tom Proctor.

"We're all friends of Broke's," said the Consul, "so I can speak quite frankly. I'm afraid you've made things a bit difficult for us, Commander."

"If I've done that I'm sorry," said the Commander. He didn't sound too penitent. "What's happened now?"

"My telephone has been ringing since eight o'clock this morning. I've had the head of the Florence bar, the President of the Institute of Advocates, and the Secretary General of the Ordine degli Avvocati e dei Procuratori di Firenze."

"An impressive bunch. What did they have to say?"

"Their complaint was that you had browbeaten and insulted one of the most eminent members of the legal faculty in Florence. In one version you had actually threatened him with physical assault. Since you were a British subject, you were my responsibility. And would I kindly see that you stopped it."

"I see," said the Commander. "And now would you like to hear the truth?"

"Certainly."

When he had finished, Tom Proctor said, "Did you ask him why he'd gone out to see Labro?"

"It was perfectly obvious why he'd been to see him."

"No doubt. But did you actually ask for his explanation? Speaking as a lawyer myself, if I had the conduct of a case and an outsider—you'll excuse my putting it so bluntly— came along with a story of a surprise witness, I might easily pooh-pooh the idea. But, equally, I might go and see him myself, to make sure that he had nothing of importance to say."

"It's possible," said the Commander. "But it doesn't account for one thing. Labro originally had something to sell.

He said so to Broke. He wrote as much to me. But when I got there, the auction was over. The lot was no longer for sale. I'd been outbid. And who by, if not by that slimy toad?"

"Calling him names isn't going to mend what you've done," said the Consul. "And I hope you realize exactly what it is. Now we shan't get any reputable lawyer in Florence to handle this case."

"Oh, come. It can't be as bad as that. Finding a lawyer is usually a matter of finding enough money to pay for him."

"And where are we going to do that?"

The Commander looked a bit blank.

"There's no legal aid system in Italy, you know. Can you think of someone who'll put up, say, five hundred pounds as an advance against costs?"

"Would it really cost as much as that?"

"At least. And a good deal more when the case got under way."

"Hasn't Broke got any money?"

It was Tom Proctor who answered that one. He said, "Yes, and no. But chiefly no. If he weren't such an altruistic sort of person he'd have quite a reasonable amount of spare cash. It comes from a trust set up by his maternal grandfather, Leopold Scott, the fashionable artist. His reputation in art circles may be a bit fly-blown now, but there's no questioning his competence as a financier. He put all his money into projects like the Hudson Bay Company and De Beers, and the investments must be worth ten times what they were when they were first made."

"And who has the money?"

"His mother had a life interest in it. On her death it went to Robert and his sister, Felicia, absolutely. Only Robert wouldn't take his share. He said it was against his principles to live on unearned income."

"So Felicia gets the lot."

"That's right."

"Wouldn't she help?"

"I don't know. If Robert is an Edwardian Englishman, Felicia is an early-Victorian Englishwoman. Although the money she lives on originally came from painting ennobled aldermen, diamond-spangled dowagers, and overfed lap-dogs, she has never really approved of the arts."

"But if she knew he was in trouble?"

"The question doesn't arise. I should need Robert's permission before I approached her, and he'd never give it."

"Hasn't the Consulate got funds for crises like this?"

"Very small funds," said the Consul sadly. "And not for crises like this. I could produce twenty pounds to send a drunken British sailor back to Pompey, but that's about all it really amounts to."

"Then we shall have to organize a whip-round," said the Commander. "I'll put in a hundred pounds for a start."

"I expect we could raise a fighting fund," said the Consul. "A lot of people would contribute, if I asked them as a personal favor. The only snag is—" He seemed to experience some difficulty in going on.

"Well," said the Commander.

"I should have to persuade them that their money wasn't going to be wasted. Before you say anything more, let me tell you something. I've had Risso round here this morning. He's the Sostituto Procuratore in charge of the case against Broke. He made no secret of what he wanted. He wanted me to see Broke and persuade him to agree to a modified plea of guilty."

"I see," said the Commander. "Having lost one ally, now that we've got rid of Toscafundi, he comes crawling round to try and get you to do his dirty work for him. I'm quite sure you refused."

The Consul said, with a suggestion of controlled anger

that was curiously effective, "I suggest, Commander, that we stop looking at this from the standpoint of sentiments like friendship and personal loyalty, however laudable, and have regard to the facts. Risso showed me the reports from the Forensic Science Laboratory at Rome. Fragments of glass were found in Milo Zecchi's hair, and, in two cases, actually embedded in his skull. They have been extracted, and fitted back into the other fragments from the fog lamp on Broke's car. The microphotographs show, beyond any question, that the fragments fit together. There is therefore no doubt at all that it was Broke's car which hit Milo. And unless we can suppose that someone else took out his car later that night, knocked down Milo, and then took the car back to the garage—which seems to me completely incredible—then it was Broke who hit him."

9

Jigsaw

"I seem," said Commander Comber, "to have put my foot in it. And not for the first time. I remember running down the Admiral commanding at the Nore, when he was out in his pinnace fishing. I got away with that, too." His gleam of cheerfulness faded. "But I'm damned if I see what we're going to do next."

The three of them were sitting around the table in the Commander's flat at the early-evening conference that seemed to have become part of their lives in the last ten days.

"Cheer up," said Elizabeth. "At least we're doing something. No one else is doing anything at all."

"But is it getting us anywhere?"

"I think it is. I think that what Tina's just told us is tremendously important."

"I did not see it at all clearly," said Tina, "because that pig, Danilo Ferri, came and slammed the door. But there was gold. That I'm sure. A necklace, and some earrings, and—a sort of—" She passed a hand over her head.

"A tiara?"

"No. It was more like a crown, I think. And there were two or three boxes. Long shallow boxes on little legs."

"Caskets."

"Yes. You could say caskets. They were made out of a smooth stone. Mercurio told me the name. I will think of it in a moment. Alabaster. And there was this lady. She had no clothes on, and she was lying in the safe, but I think she was meant to be standing up. She was made of alabaster, too."

"How long?"

Tiny gestured with her hands about two feet apart.

"And was there some sort of pedestal?"

"That I could not see. The door was only open for a few seconds, you understand."

"What we need here is a bit of expert advice," said the Commander. "Trouble is, the only expert I know is Robert and he's locked away in the Murate prison."

Elizabeth said, "There is the man who came to lunch the other day. The American. Harfied Moss. If he's still in Florence . . ."

"Action to be taken," said the Commander, making a note. "See this chap Moss. What comes next?"

"The next bit is becoming a little bit clearer," said Elizabeth. "It's these two men. The 'listening box' Annunziata was talking about would be some sort of microphone, which had been put in the Zecchi kitchen. The wires probably ran up to Dindoni's apartment across the courtyard."

"That was a bit farsighted of them, wasn't it?" said the Commander. "I mean, why should they think they were going to hear anything to their advantage?"

"Tina's explained that. The first time Robert came to see Milo they had their talk in his workshop. Only he wouldn't go on with what he was going to say, *because* he thought Dindoni was listening in."

"That is right," said Tina. "And very likely he *was* listening. His pig's ear was made for keyholes."

"So the only other place they could talk was in their own kitchen."

"All right," said the Commander. "I'll accept that. But what did Dindoni hear that was so important?"

"He heard Milo making all his arrangements for that

164

evening. How he was going up to see his doctor. How he planned to slip away from the back of the office. When and where he was to meet Broke. The whole plan."

The Commander thought about this. He said, "So what did he do about it?"

"He told those two hired bullies who were working with him. Incidentally, what have you done about them, Tina?"

"I have told the police about them."

"And what did the police say?"

"They said they would investigate the matter."

The Commander snorted. He said, "We're getting off-beam. Suppose Dindoni did hear all that stuff, and suppose he did pass it on to these two thugs. *What did they do?*"

The three of them looked at each other. "All right," said Elizabeth. "That's where *that* story runs into the sand. The next bit of the jigsaw is Labro. What was he trying to sell?"

"I don't think that's too difficult. It's obvious the Professor is working some sort of fiddle. Probably he's already broken into the main burial chamber in that tumulus of his, and taken out the pick of the stuff."

"The gold and alabaster in his safe."

"Right. And now he's postponing the offical 'discovery' until he's disposed of the top pieces abroad. *Then* he'll announce the finding of the tomb, and a lot of less valuable relics—terra-cottas and bronzes and suchlike—which will go to the national museums, and everyone will be happy. Labro probably spotted this. The other workers would be too dumb to realize what was going on—"

"Or too much under the Professor's thumb. After all, they're his farmhands. His slaves almost."

"Very likely. So now you can see why the Professor used Avvocato Toscafundi to buy off Labro. He couldn't afford to have him shooting his mouth off. Particularly *before* he's disposed of the real loot."

"That bit makes sense," said Elizabeth. "But it *still* doesn't explain what happened to Robert. Or was that just a coincidence?"

"I refuse to believe it."

"How will this help Signor Roberto?" said Tina.

Their discussions were held partly in Italian, which the Commander and Elizabeth both spoke well, and partly in English, which Tina understood very slightly. The last exchanges had been in English, and had gone over her head.

"It's a difficult question to answer," said Elizabeth. "If we could find out what really happened, and prove it—"

"And get a lawyer to put it across for us—"

"And find the money to pay for the lawyer—"

"If it is money that is needed," said Tina, "I have some. As much, perhaps, as fifty thousand lire."

"I'm afraid it isn't that sort of money."

"How much then?"

"Five hundred thousand. Maybe a million before we've finished."

"Does it cost that much to buy a lawyer?"

"They're expensive animals," said the Commander. He looked at Elizabeth, who said, "I could contribute. But not a great deal."

"I'm in much the same boat," said the Commander. "In a pinch—" The noise outside interrupted him. Someone was shouting from below in Italian. The Commander went to the door, opened it, and listened.

The noise increased in volume. Three people were now shouting.

"I think," he said, "that someone's got stuck in the lift. It's such a ropy old contraption that I usually try to avoid using it myself. Once it does stick, there's only one way to unstick it. I shall need help. Quiet, all of you!" This was bellowed down the stairs, and had no effect at all. Muffled sounds were issuing from the lift.

"Elizabeth, you go down to the next landing. What you've got to do is press the button there at exactly the same time as I press the button here. Tina, stand halfway down the stairs and give her the signal. And for God's sake stop howling down there. *Tutto è sistemato.* Everything's under control. Right, Tina. When I drop my hand. So."

There was a click, and the outer door of the lift slid open. The Commander saw a middle-aged lady, dressed in a tweed coat and skirt and brown square-toed shoes, and carrying a green umbrella. The patrician face reminded him of someone, but he could not, for the moment, place it.

"Well," she said. "I'm glad *someone's* succeeded in opening that terrible door at last." The door took instant exception to this comment and started to shut. The Commander jumped forward and grabbed it.

"Better get out while the going's good," he said.

"I quite agree with you," said the lady. "Are you Commander Anthony Basil Comber?"

"I am."

"And these are . . . ?"

"Miss Elizabeth Weighill, and Signorina Zecchi."

"Excellent," said the lady. "Precisely the three people I had planned to meet. Should we go inside? My name, by the way, is Broke. Felicia Broke."

When they were seated Miss Broke assumed charge of proceedings in the brisk way in which, Elizabeth felt sure, she had chaired countless Women's Institutes and Mothers' Unions. She said, "When I read a very brief account in the *Daily Telegraph* of what Robert had got himself involved in—he had not seen fit to communicate with me himself—I realized at once that he would be in need of financial assistance. As Tom Proctor may have told you, with a misplaced sense of chivalry Robert diverted the family money to me. I had really no need of it. It piles up in my bank account and forces me to pay a ridiculous amount of tax. However, it may now be useful. I have opened a credit of a thousand pounds at the Banco di Napoli here. There is more if it is needed. But that should be enough to start with."

"Indeed, yes," said the Commander. "But how did you do it? I mean, Exchange Control regulations . . ."

"I was given to understand that there were some regulations. I went to see the Governor of the Bank of England. He agreed that this was a crisis, and the restrictions must be waived."

"And there was no difficulty," said Elizabeth.

"None at all." Miss Broke switched her attention to Elizabeth. Her light-blue eyes were unnervingly like Robert's. "Five minutes' talk, and the thing was fixed. I have found that men of intelligence usually see my points quite quickly. I had rather more difficulty with your father. I don't imply by that that he is lacking in intelligence. But he seemed to me to be a particularly obstinate man."

"He's all of that," agreed Elizabeth.

"I pointed out to him that he had a clear duty. As British Consul he was charged with the welfare of all British subjects. His personal feelings did not enter into the matter at all."

Put her in charge of the Navy, thought the Commander, and we might still have a few aircraft carriers. "What did he say?"

"He started to talk about procedure and the laws of evidence. Unconvincing stuff. I told him that I never thought the day would come when I should hear a British Consul preaching the virtues of Italian law. Well, that's really all I came to say."

She rose to her feet. The others rose with her.

"I've given instructions to the bank to honor your signature, Commander. I shall be here for a few days and shall hope to see you again."

"If you could tell us the name of your hotel . . ."

"I am not at an hotel. I am staying with my old friend Beatrice Plant. I will wish you good day. I think I won't chance the lift. I'll use the stairs."

"If, as I understand is the case," said the Sindaco with a grin, "you now have unlimited wealth at your disposal, then your problem, although still difficult, is not insoluble. There are a number of lawyers in Florence who would be prepared to ignore the caveat of their professional organization. In the first place, because Avvocato Toscafundi is not universally popular. Secondly, because he is an avowed supporter of the Social Democrats, which brings him into disfavor with the parties of the left. The difficulty will be to avoid wasting your money on someone who will take the cash and do nothing for it."

He considered the matter, smoking his pipe. Outside in the street a loudspeaker van rolled by, blaring out election slogans.

The Sindaco arrived at a conclusion. He said, "He is not what I believe you call 'everybody's cup of tea.' But I think the man for your money is Riccasole." He scribbled something on a piece of paper and pushed it across at the Commander. "That is his wife's telephone number. Mention my name, and she will put you in touch with him."

It seemed to the Commander to be an odd way of contacting a solicitor, but he pocketed the paper and was on the point of leaving when the Sindaco said, "I am conscious that I have not, so far, been as helpful to my friend Roberto as I could have wished. I have been very much engaged in these elections. When they are over I shall be freer to help. And possibly, if the elections go well, in a better position to do so. I have, however, been able to take certain minor

169

steps which, even if they do not directly help Roberto, will at least annoy his opponents."

"I'm sure you're doing all you can," said the Commander.

Avvocato Riccasole kept no office hours, for the good and sufficient reason that he had no office. The Commander's rendezvous with him, arranged through his wife, was at a fashionable teashop in the Piazza della Repubblica.

"He will be occupying," his wife had said "the table in the corner, behind the door. He will be drinking a cup of chocolate, with cream in it."

He was also, the Commander discovered, eating a chocolate cake with cream on it. He was a small man, with bright inquisitive eyes and a flattened yellowish nose.

"So pleased to meet you, Commander," he said. "Sindaco Trentanuove has told me about you, and about your friend's difficulties. Do you mind if we do not discuss them for just five minutes. I wish to listen to the music."

There were three performers. The pianist was a middle-aged woman with iron-gray hair. The men were younger. The Commander recognized the piece they were playing. "Mozart," he said, when the applause, vigorously led by Riccasole, had subsided.

"From the overture to *La Finta Giardiniera*. A minor work. It was the execution which interested me."

"You are a performer yourself, perhaps?"

"Indeed. I was originally trained as a concert pianist. Unfortunately there was not enough money in it. I had to abandon it for the law. That woman has a real touch, don't you think?"

"She plays very well. Do you know her?"

"She was my client. I was fortunate enough to secure her acquittal. Here is the waiter. Will you take chocolate?"

"Tea," said the Commander. "Lemon, and no milk. What had she done?"

"She had killed her husband."

"Why?"

"Who knows? Possibly he did not appreciate her piano playing. But we must not divert ourselves from your problems. A slice of this cake?"

"Thank you," said the Commander, "but no."

"You are worried about your figure. Curious how many Englishmen are. Their figures, and their balance of payments. These are becoming obsessions with the English. Quite unnecessarily. There is no harm in being fat, or in debt, as long as you do not let it worry you. Now tell me your story. Beginning at the very beginning..." Avvocato Riccasole speared a further rich-looking patisserie with his fork, and added, "Omitting no possible detail."

Colonel Nobile, head of the Florence Police, studied the report in front of him. It was, in a sense, satisfactory since it confirmed his long held and deeply felt suspicions of the English. He said to the Police Inspector who had brought it in, "There is no doubt, in your own mind, Inspector, about these facts?"

"None at all, Colonel."

"And the conclusions you draw from them?"

"I conclude that Commander Comber is a member of the British Intelligence service."

"Curious," said the Colonel. "Such men are usually attached to the Embassy, to afford them diplomatic privilege."

"This one is an undercover agent. He sends messages every week. They go to a 'Mister Smith' at what is evidently an accommodation address in London and payment is received through a well-known English newspaper. Yet a curious fact emerges. No article by Commander Comber has ever appeared in that paper!"

"And this is one of his communications?"

"This is the most recent."

171

The Colonel studied the message, which was attached to the report. It started: "Fishcake, Filigree, Obal, Shoehorn, Dichotomy..." and continued in the same style, some of the words being long, some short, and many of them uncommon. The message concluded with the words, in brackets: "Frame 8B."

"And has it been decoded?"

"Our cryptography department is working on it now. The difficulty is that it is clearly a mechanical code."

"Explain."

"The recipient will have a number of different frames. He will set the words out in a prearranged form. Probably in columns, each ten letters long. The correct frame is then laid over the letters, and the message emerges."

"And the words at the end indicate which frame to use. Ingenious."

"And almost insoluble."

"If we cannot solve it we can stop it," said the Colonel angrily. "I will speak to the British Consul about it at once."

10

Harfield Moss Talks to Elizabeth

"It's an outrage," said Sostituto Procuratore Risso.

"Are you certain you are not exaggerating?"

"I am not exaggerating. It is persecution. Deliberate and systematic persecution." He laid a slip of yellow paper on the Procuratore's desk, and prodded it with his finger. "A demand for supplementary tax for refuse collection, on the grounds that the refuse collected from my house exceeds the limit laid down by municipal regulations."

"And does it?"

"Of course. All houses exceed it. But other people do not get these demands. And this." He produced a second paper. "An additional water rate on the grounds that my gardener has been observed using a sprinkler on the lawn. And this—this came this morning."

The Procuratore examined the document cautiously. He said, "It seems quite clear. Your *tassa di famiglia* is being raised on the grounds that you have installed a swimming pool. If you must indulge in these luxuries, Antonio—"

"It is *not* a swimming pool."

"No?"

"It is a goldfish pond. It has been there ever since I bought the house."

"Have you been swimming in it?"

"It is precisely seven feet long. Even the fish can hardly swim in it."

"Why do you suppose . . . ?"

"There is no mystery about it. All the imposts in question

are controlled by the office of Sindaco Trentanuove."

"You think he is conducting a personal vendetta against you?"

"I'm sure of it."

"Why?"

"In some of my recent speeches I have been forced to say things about the Communist party which he may have found it hard to forgive."

"I see," said the Procuratore. He untwisted the string and opened the flap of the folder on his desk. "You are sure, are you, that his motives are political?"

"What else would they be?"

"You have not forgotten that he is a friend of Signor Broke."

"I did not know that. No."

"A very old wartime friend."

"His motives, you suggest, might be personal."

"They might be mixed," said the Procuratore. "He would gain just as many kudos, in the eyes of his party, by defeating you in the courts as he would by defeating you at the polls. Indeed, the one might lead to the other." He had the papers out now, and was leafing through them. He said, "I think, Antonio, that we had better bring this case on without further delay."

"I entirely agree. Now that we have the scientific evidence, the indictment is complete."

"Almost complete. If the cemetery keeper reconsidered his evidence—if, for instance, he was prepared to admit that the noise of a car braking and skidding which he heard *might* have occurred about an hour earlier—then I would agree that the case would be sufficiently complete, and the papers could go forward to the Tribunale."

"It is easy for an old man to be mistaken about times," said Risso. "I will ask the investigating officers to question him again. We may find that when he is questioned verbally

174

his evidence will not be as cut-and-dried as it appears from his written depositions."

"I have known that to happen," agreed the Procuratore.

Tenente Lupo said, "And has the girl's complaint been investigated?"

"I have done what I could," said Carabiniere Scipione. "It was difficult to investigate the matter thoroughly since the complaint was so indefinite. I spoke to the girl—"

"Tina Zecchi. She would be the daughter of Milo Zecchi, who was knocked down by the car. What was her story?"

"She was in a café, near her house, in the Via Torta. It is not a place of very good repute. We have had complaints of disorderly behavior from there before. It belongs to a man called Tortoni, but he goes there very seldom. He leaves the running of it to a woman, Maria Calzaletta—"

"Who is a witness in this same running-down case."

"That is true. According to Tina's story, she was visiting the café with a young man, and they became involved in an argument with the woman Calzaletta."

"The name of the young man—"

"It was Mercurio Bronzini. He is the adopted son of Professor Bronzini, of the Villa Rasenna."

"I know the Professor. I seem to recollect that he also has some connection with this running-down. Refresh my memory for me."

Scipione said, rather sulkily, "Milo Zecchi used to work for him, and the Professor has interested himself in the case. As I was saying, there was an altercation—"

"Did it not strike you as a curious coincidence that three of the people connected with the running-down should also be connected with this incident?"

"It did not seem to me to be of any particular significance."

"I wonder."

The Tenente considered the matter, while his subordinate fidgeted.

"Do you wish me to continue?"

"Please go on. You were saying that there was an altercation. What happened next?"

"The girl says that a man came into the shop."

"Which girl says it—Signorina Zecchi or Maria? You are telling this story very badly."

"I'm sorry." Scipione's face was flushed with annoyance, and his mouth, under the line of black mustache, had for a moment an ugly look about it. If the Tenente noticed it he made no comment. He said, "The girl's statement will have been written down, I take it?"

"Of course."

"Then perhaps you had better read it to me."

"I will fetch the papers."

"No need. They are in that filing cabinet. I was reading them last night."

A wary look had come into Scipione's face. He walked across to the filing cabinet, took out a folder and extracted a paper from it, and returned to the desk. Then he said, his voice carefully expressionless, "Do you wish me to read the whole statement?"

"No. Just from the point where this man comes in."

"It is here. 'A man came into the room. I did not know him, but from his general appearance suppose him to be one of two men who have been hanging around the café for the last ten days. They are said to be Sicilians, and both have the appearance of Mafia gangsters. This one attacked Mercurio. I hit him with a billiard cue, and in the struggle the girl also got knocked unconscious, and we were able to make our escape from the room.' That is all she says."

"Very curious, is it not?"

"In what way curious?"

"That Signorina Zecchi should have been the one to make

the complaint. This unknown man, and the woman, Calzaletta, were knocked down. Yet it is their assailants who complain."

"True," said Scipione.

"And there is a further curious coincidence about the matter. The report speaks of two men, Sicilians, Mafiosi, who have been around Florence for the last ten days or so. Now, it is in my mind that we had a report from the Stazione Centrale of the arrival of two such suspicious characters. Am I right?"

"You are right."

"And you were to make a check on various hotels and *pensioni* to see if they could be located. You did that?"

"I did."

"Men of that type should not be too difficult to locate."

Scipione flushed again. He said. "They might not be staying at a *pensione*. They might have compatriots who would lodge them and conceal them."

"That is quite possible," agreed the Tenente. He seemed to have lost interest in the topic. He said, "I have had a communication from the office of the Procuratore. There are certain points in connection with that running-down case which he desires to have checked. In particular, the testimony of—now, what is his name? I have it here. Frutelli. Carlo Frutelli, the attendant at the mortuary in the Via Canina."

"I know him. A silly old man."

"His testimony appears, on paper, to be clear, and at variance with the rest of the evidence. He states that he heard a car coming down the Via Canina, fast. Then he heard the squeal of brakes."

"So? Where is the inconsistency?"

"It lies in the timing. He says he heard these sounds at half past eleven. By that time, Broke had been long back in his house and in bed."

Scipione laughed. "Is that all?" he said. "One hour! He is such a stupid old man that he would not know the difference between midday and midnight."

"I think, perhaps, you had better speak to him."

"I will do so."

"In order to clarify his testimony."

"When I have finished speaking to him," said Scipione, "his testimony will be completely clear. I can promise you that."

"It's good of you to spare me the time, Mr. Moss," said Elizabeth. "Particularly as I've come to pick your brains."

"Anything you can find there," said Harfied Moss gravely, "is entirely at your disposal. How is your father?"

"He's in very good health."

"And your sister?"

"She's all right, too."

"Fine, fine. Now tell me exactly what it is I can do for you."

"I want to find out everything I can about faking Etruscan relics."

A poker player of international repute, Harfield Moss had schooled his face not to reveal his thoughts. This was one moment when he was glad of it. He said, "Would your interest be academic, Miss Weighhill, or were you contemplating going in for that line of business yourself?"

"I'm not taking it up as a hobby," said Elizabeth. "But my interest isn't academic, either. I really want to know something about it. It's to do with the charge they've brought against Robert Broke."

"That nice Englishman I met at lunch, who had that attack."

"Yes."

"If there's anything I can do to help you, you can surely count on me. But I find it difficult, right at this moment, to see how Etruscan relics, genuine or otherwise, could be connected with a hit-and-run charge. Perhaps you can explain?"

Elizabeth did her best. Harfield Moss had disconcertingly candid eyes, which he kept focused on her as she spoke, like twin cameras in close-up. But she had a feeling that his mind was not entirely on what she was saying; that he was weighing up considerations beyond her ken, estimating the strengths and weaknesses of his own position, weighing the comparative virtues of disclosure and concealment, in exactly the way he would have done if she had been a business rival. Curiously, the feeling did not make her dislike him.

At the end of it he said, "You have two theories about this, am I right? The first is that the Professor has unearthed a genuine hoard, the pick of which he plans to sell abroad. Well, I won't deny that that fits in with certain other information I have. You won't want to press me about that, I'm sure. But I'm not in Florence entirely for my health. Can we leave it at that? The other idea is rather more alarming to me personally. And that is that *no* real discovery has been made at all. That the so-called relics are fakes."

"I wanted to find out if that was a possibility."

"Ordinarily, I would have dismissed the idea at once. There have, of course, been successful swindles in the past. Your own British Museum had a sarcophagus foisted off on it some fifty years ago, and there were the famous Etruscan warriors in terra-cotta in the twenties. The Metropolitan Museum of Art in New York is still sore about them."

"If real experts were deceived—"

"Surely. But we're talking of the dark ages, Miss Weighill. Neither of those fakes would have stood up for five minutes under modern spectrographic analysis. Just to give you an example, in the case in New York, the examination showed that cobalt, lead, and manganese had all been used as coloring agents, none of which could have been present in the genuine article. If your Etruscan craftsman wanted to produce that lovely black glaze you see on his kraters and jars, *he* did it by a three-stage firing process. He didn't employ mineral additives at all. That was demonstrated in the forties by Dr. Theodor Schumann, who actually reconstructed a kiln on the Etruscan model and fired—"

"I'm sorry," said Elizabeth, "but I'm getting out of my depth. Is what you're saying that, in this day and age, it would be impossible to fake Etruscan terra-cotta so as to deceive an expert?"

"Certainly. And the same would go for bronze or iron work. In those cases the patina or encrustation would reveal marked dissimilarities—"

"Then *is* there any material which you could use, and hope to get away with it?"

"It's precisely the point I was coming to, Miss Weighill. And it's the point that makes your story so particularly interesting—and disturbing. The materials that come most readily to mind, because they are both natural materials, and are neither of them subject to decomposition, are gold and alabaster."

"I see," said Elizabeth. "That does look a bit coincidental, doesn't it?"

"Mind you, even if you decided to work in those particular materials, your difficulties would by no means be over. First, there is the question of style. Either you would have to make an exact copy of some known Etruscan original— and that, in itself, would give ground for suspicion—or you would have to design something new for yourself. To do that with any hope of success you'd need not only great expertise but—how shall I put it?—an Etruscan mind. An Etruscan outlook."

"Right. And the second snag?"

"The second is even more difficult. It is a question of what collectors call provenance. You produce an Etruscan relic, apparently genuine in style and material. The first question I ask you is, Where did it come from? You can of course refuse to tell me. But that in itself would give rise to suspicion. The men who produced those New York forgeries were lucky. They named the site, but before any proper investigation could be made, the war intervened. By the time the war was over, and the minefields had been cleared, and travel restrictions lifted, so much time had elapsed that they were able to be a bit vague about the location. It might have been just here. It might have been a mile or two up the valley."

"I see," said Elizabeth. *"But suppose you already had a tomb.* A private tomb, on your own land. One that people knew you were investigating. You dig away like a beaver, and one day you hit on the main burial chamber. Unfortunately, it doesn't have anything very exciting in it. Just a helmet and a few arms perhaps, the man having been a pirate by trade. So what do you do? You manufacture a lot of much more valuable items—gold necklaces and alabaster boxes and statues—and then you find *them* in this burial chamber—"

"You've got a criminal mind, Miss Weighill," said Harfield Moss thoughtfully.

Carabiniere Scipione drove out alone to the cemetery in the Via Canina. As he drove, he was whistling to himself. He parked his car at the bottom of the street and walked up. Seen in full daylight, it was not a pleasant place. The pavement was narrow and irregular, the roadway cracked and dirty, with storm-water tunnels breaking the surface. On one side a row of condemned houses with boarded windows and weed-choked front courts. On the other a low wall and rusty spiked railing guarded the moldering bones of the departed below and the crumbling relics of piety above.

Scipione whistled all the more cheerfully. He was not an unimpressionable young man, being full of the cheerful vitality of the south, his black hair sleek with health, his eyes alight with the lust of of living.

He opened the gate and made his way down the path to where, behind a hedge of cypress, the cottage of the cemetery's custodian stood. It was a tiny building, smaller than many of the ancient catafalques it guarded.

As he walked, he was considering the precise technique he would use with the old man. There would be no need to terrify him. An air of authority, a hint of force in reserve. The rest would be achieved by simple suggestion. He rapped on the door and marched in.

Carlo Frutelli, keeper of the tombs, was seated in a chair on one side of the kitchen table. He was not alone. On the other side of the table, a notebook open in front of him, and a gentle smile on his face, was Avvocato Riccasole.

11

Hot

It was nine-thirty on the following morning when Sir Gerald Weighill entered the Consular offices on the Lungarno Corsini and asked the lady who officiated at the switchboard to get him a Rome number. Then he went into his private room and locked the door.

When the call came through he spoke at some length to the man at the other end, whom he addressed as Colin, and from whom he got a number of noncommittal answers. Finally he said, "Well, would you check up on him? If Comber isn't one of ours I should like to know what the devil he's up to, and let me have the answer as soon as you can. The head policeman is coming to see me this evening and I've been instructed to throw this chap out by the end of the week."

He rang off, unlocked his door, wiped his forehead, for it was already a day with a promise of exceptional heat, and was ready for his first visitors, who turned out to be Felicia Broke and Miss Plant. Neither of them was pleased with him.

"Had I been consulted at the start," said Miss Plant, "the matter would not have developed in this deplorable way. It appears to me that Mr. Broke has been allowed to become a political scapegoat. My Italian friends tell me that a conviction will go a long way toward securing a seat on the Municipal Council for his prosecutor, Risso. An extremely objectionable and bumptious young man."

"On the other hand," said Miss Broke, "we understand that his acquittal will mean votes for the Communist party. Things have come to a pretty pass when a Broke is allowed to serve as propaganda material for the reds."

"I'm afraid I don't see how I—"

"On top of all this," said Miss Plant, "it's being openly stated, in the British community, that you have *advised* Mr. Broke to plead guilty. I have no doubt this has been exaggerated, but since there's no smoke without a fire . . ."

"Oh, dear," said Sir Gerald. He said it to himself, after the two angry ladies had gone. Then he picked up his brown homburg hat, a spectacularly British piece of headgear, and set out for the Murate prison. He got back to his house in time for a late luncheon, and found Elizabeth waiting for him.

"Did you see him?" she said. "How is he? How did it go? What did you think of Riccasole?"

"Before dealing with one question, let alone four," said the Consul, sinking down into his chair and mopping his forehead, "I demand a pink gin."

"I've poured it out for you. Now then."

"Yes. I saw Broke. He appeared to be in good health and perfectly normal spirits. Alarmingly so."

"Alarming!"

"*I* found it alarming. When a man is in imminent danger of a heavy sentence for what was, on the worst view, an error of judgment, you would expect him to show some signs of apprehension. Broke seems to be entirely unconcerned. So much so that one might be driven to the conclusion that he was almost welcoming his martyrdom."

"You don't understand him. Just because he doesn't make a show of his feelings—"

"It isn't a question of showing his feelings. It's a complete lack of feeling. A mental unawareness which seems to me—I may be wrong; I'm no psychologist—to be something akin to a death wish."

Elizabeth stared at him.

"Are you serious?"

"Certainly. I think the destruction of his wife and unborn child did something to him. Something possibly irreparable. He's like a clock with a broken mainspring. No. That's a poor simile. If the mainspring were broken, the clock would stop altogether, and Broke hasn't done that. Outwardly he seems perfectly all right—apart from occasional fits of amnesia. But inside, something's dead."

"Not dead," said Elizabeth. "Frozen. Given time, it'll melt."

"I wish I could be sure about that." The Consul swallowed his drink and handed the glass to his daughter, who poured him out a second one, and they sat in companionable silence for some minutes.

"He's got a new lawyer—but you know that. I met him at the jail and we went in together."

"What did you think of him?"

Sir Gerald laughed. "He's quite a character. Most of the time I was there, he and Broke were talking about music."

"Music?"

"They were arguing about whether a phrase in one of Beethoven's symphonies should be dah-di-di-dah or dah-dah-di-dah."

Elizabeth said, "That was a nice change, anyway."

"I don't think Riccasole's a fool. He'd done one thing which was really quite obvious, but no one had thought of doing to date. He went to see the doctor."

"Which doctor?"

"The one that old Milo Zecchi had planned to visit on the night of the accident, remember? He was planning to sneak out of the back door of his office to go and meet Broke."

"And did he?"

"No," said the Consul. "He didn't. He never got to the doctor's at all."

At one o'clock Avvocato Riccasole pushed open the door of the café in the Via Torta and peered in. The outer room was empty except for Maria, who was seated behind the counter, reading a newspaper. She had a broad strip of adhesive tape over her right temple, and her face looked paler and sulkier than usual. She did not look up when Riccasole came in, and he had to cough to call attention to himself.

"Well?"

"It is the Signora Maria Calzaletta I am addressing?"

"It is. And if you are from the newspapers I have nothing more to say."

Riccasole slid a card across the zinc counter. Maria looked at it with apparent indifference.

"So! A lawyer. And what can I do for you?"

"First, a Cinzano soda, with a lump of ice in it."

Maria got down the bottle, poured the contents into a glass, and added a cube of ice from the refrigerator under the counter. Riccasole leaned one elbow on the bar and watched her. Then he took something from his wallet. Maria's eyes widened at the sight of the pink-and-brown ten-thousand-lire note.

"I'm afraid I haven't enough change. . . ."

"Then don't bother to change it," said Riccasole softly.

"I—thank you." Her eyes shifted uncertainly.

Riccasole smiled dreamily. He took a second card from his wallet, drew out a thin gold pencil, turned the card over, and wrote on the back. "If it is difficult for you to talk here, come to this shop any evening at six."

When he had finished his drink and drifted out into the street again, the curtains parted and the stout man came out.

He said, "What was all that about? Who was he?"

"He was a lawyer." She pushed across the first card that Riccasole had given her. The second seemed to have disappeared. The ten-thousand-lire banknote also.

"What did he want?"

"A drink."

"Why should a lawyer come to a dump like this for a drink? And why did he leave his card?"

"Perhaps he was touting for business."

"Perhaps you are lying," said the stout man.

"Why should I lie?"

The fat man looked at her thoughtfully. He detected a hint of defiance in her manner. He distrusted it. He said, "You wouldn't be thinking of doing anything dishonorable, I hope."

Maria said, "You're making something out of nothing."

"I hope so," said the stout man. "Because if you did anything so stupid"—he leaned forward comfortably on the counter—"I myself would take great pleasure in teaching you a lesson that you would never, never forget."

At three o'clock, under a merciless sun, Avvocato Riccasole picked his way down the Via de' Malcontenti, crossed the Ponte San Niccolò (with the smart new balustrade replacing the one swept away by the flood), and climbed the tree-shaded slope of the Viale Michelangiolo. When he got to the cul-de-sac in which Broke's house stood he paused for a whole two minutes, rocking slowly backward and forward on his pointed shoes, his eyes half shut.

Then he seemed to come to a decision. Instead of making for Broke's house, he turned into the garden of the house next door.

A fat Alsatian padded up and sniffed at his trousers.

Riccasole smiled nervously at it and rang the doorbell.

"Signora Colli?"

"Yes. Down, Benito! He is a good dog really."

"I am sure of it," said Riccasole. "He has a *most* amiable face." He took out his card and handed it to the woman. "Allow me to introduce myself. I have been retained by friends of Signor Broke to see to the conduct of his defense."

"Ah, the poor man. What they say of him is nothing but lies. Such a gentle soul. So kind, so considerate. How could he be thought to have done such a thing?"

"I am encouraged to hear you say so, signora. Such, of course, is my belief, too, or I should not have undertaken this task. However, there is one point on which you could perhaps help me."

"Anything in my power. Anything at all."

"It concerns your dog."

"Benito?"

"Indeed. Would you say that he is a good sleeper?"

Signora Colli looked in astonishment, first at the lawyer, then at the dog, who made a noise like a very old man clearing his throat. She said, "Indeed, yes. As you see, he has a comfortable figure. He eats well, and in consequence he sleeps well."

"Then he does not bark a lot at night."

"Hardly ever—but wait. It is true, now that you bring it back to my mind. He did bark a great deal on the night on which this accident happened."

"Could you, I wonder, be even more precise. Did he bark all through the night?"

"Not all through it. No. We retire early in our household. We are in bed by half past ten. He was barking for perhaps an hour. Then my husband went down and spoke to him, and after that he stopped."

"Between half past ten, then, and half past eleven?"

"That is right. Though you might not judge it from his appearance, Benito has a very sensitive nature. Do you suppose—is it possible that he may have sensed that Signor Broke was in trouble?"

"With a sensitive dog," said Avvocato Riccasole, "anything is possible."

Benito looked gratified, and waved his tail.

"I shall have to insist," said Sostituto Procuratore Risso angrily, "that the prosecution witnesses are given police protection."

"You think that wise?" said the Procuratore.

It was half past four, and the heat was still as intense as it had been at midday.

"Wise and necessary. I have information that they are being subjected to most improper interrogation. Possibly also to bribes."

"By whom?"

"By Avvocato Riccasole."

"I see. He is, of course, entitled to ask them questions. Is there any actual evidence that he has offered them bribes?"

"You know Riccasole," said Risso contemptuously. "He's the slipperiest fish in Florence. He should have been disbarred years ago. Half a dozen times he's come within an inch of a charge of bribery, intimidation, and interference with the course of justice."

"And half a dozen times he has wriggled his way out."

"Or bought his way out."

The Procuratore thought about it.

He said, "In principle I agree. But we must proceed with care. This case is in the public eye. If it came out that we had tried to use the police to prevent the defense from questioning witnesses, it would look very bad. Very bad indeed. It might, in fact, give them a handle which they do not possess already. You realize that this may be why Riccasole is behaving in this way. He has visited these people quite openly?"

"Openly, yes."

"Have you considered that he may be doing it *in order* to provoke us to precisely this action. Had you thought of that?"

"I should not put it past him," said Risso, chewing his upper lip as if he hated it.

"Nevertheless, on balance, I think you are right. What is called for is a discreet form of surveillance. The carabinieri will be more adept at this than the police. Make all arrangements with Tenente Lupo. *But warn him to be very careful.*"

The voice on the telephone said, in tones of cold anger, "My instructions were clear. You were to behave unobtrusively until some definite action was called for."

"I agree," said the stout man.

"Not to call attention to yourselves. Not to indulge in brawling. Not to get your presence reported to the police."

"We were not inviting trouble. We were attacked."

"By a young boy, and a girl. And you had to make such a drama out of it that the police are brought in."

"Listen," said the stout man. He, too, was getting angry. "We did not start the trouble. And we did not send for the police."

"It seems possible," said the voice, and its previous coldness was as nothing compared to its icy quality now, "that you are not the right men for this job. I should be sorry to have to report to your superiors that you had failed."

There was a long silence. Then the stout man said, in tones of surprising mildness, "I do not think you need worry. There will be no difficulty with the carabinieri. Our contact there is reliable. I can promise you that."

"There had better not be. It may, in any event, be too

late to replace you. But you will act with more discretion, and remain out of sight *until you receive orders.*"

"Very well," said the stout man. It had been hot inside the telephone booth but hardly hot enough to account for the fact that he was sweating so freely when he came out.

"It is good of you to call, Colonel Nobile," said the Consul. "And I am delighted to be able to set your mind at rest."

"You have advised Commander Comber to leave Florence, then?"

"I have not spoken to Commander Comber."

"So?"

"But I have spoken to the authorities in Rome who know about such matters. They were able to assure me that Commander Comber has no connection whatever with any British intelligence organization."

"Then perhaps you can offer me a rational explanation of certain of his messages which have been intercepted."

"If you have one of them with you," said Sir Gerald with a smile, "I might be able to do just that."

The Colonel extracted a piece of paper from his briefcase and laid it on the desk.

"Fishcake, Filigree, Obol— Yes, I fancy that was last Thursday. Let me see if I can find it. I had a good deal of trouble with that one myself, I remember."

He was looking through the collected set of *The Times* that was stacked on a side table beside his desk. "This is the one, I think."

"What is this?"

"It's the solution to the crossword puzzle which was set in last Wednesday's paper."

"A crossword puzzle?"

"As I understand the matter, they are set by several different people. Commander Comber constructs one each week. He is better at the actual putting together of the diagram than at thinking out the clues. Those are done for him by an old naval colleague, Commander Robin Smith, in London."

"I see," said Colonel Nobile.

"His clue to 'dichotomy' was particularly apt, I thought. 'A backward police force has roast duck. And goodness me! A split.'"

The Colonel looked baffled.

"'CID—reversed. Then 'hot.' 'O,' of course, stands for a duck. Then we have the expression 'My!' Clever, don't you think?"

"Amazing," said Colonel Nobile. It seemed to him to confirm, in every particular, his previously held opinion of the English.

"Well now. The sun's over the yardarm at last. And what a day it has been, to be sure." As he spoke, the Consul was unlocking what appeared to be a filing cabinet and was really an icebox at the side of his desk. "Perhaps you would care to join me in a little drink? Whiskey with ice and soda water? Admirable!"

And the sun went down at last, a circle of liquid fire, turning first to bronze and then to a deep blood orange as it slid toward the horizon, its rays refracted by an evening mist that promised further and greater heat to come.

Avvocato Riccasole drove home through the cooling streets in his baby Cinquencento. A mile out on the Bologna road he turned right into a lane hardly wide enough for one car, and then maneuvered to the left, through an open pair of gates, and into a quiet backwater of villa residences.

Each one was flanked by iron railings, the railings topped with spikes and interwoven with climber roses in full bloom. Riccasole stopped his car facing high iron gates at the far end. A notice on them said: "Cane Mordace." He touched the horn and waited. There was a sound of bolts being withdrawn and the gates creaked open.

The maid who took charge of his hat and briefcase was rewarded with a smile. Riccasole walked down the path, through the open front door, along a passageway, and out to the stone-flagged court at the back where chairs were set under a lime tree. His wife, Isabella, awaited him with a long drink already poured. Her husband sat down beside her, picked up one of her plump hands, counted her fingers, as if to see that they were all there, then put the hand down again gently.

A dog padded up to them through the shadows. Bernado was a coal-black Molossian, a Neapolitan guard dog, weighing a full hundred and twenty pounds. The amber eyes, fixed on Riccasole, were gentle. When aroused, the dog could retract the outer iris, revealing the inner eye blood red. The breed had been developed by the dukes of Padua to hunt men.

Bernado subsided onto the ground with a windy sigh. Silence settled. Isabella broke it. She said, "Has it gone well? What success have you had? Can you help the poor man? Did he do this terrible thing, or is he innocent?"

Riccasole pondered. A thrush, which had floated down onto the lime tree, had its head on one side. Woman, dog, and bird all seemed to be listening for the answer.

Riccasole said, "I am very sad. He is quite innocent. But I very much fear that he will be found guilty."

12

Hotter

Mercurio came out from under a shower, toweled his beautifully bronzed naked body, encased it in a white shirt, navy-blue shorts, and sandals, spent five minutes combing and brushing his hair, and then left his bedroom and padded down to the floor below. In the central living room Arturo was busy with an electric polisher.

"Your father," said Arturo, "he is in his business room. He is writing letters. He has asked not to be disturbed."

"*I* shan't disturb him," said Mercurio. "He is always glad to see *me*." He took a quick sideways glance at himself in the long mirror by the door.

Arturo smiled. He said, "You look very well."

"I feel very well. Feeling well, Arturo, is a matter of the mind being in consonance with the body. At this moment, it is remarkably consonant."

He made his way down the passage, breaking into the quick double shuffle of a dance step as he did so. Then he opened the door at the end of the passage and went in.

The Professor, who was writing, looked up with a scowl, which changed into a smile as he saw the boy.

"Come in and sit down," he said. "I have nearly finished. A business letter." He signed his name with a flourish, blotted it, and pushed the paper away. "What can I do for you? You need more money? Don't tell me. You're an extravagant animal."

"Not money. Information." Mercurio sat on the edge of the desk and swung his long bare leg, admiring the shape of the calf and the way the golden hairs lay on his thigh.

"On any particular topic?"

"I desire," said Mercurio, "to know exactly what you are up to, my Father."

"Up to?" Professor Bronzini sounded neither surprised nor alarmed. An onlooker would have supposed that he was flattered by the interest this beautiful young man was showing in him and his affairs.

"As your adopted son, and your heir, I have the right to ask, have I not?"

"Hmm."

"Is it criminal?"

"Come, come," said the Professor, with a touch of asperity. "If it were criminal, do you imagine I should have anything to do with it?"

"If it is not criminal, why have you brought two Mafiosi thugs to Florence? They are not here to admire the pictures in the Uffizi and the Pitti, I imagine."

The Professor looked genuinely surprised. "I knew nothing of this," he said. "Thugs. What thugs?"

"Never having been formally introduced to them, I am afraid I cannot tell you their names. But one of them is short and thick, and the other is long and thin. And the stout one has stained his hands with blood, many times. That I detected when he touched me."

"But when did you encounter them? And how?"

"The pair of them have been hanging around the Via Torta for the last two weeks."

"And what have *you* been doing in that quarter?" There was a twinkle in the Professor's eye. "Some girl, don't tell me."

"There is a girl. I intend to make her my wife."

"Wife! You are not old enough to think of such things. At your time of life it should be girl friends. Lights of love.

Passing fancies. When I was your age..." The Professor chuckled.

Mercurio said, coldly, "We are not discussing your sexual adventures, nor mine. We are talking of more serious things. Things in which you are involved. Why have you changed the combination on your wall safe?"

"Because Danilo told me that you knew it."

"And why was it particularly important that I should *not* see the inside of your safe at this moment? It has never bothered you before. Well?"

The Professor said nothing.

"It contains, as I have now seen with my own eyes, two or perhaps three alabaster chests of the type which might hold ashes. Also the alabaster figure of a goddess. Such a one as might preside over the resting place of the noble dead. Two heavy chains of worked gold. A gold headpiece. And a number of golden ornaments. There were other objects. I had no time to inspect them."

"You seem to have made good use of the short time you did have. Did that transitory glance tell you anything else about these things?"

"Yes," said Mercurio. "It did." He was leaning forward a little, and his blue eyes were fixed disturbingly on the Professor's brown ones.

"I have, as you know, certain powers of extrasensory perception. For instance, I can always detect where human blood has been spilled. In some cases I can foretell the hour of death. Also, in certain matters I can infallibly distinguish between truth and falsehood."

"You have wonderful powers." The old man muttered the words, scarcely parting his lips. "Wonderful."

"The objects in your safe are very beautiful. They were designed by a master of Etruscan lore, and fashioned by the hand of a most expert professional craftsman. Yet they are false. Every one of them."

196

The Professor still said nothing. He seemed to be mesmerized by the boy, in almost willing subjection to his voice and eyes.

"Ordinarily," Mercurio continued, "I should have nothing to say to such matters. I have sensed, for some time, that all of this"—a wave of his hand indicated the Villa Rasenna and the comfortable life around him—"all of this was founded on fraud. You have used your knowledge and your reputation to sell to collectors pieces supposed to come from tombs on your private property. That I divined. But I asked myself, Who suffered? The collectors were happy. Many of them were foreign institutions, to whom money meant nothing. The private individuals were millionaires, indulging a whim. The only loser was the Italian State, for whose regulations I care as little as you do yourself. But now, at last, something has happened which forces me to take a different view."

His tones were those of a schoolmaster talking to a boy.

"Your practices involved old Milo Zecchi. His was the hand that carved the alabaster—to your designs, no doubt. It was in his workshop that the golden ornaments were fashioned. For long he was faithful to you. You had secured his silence, with your patronage and with your money. But in the end something happened. Something which comes to all of us, sooner or later."

As he said "sooner" he turned on the old man a look of clinical analysis and paused in what he was about to say. The Professor shook himself, like someone waking out of a deep sleep, and said "No" in a strangled voice.

"Indeed, yes," said Mercurio slowly. "He felt the hand of death upon him. He saw it, as an old man always sees it, in the early hours of the morning when he woke from his thin sleep. He was not afraid of death, but he did not desire to die with sin unconfessed. So he sought advice. And he was honest enough to seek it first from you. You were his patron. But you put him off. So he sought it elsewhere. From the Englishman, Broke. *But by this time, you had taken fright*. The greatest coup of your life was in jeopardy. The treasures of the inner tomb of Thryns. A second Regolini-Galassi. Objects of untold value. But of a value which the least breath of suspicion would destroy. So you took your precautions. You sent for these men. These animals. You had him watched."

"I—" said Professor Bronzini, and stopped.

"Yes," said Mercurio. His eyes had never left the old man's face. He seemed to be sucking the strength out of him.

"I didn't—" The Professor stopped again. The house was very quiet. "It wasn't my idea at all. I was fond of Milo. I was convinced he would do nothing to harm us."

"If it was not you, who was it?"

"Not me."

"Who then?"

The door opened very quietly, and Danilo Ferri came in. He said to the Professor, "I am sorry to interrupt you, but you are wanted on the telephone."

The fans in the carabinieri office were turning sluggishly, hardly disturbing the hot and heavy air.

Tenente Lupo pushed his uniform hat back on his head and wiped his forehead with the back of his hand. "We cannot possibly guarantee it," he said. "Surely it is a matter for the Polizia Giudiziaria generally. Not for the carabinieri alone." He looked across at Scipione for support.

Antonio Risso said, "The Procuratore has particularly asked that your office should attend to it." He was the only one of the three who seemed unaffected by the heat.

"The city police—"

"Usually we would ask them to assist. But these elections are occupying their full attention. Last night, a loudspeaker van was overturned in the Piazza della Libertà and set on

198

fire by the Communists. This morning, in retaliation, three Communist speakers were attacked and beaten. One of them is on the danger list. Every man of the police will be on duty twenty hours a day until the ballot is closed."

Scipione said, "If I might make a suggestion . . ."

"Yes?"

"I do not know a great deal about legal proceedings, but it appears to me that, apart from the experts, the only witness whose testimony is likely to be of great importance is the woman, Maria Calzaletta."

Risso considered the matter. He said, "There is also the cemetery keeper."

"There, I fear, we may be bolting the stable door after the horse is gone. He has made and signed a statement for the defense lawyer."

Risso's face darkened. He said, "I heard of it. There was, I consider, some inexcusable carelessness there."

"What would you have us do?" said the Tenente. "We would like to keep your witnesses on ice for you, fresh and uncontaminated. Unfortunately they are not only witnesses. They are also people. They cannot be stored in a refrigerator and brought out when required."

"You must ensure, at all events, that they do not get at Maria. You can spare this man, until the trial, to see to that?"

"I could do that, yes."

Scipione said, "The girl works at a café in the Via Torta. She sleeps above the café. For the last few days, a man has been lodging there, too."

"What man?"

"His name is Dindoni. He used to work for Milo Zecchi, and he had a flat above the workshop. Then the widow Zecchi threw him out. He and Maria are . . . friendly."

"So it would appear," said Risso, "if they occupy the same house. Why do you mention the man?"

"I have a certain influence with him. It occurred to me that he could assist in ensuring that Maria did not get into undesirable company."

"Well now, I think that is a very practical suggestion," said Risso.

The blazing afternoon was lengthening slowly toward evening when Maria finished polishing a row of glasses and put the last one back on the shelf. No customer had entered the place in the past hour. Dindoni, sitting on one chair with his feet on another, was half asleep. A fly rose off a smear of martini on the zinc bar, and settled on Dindoni's face. He grunted, brushed it off, and sat up. Then he said, "What's this? Are you going out?"

Maria had her hat on and her handbag in her hand.

"Certainly. I am going shopping, and you are going to watch the bar."

"Who says?"

"I say. If you are lodging here free, you are to work for your living."

"What about those other two? They are almost living here now. I believe one of them sleeps in that little room."

This was true. The fat man and his thin friend had cleared out a little room behind the bar that had once been a storeroom and had installed a table and chairs and a pallet bed.

"They have squared old Tortoni," said Maria indifferently. "I think the police are looking for them, and they are keeping under cover. It has nothing to do with me."

"He will get into trouble himself if the police find out."

"That will be his sorrow," said Maria. "I shall be gone for about an hour. Behave yourself."

As she left the café a man who had been sitting in the seat of a car parked in the shade farther down the road got out. He closed the car door carefully, taking care not to slam it, and started after her.

Maria walked slowly. The streets were filling as people came out of their offices. This was the hour for shopping, gossip, and the *aperitivo*. Maria seemed content to drift with the crowds, window-shopping as she went. The man drifted behind her; up the Corso Borgo degli Albizi, across the Piazza della Repubblica, and into Via Strozzi.

Here Maria seemed to seek, at last, what it was she had come out to buy. She turned into a shoe shop. It was dark in the interior. As she stood blinking a young man came out from behind the counter and said, "What can we do for you?"

Maria opened her handbag and took out the card that Avvocato Riccasole had given her. The young man scarcely glanced at it. He said, "I am sure we can fit you. If you would take a seat in here . . ." He held open the door of a cubicle and followed Maria in. She then noticed that there was another door at the back of the cubicle. He held this open for her, too, and she went through and found herself in a small sitting room, furnished with a circular mahogany table, three or four chairs, and a cage of stuffed canaries.

Avvocato Riccasole was seated behind the table, sorting over a folder of papers. He said to the young man, "Choose a nice pair of shoes for the lady, Carlo. Tell him what size you take, Maria. Pack them carefully, and have them ready in half an hour exactly. Sit down, Maria. We have no time to lose. My client's proposition is a very simple one. He will pay you two hundred thousand lire for your full co-operation. And a further hundred thousand in the contingency that you have to give evidence in court."

"Cooperation. What does that mean?"

"It means that you have to give me all the information you have. Names, details, matters which can be confirmed."

Maria thought about this, her peasant eyes bright with mingled greed and apprehension. "If I now have to say that I lied to the police, I shall be in trouble. Possibly I shall be imprisoned. No money would pay for that."

"Tcht," said Riccasole. "There's no question of that at all. You told the police you saw a car coming down the street. An English car, of unusual make. You noted its number. You told them also that you heard a car skidding, its brakes squealing. But that was a little later. It was not the same car. They muddled you with their questions, that was all. A girl cannot be sent to prison because she was confused. I promise you that."

"I am afraid."

"If you cooperate with me, there is nothing to fear. For both stories are equally untrue, are they not?"

Maria stared at him.

"You were nowhere near the Via Canina that night. What you said to the police is what you were taught to say by that creature Dindoni. I have proof of that. So consider. If you stick to your original story, you will be in very bad trouble. You may, indeed, go to prison. If, on the other hand, you modify your story, you will be supported by other witnesses. The truth of what you say will be established. *And* you will be the richer by two hundred thousand lire."

"Dindoni will be very angry."

"Dindoni will be very happy. He, too, has a great deal of information which will be useful to me, and which I am prepared to purchase. More, perhaps, than you have, since he is more deeply involved in this plot."

"I shall have to talk to him."

"Of course," said Avvocato Riccasole indifferently. He took out a wallet, extracted five notes of ten thousand lire each, and held them for a moment in his hand. Maria watched him greedily.

Leisurely he folded them, first into halves and then into quarters. Then he placed them on the table and pushed them across toward the girl, whose fingers folded over them. He said, "As soon as Dindoni is ready to talk to me, telephone me at this number." He scribbled on the back of the card. "The person who answers will know where I can be found. And I think it would be wise not to waste too much time over your deliberations. Say this to Dindoni: As soon as the information which I am certain he possesses is in my keeping, he will himself be a great deal safer. Until he has seen me, he stands, I think, in great peril."

13

Hottest

"Oh, dear," said Dindoni. His mean little face was pinched with indecision, fear, and cupidity. "Blessed Mother of Christ. If only I knew what to do."

They were in his bedroom, on the top floor of the café. Maria sat on one end of the bed, he on the other, dangling his brown booted feet. The left boot had a thickened surgical sole.

"Just listen to me," said Maria.

"I have listened, and I am still uncertain. Both courses are dangerous. Saints in heaven, I do not know which is the more dangerous."

Maria suddenly lost her temper. She said, "If you would stop whining to the Virgin Mary and the Congregation of the Blessed, and would think for yourself, you would see your way clearly enough. On the one hand, money and protection. Enough money to start up that business of your own you are always babbling about. Enough protection to keep your miserable carcass out of jail."

"Protection," said Dindoni, licking his lips. "Protection by whom?"

"By the authorities, if you admit the past and speak the truth. By the Sindaco of Florence, who is a friend of the Englishman, and pulling every string which he can pull on his behalf."

"Sindaco Trentanuove?"

"No other."

Dindoni pondered. He said, "Sindaco Trentanuove is of

the Communist party. If they make substantial gains in the local as well as the national elections—the one usually follows the other—his power will be even greater than it is now. Yes?"

"Certainly," said Maria. "His power to help—and his power to punish."

There was a long silence, but Maria sat composedly. She knew that the battle was won.

"If—I only said *if*—I desired to help, what would I have to do?"

"See Avvocato Riccasole, and tell him all that you know."

"When?"

"As soon as possible. Tonight if you wish."

"How would it be arranged?"

"He has given me a number to telephone. From there a message will be sent to him. He will arrange the meeting place. With me, it was a shop. With you—who knows. But it will be cleverly done. No one will suspect."

"And he will pay me money?"

"So much for the information. So much more if you have to speak in court."

Still Dindoni hesitated. He said, "How do we know he has this money? Where does he get it all from?"

"There is nothing in that," said Maria impatiently. "He gets it from the Englishman's sister. They say she has come to Florence, stuffed with money, to aid her brother."

"Very well," said Dindoni at last. "Telephone. But not from here. Not with those two men downstairs. Are they there now?"

"I do not know, nor do I care. They will not touch us now. They are themselves hiding from the police. They never come out by day."

"It is *not* day," said Dindoni. "It is night," and he shivered.

"Day or night," said Maria. "What does it matter, if they do not know?"

All the same, she closed the room door very softly when she went.

Alone in his attic room, Dindoni found it beyond his power to keep still. He walked to the window and peered down over the slates. The Via Torta was empty, and ill lit. But there was a car parked twenty yards up on the right, and he saw the sudden glow of a cigarette. Someone was sitting in the driver's seat of the car, waiting. Waiting for what? Dindoni swallowed, his mouth suddenly dry.

He walked over to the door, opened it an inch, and listened. No sound at all.

It was when he was walking back toward the bed that he saw it, and his heart turned over in his chest, then tripped and started to pound furiously. There was a red mist in front of his eyes and as his legs gave way he gripped the head of the bed to steady himself.

God in heaven, what a fool he had been! What a blind stupid fool to listen to that whore Maria! What in the name of mercy was he to do now?

As these thoughts—hardly thoughts; promptings of panic—raced through his mind his eyes kept jerking back, as if hypnotized, to what he had seen.

It was a small black metal box.

It was inconspicuously placed, under the corner of the mantel.

He knew exactly what the box was. He had fixed it with his own hands in Milo Zecchi's kitchen and had reeled out the threadlike, almost invisible black wires through a crack in the window frame.

He knew that if he looked, he would find the wires here. And he knew where they would lead. They would lead to a little room behind the bar that had once been a storeroom, and which now contained a table, two chairs, and a trundle bed.

"I must get out of here," said Dindoni. The words were spoken inside his own head. With that treacherous black box listening, it was not safe even to whisper.

He opened the door, and listened. Still no sound. Hope began to stir. If the men had been in their room, if they had overheard anything, surely they would have moved by now. Maybe they were both out, maybe that infernal machine was switched off.

Dindoni reached the bar, crossed it, and had put out a hand to open the street door, when it burst open. Dindoni cowered. A red-faced man whom he had never seen before strode into the room, rapped on the zinc counter, and said, "Service. Why the hell can I never get any service in this dump?" He glowered at Dindoni, who muttered, "The girl—she will be back in a moment," and shot out into the street before the man could say any more.

The stout man and the thin man were standing behind the beaded curtain that partitioned off the inner room.

"So," said the stout man. "I wonder if perhaps he has spotted the box, and is bolting."

"If so, all the better," said the thin man.

Together they crossed the bar.

The red-faced man said, "Service?" hopefully, but they ignored him and went out into the street. Dindoni was turning the corner.

"He will make for the crowds," said the stout man comfortably.

"He will feel safe in a crowd," agreed the thin man.

They, too, reached the street corner.

Behind them a car door opened and shut quietly.

As Dindoni got clear of the house, and the pounding of his heart slowed down, he began to recover the power of thought. His first step must be to contact Maria and warn her. She had gone out to telephone. The nearest boxes were in the Piazza della Signoria. He would look for her there. But if he failed to find her . . . could he possibly return to the house?

Dindoni shuddered.

He would never return to the house, except with a strong guard of policemen. As this thought crossed his mind, he began to realize the difficulty he was in. For what could he possibly say to the police? Could he tell them that he had accepted instructions, and money, from two criminals? That he had then been persuaded, by further promises of money, to betray them? That they might have got to know of his intentions, and if so would have only one objective, to silence him? What would the police say to all that? They would laugh and tell him to stop reading *i gialli*.

It was at this point in his desperate deliberations that Dindoni stepped out of the side road into the Via dei Leoni, and realized, for the first time, that something was happening.

A wave of men and women was sweeping up from the Lungarno. It was like the flood, but composed, not of the waters of the Arno, but of a great crowd of citizens. The front rank, as it were the crest of the wave, carried white banners. Behind them rolled a disorderly mob of men and women, singing, bawling slogans, and waving clenched fists aloft.

A glance at one of the banners showed Dindoni that this was a phalanx of the Communist party, celebrating the closing of the polls and a conviction of victory.

It was a question of going with them, or going under. Dindoni was sucked into the throng. They seemed to be heading for the Piazza della Signoria, traditional ground for demonstrations.

Had he been able to keep up with the leaders, all might

have been well. Hampered by his crippled leg, he could not manage this and, like an inexperienced surf rider, fell back from the crest of the wave, and was sucked into the trough behind.

Hands grabbed at him. He tripped and nearly fell. Tripped again. His one thought now was to get out of it, to get to the pavement, to cling onto something solid. He staggered and nearly went down again.

This time a strong hand had him by either arm, holding him up, edging him out of the crowd.

He turned his head and found himself looking almost down the throat of the thin man, whose discolored teeth were showing in a grin of pure enjoyment.

Dindoni screamed.

A woman in front of him turned her head and bawled, "That's right! Up the Communist party!"

A mist was clouding Dindoni's eyes. The strength had gone out of him. His legs were refusing to answer the last flutterings of his will. By the time the two men had dragged him clear of the crowd and into the comparative calm of a side street, his knees had buckled and his eyes were glazed.

"The gentleman would appear to have fainted," said the stout man. "What shall we do with him?"

"It would be an unthinkable waste of energy to carry it," said the thin man, looking down at the crumpled bag of clothes moaning and twitching on the pavement.

"We could borrow a car," suggested the stout man.

"There will be any number to choose from on a night like this. Watch him. I will be back within five minutes."

"And what do I say if a policeman comes along?"

"Tell him the excitement has been too much for the poor gentleman."

Dimly, the noise of the rioting crowds floated up to Commander Comber's flat, where he, Elizabeth, and Tina sat at their regular evening conference. Tonight the confederacy had an air of optimism. They were discussing their new champion.

"Extraordinary fellow," said the Commander. "Looks like an old pansy."

"Pansy?" said Tina, recalling her conversation with Broke. *"Finocchio!"*

"Yes. But actually nothing of the sort. If half the stories I hear about him are correct, that is."

"He's clever," agreed Elizabeth. "Pretty unscrupulous, too. I gather he's simply using Miss Broke's money to bribe Maria and Dindoni."

"Not exactly bribe. What he says is that before he can plan the defense he's got to find out what happened. And the only person who can really tell him that is Dindoni."

Tina said, "Dindoni is a— I can tell you the word in Italian, but I cannot translate it." She told him the word in Italian.

"Better leave it untranslated," said the Commander. "What a row those chaps are making." He moved across to the window. There were lines of tossing lights where torchlit processions wound through the streets, and a more solid glare from the direction of the Palazzo Vecchio.

"If they don't look out," said Elizabeth, "they'll set the town on fire."

Miss Plant was saying the same thing to Sir Gerald Weighill. She had narrowly escaped a crowd pouring down the Lungarno, and had dived into the Consulate for sanctuary.

"It's so stupid. They don't even know the result of the polls yet. That won't be out until tomorrow."

"That enables all parties to rejoice tonight," said the Consul. "Anticipation always beats realization."

"It's *my* anticipation," said Miss Plant, "that we shall have a conflagration. It might be very serious. This dry weather has made everything like tinder. A fire to windward could burn down half the city."

"I don't think that's very likely."

"People didn't think the flood was likely," said Miss Plant.

The Sindaco sat in his office with the window open on the street. He had studied the straw votes and opinion polls, and the smell of victory was in his nostrils. It would not be an out-and-out victory. Indeed, such a thing would have been embarrassing. The Communist party was not equipped with talent or experience to run the whole government. But an increase in votes would automatically mean an increase in offices and influence. They might become the dominant partner in a coalition.

The Sindaco stepped up to the window. A passing band of youths recognized him, and threw up hands in greeting.

The Sindaco raised his own clenched fist in reply.

To Broke, in his cell in the Murate prison, the noise of rejoicing came muted, like the surge on a distant shore. It did not register as a matter deserving any particular attention. It was, as he was coming to realize, one of the compensations of imprisonment that what went on in the outside world affected you very little.

Even that great question which should have occupied his mind day and night, the outcome of his trial, had ceased to be a matter of paramount interest. Things of more immediate concern were crowding it out. What food would he get at the next meal? When would he be allowed his next bath? Might he be forced to share a cell with another prisoner? He sincerely hoped not. He was entirely satisfied with his own company and the solace of books.

Paradise Lost was open on the bunk beside him. In his leisurely reading he had got as far as Book Eight.

> *What callest thou solitude? Is not the earth*
> *With various living creatures, and the air*
> *Replenished? And all these at thy command*
> *To come and play before thee. Knowest thou not*
> *Their language and their ways?*

That was really more Robinson Crusoe with his cat and his parrots. There were prisoners who had made friends of mice. Even of spiders, he had read. It would take a very long time to understand *their* language and their ways.

> *They also know*
> *And reason, not contemptibly, with these*
> *Find pastime and bear rule. Thy realm is large.*

"Thy realm is large." Broke repeated the words to himself, over and over again. He felt a curious form of contentment. He recognized that it might only be numbness; a lack of feeling as the anesthetic took charge.

Probably it was wrong to let go. Certainly he was letting down all those good friends of his outside who were rallying to his cause. He must not forget them. He must get a grip on himself.

He picked up the book and continued to read.

By midnight Florence was aglow with lights and bonfires, but the night was calm, and there seemed no danger of the general conflagration that Miss Plant had feared. It was all the more inexplicable that farmer Pietro Agostini, whose holdings lay a full three miles outside the city bounds, coming out for a final inspection of his outhouses, should have found a hay-and-fern stack already well alight.

He bawled for his wife, who came running.

"Telephone for the fire brigade."

"What use?" said his wife. "The brigades will all be fully occupied in the town. It will burn out. We are well insured."

"As long as the sparks catch nothing else," said Agostini. He moved nearer to the rick, and sniffed.

"How do you suppose it happened?" said his wife. "Perhaps one of the men was careless with a cigarette. I have warned them before. What is the matter?"

"The matter," said Agostini, "is that I can smell gasoline. Come closer."

He shielded his hand against the heat that was building up. His wife sidled up to him. She, too, could smell the pungent reek.

Her scream and her husband's shout of horror came together. A truss of blazing straw fell away and showed them, projecting from the heat of the fire, a single human leg.

Agostini darted forward, realized that he could do nothing, and fell back, swearing.

He could see, more clearly as the flames threw up more light, that the foot at the end of the leg wore a curiously shaped brown boot with a built-up surgical sole.

PART THREE

The Wheels Turn

1

Colonel Doria

On July 17 the political correspondent of *Osservatore Romano* reported that the President of the Republic had spent two hours in conclave with Dr. Pasquale, head of the Christian Democrat party. He gave his readers a summary of the discussions that had taken place behind closed doors at the Quirinale. Since the political correspondent had certainly not been invited to be present at this discussion, much of the report must have been intelligent guesswork, depending on the device, well known to political correspondents, of stating as fact matters that, given certain premises, must logically transpire.

The elections, so recently and hectically concluded, had produced no clear-cut mandate for any party. The Christian Democrats had suffered marginal losses. Their normal allies, the loosely knit collection who called themselves, with singular inaccuracy, the United Socialists, had lost nearly a third of their seats. Almost the whole of these had gone to the Communists, who were now, by some way, the largest minority party in the Chamber of Deputies.

The United Socialists had apparently concluded that this electoral setback was due to acting for too long as fifth wheel to the chariot of the Christian Democrats, attracting to themselves most of the unpopularity that tends to gather around a coalition. They had therefore refused to take part in the caretaker government that, as was customary, followed the elections.

The problem before the President, said the *Osservatore*'s

correspondent, underlining the obvious with a heavy pencil, was to persuade the leader of the Christian Democrats to form at least a loose alliance with the Communists, in order to produce a government that would not be outvoted in the Chamber every day of the week. It would not be a coalition. Neither party was ready for that. It would be a working arrangement.

What was, however, quite clear was that the Communists would not cooperate unless they were given some substantial inducement to do so. This inducement must include one or more of the key ministries. The price that the Communists were thought to be demanding was the Ministry of the Interior.

"Was that," asked the writer, "too heavy a price to pay?"

Since the two hours of discussion resulted in no apparent moves, he concluded that it was. But stalemate had not yet been reached. After all, there were other ministries. The Exterior. Grace and Justice. Defense. Agriculture.

"The next few days," the correspondent had written in the original version of his article, "will no doubt reveal which of these important posts is to be handed over to a party which has, in the past, openly dedicated itself to the destruction of the machinery of government and justice."

The editor, however, reflecting that they might yet see a Communist as Minister of the Interior, had prudently deleted this final comment.

"I cannot disguise from you," said Avvocato Riccasole sadly, "that it constitutes a heavy blow to our hopes. If we had available to us the testimony of Dindoni, however unwillingly given, I should have rated our chances high. Now that he is gone, I scarcely like to give you too much encouragement."

"I take it there's no doubt that it was Dindoni," said the Commander.

The conference was taking place in his flat. Elizabeth looked depressed. Tina had been crying.

"It is true," said Riccasole, "that by the time the fire was finally brought under control, early the following morning—this I had from the farmer—the body was almost entirely consumed. But three facts are inescapable. First, that Dindoni has completely disappeared. Secondly, that an examination of the bone structure of the body shows a deformed hip. And finally, that the farmer, in the instant before the fire took control, clearly saw a brown boot with a surgical sole such as Dindoni was wearing."

"I think we should be deceiving ourselves," said Elizabeth, "if we went on any other assumption. Dindoni is dead."

"Agreed," said the Commander. "But because we've lost a battle it doesn't follow that we've lost the war. What about Maria?"

"When Maria went back to the café and found that Dindoni—for reasons, incidentally, which are still unexplained—had left the house, she was sensible enough to telephone me at once. I invited her to my house. She was in a state of hysteria, but my wife succeeded in calming her. The following morning I took steps to place her in safe custody."

"Where is she?"

Riccasole hesitated.

"All right," said the Commander. "We're all on the same side here. But I agree. The less people who know, the less chance of it getting out. Let's leave it that you've got her safe for the moment. What's the next step?"

"The next step, which I already put in hand, is to arrange for Maria to make a sworn statement of all that she knows in front of a notary. Then, should anything unfortunate happen to her, too, we shall at least have a statement in a form which would be admissible in a court of justice."

"Surely you'll have more than that," said the Commander, springing up. "It will take us a long way down the course. Almost into the straight."

Riccasole, a student of human nature, took pleasure in observing the Commander: his abrupt but decisive movements; his naval and sporting metaphors; the piratical jut of his beard, all corresponding so exactly to his conception of an officer in the Royal Navy. Now, however, he shook his head sadly. "It will not," he said, "get us to the winning post. It will scarcely get us past the first flag."

"They were confederates," said the Commander. "Either of them can tell us as much about it as the other. It might only be secondhand evidence in court, but we shall at least know what happened."

"You forget," said Riccasole, "that I have already spoken to Maria. To have the statement recorded is only a formal precaution. What she knows I already know, and it is not very much. Her part in the plot was necessarily a small one. Consider that the men took a chance in using her at all. I think they did so because she was the only person available to them. They could use her through Dindoni. But they took good care to tell her very little of their plot."

"Plot!" said Elizabeth, looking up. "That's the first time I've ever heard anyone use the word. Then Robert didn't do this thing. There *was* a plot."

"Certainly there was a plot. A very carefully worked out plot, involving more than one person. A plot composed by professionals, who took great care that each person involved knew only sufficient to play his own part. Maria, for instance, had a small but important role. It was necessary that the police should get to Signor Broke without any delay. For consider: if there had been a delay only of a few days, he might have taken his car to the garage to have it serviced and cleaned. To have the broken fog lamp repaired. What more natural? But by so doing he would have destroyed,

quite innocently, the main part of the evidence against him."
He swiveled around in his chair, turned his soft brown eyes
on Elizabeth, and repeated, "Quite innocently, you understand?"

"Yes," said Elizabeth.

"The only convincing way to direct the police immediately to Signor Broke was that someone should have been
passing in the street, and should have noticed the number
of the car. But *why* should a casual passerby notice it? True,
it was an English car, of uncommon make. But that is not
very convincing. *But if one saw, and heard, the accident* . . . The squeal of brakes—that would make one take
notice. Yes?"

"It would also fix the time of the accident," said the
Commander. "I mean, it would appear to fix it. At a time
when Broke was known to have been driving down the
road."

"That is so."

"Whereas the cemetery keeper, who had absolutely no
reason to lie, puts the whole thing an hour later."

"Also true."

"Well, I mean to say, that clears the whole thing up,
doesn't it? They simply took Broke's car out of the garage,
after he was in bed—the dog heard 'em doing it, and kicked
up a fuss—and used it to run over Milo."

"Yes, but—" said Elizabeth.

The Commander had evidently begun to see some of the
difficulties, too.

"Remember," said Riccasole, "that two facts are clear
from indisputable scientific evidence. First, that Milo was
hit by the car. Second, that he did not die for some two
hours *after* he was hit. How did they induce him to be at
this particular point at half past eleven at night? It is certain
that he would never have gone there willingly. Do you
suggest, perhaps, that they bound him, hand and foot, laid

him in the road, ran over him, and then removed the bonds?"

"I wouldn't put anything past those two thugs we've heard about," growled the Commander.

"I agree. But it would be scientifically impossible. First, the signs of the ligatures would have been quite apparent. Secondly, he was *not* run over. He was *hit* by the car. Thirdly, if they left him alive after the accident, they were surely taking an appalling risk. He might have recovered. If not entirely, certainly enough to speak."

"I give you the last point," said the Commander. "But as for the first two, there was no need actually to tie him up. Could they not have threatened him, with a knife or a gun, and made him walk down the road?"

"Never," said Tina. "Never would he have done it. However many guns they had pointed at him, he would have fought and struggled. He would not have gone like a lamb to the slaughter."

"Also, it would have been entirely impractical," said Riccasole. "You are threatened with a gun and ordered to stand, just so, in the middle of the road. You hear a car coming. Do you continue to stand? Certainly not. You jump to one side. If you are shot, what matter? It is no worse than being run over."

Elizabeth said, "That's not the real difficulty. If we now think that Milo was killed and Robert was framed *for the same reason*—I mean, because they had to be stopped from having this talk, or the whole story of the Etruscan tomb and the planted 'relics' would have come out—then it means that the mastermind behind this plot must have been Professor Bronzini."

"Well?" said the Commander.

"I've never met him myself," said Elizabeth. "But I've heard plenty of stories about him, and you've met him more than once, Commander. Could you honestly describe him as a master criminal capable of organizing—how did you describe it, Avvocato?—a carefully worked out plot, a plot composed by professionals?"

The Commander said, "Perhaps he's a damned good actor." But he said it without a great deal of conviction.

It was at about the time this conversation was taking place that Carabiniere Scipione received a shock.

He was sitting in the office in the Via de' Bardi filing the nightly returns from hotels and boardinghouses when the door opened and a stranger walked in.

This was a middle-aged man, of medium size, with black hair, soberly dressed. Scipione said, "Well?" and continued with his work. The stranger said, "I would like to see the officer in charge of this station."

"Tenente Lupo is busy. Perhaps you will tell me your business."

"And perhaps I will do nothing of the sort," said the stranger.

Scipione looked up. Although the man was smiling, there was an undertone to his voice that sounded a warning. He said sharply, "Your name and business."

The man put his hand into his pocket, took out a card case, extracted a card, all with due deliberation, and laid it on the table.

Scipione sprang to his feet. In his agitation he nearly knocked over the table. He said, "A thousand apologies, Colonel. I will go myself." As he reached the door it opened, and Tenente Lupo came in. Without a word, Scipione thrust out the card. The Tenente read it and came forward with a smile.

"Colonel Doria," he said. "You are from Rome. Your name is known to me, although we have never met."

"The omission has now been remedied," said Colonel Doria. He sat down and motioned the Tenente to be seated also. Scipione remained standing stiffly at attention. "I should perhaps tell you why I am here. I have a letter from our Comandante in Capo, at Rome, which will establish my credentials. That is not important. It will not explain that he himself is acting under orders. The orders of the Minister of Defense." Colonel Doria paused, and added deliberately, "The *new* Minister of Defense."

"The new Minister?"

"I see that you have not yet got the midday edition of the *Osservatore*." He took a folded newspaper from his pocket and laid it on the table, indicating the passage in question. Tenente Lupo read it quickly. When he spoke, the words were carefully neutral, but it was clear that he had suffered a shock.

"The Ministry of Defense in the new government has been offered to Marcello Lungo."

"Not only offered. Accepted, I understand."

"He is of the Communist party."

"Our new master," said Colonel Doria, selecting his words with equal care, "is of that party. He has, I believe, known for some time that he would be selected for this post. That has enabled him to make certain immediate decisions. He has, for instance, expressed himself as dissatisfied with the handling, by his predecessor, of this case of the Englishman, Broke, which has attracted such publicity in the press. He has studied the papers personally, and I have been ordered to take charge of the investigation."

The silence in the room was broken by a slight movement from Carabiniere Scipione, which seemed to call the Colonel's attention to him. He said, "Perhaps we could continue this conversation in your private office, Tenente?"

Scipione held the door open for them. His face was as crimson as if it had been smacked.

When they were resettled, Colonel Doria said, "As a first step, it will, I fear, be necessary to remove that young man from the case."

"An excellent man in every way," said Tenente Lupo stiffly.

"No doubt," said the Colonel. "But a Sicilian."

"The implication being . . . ?"

"I imply nothing. But I, too, have read the papers. There are, at this moment, two dangerous professional criminals in Florence. They arrived some three weeks ago. Their arrival was reported to you by your office at the station."

"That is true," said Tenente Lupo. "And I ordered an immediate check of the registers of all hotels, *pensioni*, and boardinghouses. It was unsuccessful."

"And it was carried out by whom?"

"By Scipione. But surely—"

Colonel Doria held up one hand. He said, "Do not let us jump to conclusions. We must simply remember that many Sicilians who are not themselves members of the Mafia have nevertheless affiliation sympathies. Let me turn to another point. It was to Scipione that you entrusted the surveillance of the witness Dindoni, now believed to have been killed, possibly by these two men. What report did he make on the matter?"

"He lost sight of Dindoni in the crowd. It was the evening of the voting, you understand. There was great confusion. I could not altogether blame him."

"I do not blame him myself," said Colonel Doria. "But it was unfortunate. This is not a case in which mistakes will be lightly forgiven, you understand?"

Lupo understood very well. Where a minister, to enhance his own prestige or to discredit his predecessor, expressed personal interest in a case it was essential to the well-being of all concerned, from the Comandante in Capo di Carabinieri in Rome down to the humblest *tenente* in Florence, that the matter should be smoothly and successfully concluded.

He said, "What do you plan to do?"

"First, these two men must be found. I have here full details from the records in Rome. They can be held, for the moment, on some technical charge. Failure to register will be as good as any. Then I wish to see all the witnesses myself. The man Labro, the cemetery keeper, the woman Maria Calzaletta."

The Tenente's face clouded. He said, "The first two will present no difficulty. But Maria has for the moment disappeared."

"Then she must be found," said Colonel Doria.

A door in the upper story of the far wing of the Villa Rasenna opened, and Danilo Ferri came out. He shut the door quietly behind him and walked along the corridor, his footsteps silent on the matting that lined the floor.

No one looking at his dark composed face would have supposed that he had any troubles in the world. A man of order and method, under whose capable hands the complex machinery of the villa ran smoothly and silently.

He descended the main staircase with a curiously neat and catlike tread, and found the giant Arturo lifting the great vases of flowering shrubs onto the terrace for their daily watering.

He stood watching him for a moment. Then, almost as though it were an afterthought, he called to him, "Arturo."

"Signor Ferri?"

"There is one matter I should like you to see to. It is a matter of confidence, which I do not wish to have discussed with the rest of the staff."

"I am no chatterbox."

"I know it. The matter is this. We have two unexpected guests. I received them myself last night, and lodged them in the end room in the north corridor. They will be with us for a few days. Since it is not desirable that others should know of their presence, it follows that they cannot leave their room. They will need food and drink. Can you see to it yourself? If you use the back stair, from the little court-yard, no one need see you."

Arturo smiled a lazy smile. He had been standing all the while with a huge earthenware pot of azaleas in one hand, as if unconscious of its weight. Now he placed it gently on the ground and said, "There will be no difficulty. I myself will take care of them."

2

The End of a Dream

Colonel Doria had been allotted a handsome room on the first floor of the carabinieri station in the Via de' Bardi and it was here, on the morning of the next day, that he spoke to Avvocato Riccasole.

The two men were alone in the room. The windows were wide open and an electric fan fluttered in the corner, but it fluttered ineffectively, for the heat was of a character and a quality beyond the attention of electric fans. It had weight as well as temperature. The sky above Florence was still a fiery blue, but thunderheads were building up in the mountains behind the city.

"It was good of you to come so promptly to see me," said the Colonel. "You appreciate, I hope, that there need be no reticence between us. We are both, if I may so express it, on the same side."

"We are both on the side of justice," said Riccasole softly.

The Colonel considered this reply as carefully as if the whole conversation were being recorded for posterity. Then he said, "That is a correct statement. But it is an incomplete one. For there is also the interest of the state to be considered, an interest more important, in my opinion, than that of any individual. This case has become one of national, almost international, importance. I cannot tell you why. Intrinsically it is nothing. Perhaps it is the standing of the accused, perhaps the coincidence of the elections. Perhaps it is a feeling, an instinct, which journalists possess that there is something more, something unrevealed, which lies behind a simple running-down case. This does happen. You will remember when the accidental drowning of a young lady near Rome nearly upset the government of the day."

"I remember it well."

"This case may not be as important, but it has some of the same elements. And I can assure you of one thing. When it comes to trial—if it comes to trial—you will have reporters here from every important newspaper in the country. You will be on your mettle."

Riccasole smiled faintly. He said, "I would not presume to conduct so important a case in court myself."

"So! You will have a leading advocate from Rome?"

"Not from Rome. The case in court has been accepted by Sindaco Trentanuove. You will recollect that he is a qualified advocate."

If the news surprised Colonel Doria he was too experienced to show it. But he sat back a little in his chair to consider it. He said, dryly, "That will not diminish the public interest in the case, I should imagine."

"I should imagine not, no."

"It leads me to the next thing I have to say. It is important that the full truth should be established *before* the matter comes to court. So far we have half-truths." He tapped the bulky folder on the table in front of him. "There has been inefficiency at certain levels of the investigation. Not, I think, anything worse than inefficiency."

His eyes challenged Riccasole, who did not accept the gambit, but mopped his forehead with a large white handkerchief.

"The first step will be to question the witness Maria Calzaletta."

"Yes."

"I have reason to believe that you know where she is."

"Yes," said Riccasole sadly.

"Then I must ask you to bring her here."

Riccasole considered the matter while he continued to mop his forehead. He said, "It would be better, I think, if you would consent to go and see her. She is in a very disturbed state following the death of Dindoni. She was not greatly attached to him, but they had been ... closely associated."

"They were lovers?" said the Colonel bluntly.

"Yes. They were lovers." Riccasole considered the oddly assorted couple and sighed. He said, "She is being looked after in a convent near here. She has been given work by the sisters. I have some influence with them. I was able to do them a small service over a matter of taxation. Here is the address."

The sky was darkening as the clouds rolled up from the south and the west. Little gusts of wind made the leaves dance in the gutter and rustled the dry stalks on the walls of the Villa Rasenna until they scratched, like ghosts seeking entrance.

Professor Bronzini was facing Mercurio across his writing-room table. They had been sitting there since two o'clock and now it was nearly four. The argument had gone around in circles, like the leaves in the gutter. Mercurio said, "You're dodging the issue. If you know nothing about it, what are those two men doing in this house? I know they're here. I've seen Arturo taking them food. I've listened outside the door and heard them talking."

"They are friends of Danilo Ferri."

"They are criminals—Mafiosi—wanted by the police. A telephone call would bring a police car out here in five minutes. They would be removed. Are you afraid of them?"

"Certainly not. But Danilo—"

"Where *is* Danilo?"

"He went to Switzerland, on business, early this morning. He will be back tonight."

"*What* business?"

"Private business."

"His own, or yours? Is he your servant or your master? Is it you who dance to his piping? Does he crook his little finger and you come running?"

The Professor looked very old, and very tired. The cheerful silenus look had gone and had been replaced by a mask, with sunken holes for eyes and sagging parchment for cheeks. Looking at him Mercurio felt an unexpected twinge of pity. He leaned forward across the table and said, without any hint of his previous mockery, "Listen to me, please. I have not perhaps been very grateful to you in the past. I have sometimes behaved badly." The old man made a timid gesture with his hand, but said nothing. "Now perhaps I can repay you, if only with advice. Go to the authorities. Tell them everything. They say there is a new man here, from Rome. He has charge of the investigation. Go to him before he comes to you."

There was silence in the little room, broken only by the sound of the wind outside, coming now in gusts with some force behind them.

Mercurio said, "What have you to lose? You have had some beautiful Etruscan objects manufactured for you. But you have not yet sold them. It may be suggested that you intended to do so. But intention is no crime."

"There were others in the past."

"Certainly. But who will trouble their heads about them? Suspicion may be cast on them, but their owners will not be anxious to have their collections doubted. They will be the last people to attack you. Danilo Ferri must be given up to justice. For he is the true criminal. He, the quiet man, the steward, the organizer. It was he who brought these men to Florence. It was he who gave them their instructions. Did he consult you? Did he tell you what he was doing?"

The Professor hesitated, and then shook his head.

Mercurio said triumphantly, "I thought as much. Then how can you be blamed? It was he who organized the whole conspiracy. It was he who caused the death of old Milo, and the accusation to be made against the Englishman. Why should you shoulder the blame for something you have not done? Tell me that?"

The Professor said nothing.

"There is a difference between artistic faking—and murder."

Mercurio let the last two words hang, and then brought them out with deliberate brutality.

The Professor said, "I know nothing of that. I was promised that there would be no violence. The death was an accident."

"And the death of Dindoni? Was that an accident? Did he break his own neck and place himself on the bonfire?"

The old man shuddered. Mercurio, seeing his advantage, pressed it home. "You shall make your choice," he said. "The production of Etruscan relics—that is, perhaps, a minor matter for the civil courts. But a double murder! Will you accept the responsibility for what these animals have done? Animals hired and paid behind your back, by your own steward. Well?"

"If I speak, it will involve Milo Zecchi also. He had a part in it. And he is no longer here to speak for himself."

"Do you imagine that they will dig up his bones and hang them in the gibbet for carving a few bronzes on your instructions?"

"His family survive, and will be ashamed."

"That is true. It is an argument which I accept. But if his family themselves, his widow and his daughter, tell you

232

with their own lips that they would rather the truth came out, what then?"

The question was answered by a low rumbling of thunder. The old man was silent. His thoughts were a long way away. Many centuries away. He was walking again on the Etruscan hills, at the dawn of the first civilization, when men and women moved unencumbered, and the gods walked beside them, when life was wonderful and death only a pleasant postscript.

"Well?" said Mercurio impatiently. "If I do this, will you agree?"

"Shall an Etruscan Lucumo betray his own servant to the magistracy?"

The thunder rolled out again, on the left, a menacing drumbeat of sound. It was as though Thor, the Lord of Thunder, had himself answered the question.

Mercurio got up and moved across to the door. Still the Professor sat on in silence, unmoving. The look on Mercurio's face as he went out was one almost of pity.

He crossed the hallway of the silent house, opened the front door, and walked out into a world that was cowering before the coming fury. The light was pearly. So far only a few lazy drops of rain had fallen, but the strong wind that runs before the storm had bent the tops of the cypress trees over, like acolytes bowing all in line. Mercurio got into his car and drove down, through empty streets, to Florence.

As he reached the Zecchi house the storm broke in a fury of rain, driven horizontally down the street. In the few seconds that he had to wait for the door to be opened, he was soaked right down to the waist.

The two women were both there. Tina chirruped like a bird when she saw him, standing there, dripping. Annunziata, more practical, bade him take off his coat and shirt and gave him a towel to dry himself. Then she found a clean shirt that had belonged to Milo and popped it over him. Regardless, for once, of his appearance, Mercurio sat down in their kitchen, his head crowned with a mop of tousled hair, sticking through the collarless neck of the flannel shirt. While the storm raged outside, he talked. And as he talked, both women drew nearer to him, to hear, over the rolling and rattling of the thunder, exactly what it was he had to say. When he stopped speaking, Annunziata's piled gray crown of hair and Tina's sleek black head were nodding in unison.

When Mercurio left them, more than an hour later, the two women sat in silence for some moments. It was still raining, but steadily, and without ferocity.

Annunziata said to Tina, "That boy is growing up."

"I have noted it," said Tina. "Since the fight in the café he has become a different person altogether. Possibly he had never won a fight before."

At four o'clock the giant Arturo made a tour of the Villa Rasenna, carefully closing all open windows and fastening shutters and doors. He saw Mercurio depart in his car, and then stood at one of the windows, watching the rain advance like an army with spears.

The storm did not disturb him. He had seen many summer thunderstorms break over the house and pass on their way leaving the world fresher and brighter. This one was exceptional only in its violence. He was sorry for the flowers in the garden, which would be beaten to the ground and lose their blooms. But other flowers would grow.

When he came to consider the matter afterward he had no real idea how long he had stood there looking out, when he was disturbed by a crack of thunder, not louder than those that had gone before, but different in quality—and seeming to come from inside the house.

He decided that he must have been mistaken, but made

a tour of the ground floor to see whether, perhaps, a shutter had been blown off its hinges. Finding everything in order, he returned to his post. But he was still disturbed. Something was amiss. The noise had come from so far under his feet that it suggested some disturbance in the very lowest part of the house.

Arturo considered the matter. His mind worked slowly, but methodically. If this alarming noise had originated somewhere below the ground-floor level, there were four places it might have come from. There was the boiler room; and the coke store; there was the storage cellar, where wine and olive oil were kept; and there was the sacred room, the room of mysteries.

On balance, the most likely place seemed to be the boiler room or the coke store, and Arturo went there first. All was in order. In the cellars he found that some water from the recent deluge had made its way through one of the gratings and formed a pool on the floor. It would have to be mopped up. The only remaining possibility was the sacred room. Arturo had no key for this, and, in any event, was chary of entering it without his master's orders. Pausing outside it, he noticed that the door, usually so tightly shut, was standing very slightly ajar.

Arturo put out his hand and pushed it open.

The explanation of the noise he had heard was at once apparent. The door of the wall safe had been blown off its hinges, and the air in the unventilated room was pungent with the fumes of explosive.

But Arturo had no eyes for it. His attention was concentrated on the thing that swung by a short length of rope from a hook in the ceiling; a thing with bloated face, exploded eyes, and protruding blackened tongue; a thing that had once been his beloved master, Professor Bruno Bronzini.

3

Arturo

There was a high stool lying on its side underneath the body. Arturo stood it upright, clambered onto it, and raised the body with one arm. Then he reached up with his free hand and unknotted the rope from the hook. Climbing down, he laid the old man's body tenderly on the stone shelf that ran along one side of the room. As an afterthought, he took the clean white handkerchief out of the Professor's top pocket, and spread it over the distorted face.

He stooped for a moment, thinking. His eyes flickered over the safe door, hanging forlornly from one hinge, and over the empty shelves behind. The sight seemed to determine his next moves for him.

He walked back to the boiler room, his actions still slow, but purposeful. From the rack inside the door he selected a steel bar, eighteen inches long, flattened and slightly curved at one end. It was used for opening the dampers at the bottom of the boiler.

From the end of the basement passage shallow concrete steps led up to a landing. On one side a door opened out onto what was known as the small courtyard. Here, under a lean-to, stood a jumble of garden equipment, the bicycles of the kitchen boys, and, at the far end, the van in which Arturo did the household shopping.

The inner side of this landing gave onto a second flight of stairs, which led directly up to the top story of the house, where the domestic staff had their rooms.

It was up these stairs that Arturo had, for the past two

days, been carrying meals to the two strangers in the room at the end of the corridor.

As Arturo climbed the stairs, he was thinking about them. He had no doubt that both of them carried guns. He thought, however, that in an emergency they would rely on their knives.

He knew enough about Sicilians to be certain that two of them, armed with knives and knowing how to use them, would be too much for him. At the first warning of danger they would separate, and would come in from opposite sides. He might kill one. The other would most certainly kill him.

The door of the room had always been locked when he had brought them their food, and would be locked now. If they were still there . . . He stooped to listen. There were sounds of movement from inside the room. Something was being dragged across the floor, and one of the men was speaking.

Arturo considered the position. No doubt he could break down the door with a single kick, but this would give the men just those seconds of advantage that he could not afford. The safest plan would be to wait until they opened the door to come out. There had to be weighed against this the chance that, at any moment now, the alarm might be raised, and surprise lost. He decided on a straightforward course. He knocked on the door.

All movements inside the room ceased. Then a voice, which he recognized as belonging to the stout man, said, "Who is there?"

"Arturo."

"Well?"

"We have trouble in the house."

"Trouble?" The voice sounded much closer. The stout man had moved up to the door. "What sort of trouble?"

"It is the police. They are asking for my master. He cannot be found. Also"—Arturo purposely dropped his voice—"they seem to have some knowledge of you. I thought—" As he dragged the sentence out, he heard the click of the lock being turned, and the door was opened.

Arturo threw his weight against it, and jumped into the room.

The swing of the door going in had knocked the stout man off balance, but not off his feet. Arturo ignored him. Gripping the steel bar, he made straight for the thin man, who had been kneeling beside an old leather suitcase, strapping it shut.

The thin man flung himself sideways, steadied himself with one hand on the floor, and with the other went for his knife. These reactions to the unexpected attack were smooth, automatic, and dispassionate. They were also a fraction of a second too late. Arturo did not risk a downward swipe, which might have missed the moving head. He swung the steel bar sideways in a chopping sweep, which landed just above the shoulder at a point where the angle of the jaw ran into the neck. The force of the blow was such that it fractured jaw and spine simultaneously.

If the stout man had been on balance when Arturo started his bull-like rush, he would have had his knife in the big man's back by now. As it was, when Arturo whirled around he was already coming for him, knife held left-handed and low.

Arturo knew that to hesitate would be fatal. Despite his great strength, the odds against him were too high for deliberate maneuvering. He simply threw himself at his opponent, using his own big body as a missile, twisting sideways at the last moment.

The knife went into the upper part of his right arm, but the twist jerked it out of his opponent's hand.

Then his own hands closed around the stout man's throat.

The strength was ebbing from his right arm, but either of those great hands was sufficient for the job. As the stout man's knees buckled, he fell on top of him, never for a moment releasing his grip.

Minutes later Arturo got to his feet. The blood had been running in a steady stream from his arm and out at the wrist. A lot of it had dripped onto the stout man, who lay with his distorted face almost touching the feet of his long companion.

Arturo took no further notice of them. He had first to attend to his own hurt. He opened one of the two suitcases that stood, ready packed, beside the bed, and dragged out a silk shirt. He tore this into three strips, using his teeth, folded one of the strips into a pad, and bound the other two tightly around it, stanching the flow of blood. He would have liked to fashion a sling, but there was work for which both arms would be needed.

He went to the door and listened. Then he padded down the stairs to the courtyard door and opened it cautiously. The thunder was still rolling around the hills, and the rain was coming down steadily. The only windows overlooking the court were closed and shuttered.

He went out, got into the van, and backed it up to the door. The next bit was going to be dangerous, but there was no way of avoiding it. He had to make three trips. On each of the first two he carried a body, slung easily over his left shoulder. On the third he carried two suitcases in his right hand, and under his left arm a heavy wooden tea chest, corded and nailed. There had been no need to force it open. He knew very well what was in it.

The tea chest went into the back of the van, on top of the bodies. Still he had not finished. He walked back to the lean-to, blessing the rain that was soaking him to the skin, the rain that was keeping all other members of the household indoors, the rain that was washing away all traces from the stones of the courtyard. From the back of the lean-to he selected two gasoline drums, and carried them to the van. They were wedged in place beside the tea chest, between the thin man's legs.

Arturo drove out of the court, down the long drive, and onto the highway.

The side flaps of the driver's cab were misty talc. The windshield was running with rain, with a single clear patch under the wiper. Arturo was happy. If anyone else on the road noticed the van, they would certainly not be able to identify the driver.

His course took him steadily uphill.

Short of the Borgo San Lorenzo turning he left the main road for the secondary road leading to Pratolino. A little farther on he turned left again and was now on a minor road, hardly more than a farm track, which led up, in a series of zigzags, over the shoulder of the mountain, served two farmhouses, and then descended again to rejoin the secondary road.

The going, difficult in ordinary weather, now demanded all Arturo's skill and attention. About a half-mile later, with the track still rising, he came to a point where he could go no farther. The torrential rain of the last few hours had swollen a mountain stream, which had overflowed the path, washing the outer half of it away.

Here he stopped. On the right the ground ran down sharply, almost precipitously, to a tangle of rocks in the stream bed, covered now with white frothing flood water. Anything sliding over the edge might tumble into the river bed, or might crash into and be held up by one of the trees or rocks in the path of its descent.

Arturo dismounted. The next moves had to be made with great care.

First he took out the gasoline drums, which had already leaked a little in the racketing of the journey, unscrewed the caps, and emptied them, slowly and methodically, into the back of the van, covering the bodies, the suitcases, the tea chest, soaking the seats, forming puddles on the floor. He replaced the empty cans in the back of the van, but without their tops.

Next he moved around to the driver's seat and restarted the engine. Then he dismounted and, crouching by the open door on the uphill side, held down the clutch with one hand and put the car into first gear. Still keeping the clutch depressed, he opened the hand throttle until the engine was racing, then released the clutch.

The van lurched forward onto the broken section of the path, then, its wheels spinning, slid to the right, hesitated for a moment, and toppled off the path, turning over twice, cracking into a large rock, which held it for an instant, then toppling over this, and coming to rest just above the stream bed.

Arturo picked his way carefully down after it, moving from rock to rock so as to leave no trace.

When he got there he found that the bodies and the suitcases were still in the van. The tea chest had been thrown out, had hit a rock, and disintegrated. Its contents were scattered over the hillside. A circlet of gold had lodged in a bush, a scattering of ornaments gleamed from the weeds and grass. Both of the alabaster chests had fragmented and spilled their treasures broadcast. The goddess had been decapitated, and lay in the stream. The head, by some freak, had lodged on a rock above the water and gazed inscrutably at her destroyer.

Arturo felt in his pocket for matches. Great care would be needed here. He knew something of the properties of gasoline when aroused.

Shielding the flame from the wind, which had risen as the rain eased off, he lit a long spill of paper, waved it until it was well alight, pushed it into the back of the van and jumped clear. He stumbled on a rock, and was on his knees when the van went up in an explosion of white fire.

He climbed back to the path, glancing, as he did so, at his watch. It was six o'clock. It seemed unbelievable that so much could have happened in a single hour. He was six miles from home. The wound in his forearm had started to bleed again, and was throbbing unpleasantly. He had hurt his knee when he fell. And he was soaked to the skin with rainwater and sweat. But he was content.

At six o'clock Mercurio arrived back at the villa. The rain had almost stopped, and the clouds were shredding away under a strong wind. The earth was refreshed. A few birds were creeping out to shake their draggled feathers and tune tentative notes.

Mercurio went straight up to his room, had a shower, and put on a complete outfit of new clothes. It was a measure of the urgency he felt that he spent barely a minute on his hair. Then he marched down to find the Professor.

He drew a blank in the study, and all other likely places, and rang for Arturo. Arturo could not be found. One of the houseboys thought he might have gone out. He said that he had heard the van start up and drive off.

Mercurio was annoyed. The new-found and altogether agreeable feeling of self-confidence, of mastery of the situation, which had been growing as he talked to the Professor, and had reached full flood in his interview with Annunziata and Tina, was now demanding action. If there was to be a palace revolution, all the plans for it *must* be ready by the time Danilo Ferri got back from Switzerland.

It was well after seven when his impatience drove him down to inspect the one place he had so far overlooked.

The telephone purred in Tenente Lupo's office. He swore quietly to himself as he lifted the receiver from its rest. It was a quarter past seven. He had been planning supper, a quiet evening, and early bed. Now what?

He listened to the excited voice at the other end, said, "Speak more slowly, please," and, "Yes, of course I will come," and rang off.

He thought for a moment, then went out into the passage, opened the door opposite, and looked in. Colonel Doria was still at his desk, studying a long typewritten report, making tiny notes in the margin. He looked up.

"Something has happened," said the Tenente. "It might be of significance. I do not know."

"Tell me."

"I have had a message from the Villa Rasenna. The body of Professor Bronzini has been found."

"Found? Murdered?"

"I am not sure. Mercurio—he is the adopted son—discovered the body. He was not very clear. The shock—"

"The shock must have been severe," agreed Colonel Doria. "You are going up?"

"Yes."

"I will come with you."

"I do not wish to distress you unduly," said Tenente Lupo. "But you will see that the present situation is not very satisfactory."

"I have told you all I know," said Mercurio. Shock had given place to something harder, something more calculated. Lupo was sufficiently experienced in interrogation to recognize this. He also appreciated the need for care. He was dealing with important people, and the situation was explosive. He said, "You have told me that you left here before four o'clock, to visit the Zecchis—"

"Which you can confirm."

"I have no reason to doubt your word," said Lupo.

As Colonel Doria, who was sitting quietly in the corner,

well knew, an officer had already gone down to the Zecchi house. "You got back here at six o'clock, as your servants have confirmed. Death, we are told, took place sometime after four. There can be no question of suspicion attaching to you. I say this bluntly, to make it plain that you have no possible motive for not answering our questions."

"I have answered them."

"You have answered a great many, very patiently," said Lupo with a smile. "But there is one point on which I am not yet clear. Had your father—your adopted father, I should perhaps say—any reason for taking his own life?"

"None at all," said Mercurio. He said this with almost too much emphasis, and Lupo persisted. "No reason? He was then in good health and spirits?"

"You're wasting time," said Mercurio. "My father was murdered. *And* you know who murdered him. *And* why. Nothing could be clearer."

"These two men?"

"Of course. You have seen the safe door. Who but men like this would have had the equipment to blow it off? One of our vans is missing. No doubt they have stolen it, and used it to carry off the loot. If you would take steps to catch *them* instead of spending all these hours here talking to *me*—"

"All steps are being taken, be sure of that. The description of the van has been circulated, and roadblocks have been established. Indeed, if these are the men we think they are, we shall be very interested to interview them. And not only in connection with this affair. They will have much to answer for. But one point seems to me to require explanation. Why were they here at all?"

"My father was softhearted, and in some respects credulous. I have no doubt they told him some story."

"Did *you* know they were here?"

"I knew, but did not approve."

"Did any of the servants?"

"If anyone knew, it would be Arturo. He was in my father's confidence."

"Would you send someone to fetch him?"

Colonel Doria said, "What was in the safe?"

"It was my father's private safe. It had, as you see, a combination lock and the combination was known only to him."

"Then you have no idea what was in it?"

"I can only tell you that it would not be money or securities or papers. These were all kept at the bank. It would probably be valuable Etruscan relics. Gold and silver, and possibly precious stones— Ah! Arturo?"

"I must apologize," said Arturo gravely. "Earlier this afternoon I badly strained my right arm." He touched the sling with his left hand. "I was trying to start up the big tractor and it backfired. It was very painful. I lay down in my room, and must have fallen asleep."

He said this with his eyes fixed steadily on Mercurio, who looked as steadily back. The boy who had fetched him was well aware that he was lying. He himself, when the alarm had been raised an hour before, had gone up to Arturo's room and found it empty. The Etruscan discipline of the Villa Rasenna was strict. It did not occur to him to open his mouth.

Mercurio said, "I am sorry. It must indeed have been painful. The Tenente was asking about two men, guests of my father, who have been in the house since the day before yesterday. You knew about them, I imagine."

It occurred to Colonel Doria that if he had been asking the question he would have put it rather differently, but he did not interfere.

Arturo said, carefully, and still watching Mercurio, "Yes. I knew of them. My master had invited them here, but desired that their presence should be a secret. I attended to

245

them myself. They are occupying a single room at the end of the upstairs corridor. If you would wish to speak to them I could fetch them for you."

"I wish that were true," said Lupo.

"They are no longer there?"

"They are no longer there. And would appear to have left in a hurry."

"Is it permitted to ask," said Arturo, looking slowly around the little group of men, "has some crime been committed? Something involving them, perhaps?"

"Why do you ask that?" said Lupo.

"It seemed to me that these men were not of good character. That they might, perhaps, be of the criminal class . . ."

He paused. Mercurio looked at Lupo, who nodded slightly. Mercurio said, "Your master is dead. He died by violence. Whether by his own hand or the hand of others we do not know."

In the silence that followed the only movement was made by Arturo. He crossed himself.

Tenente Lupo and Colonel Doria drove back to Florence together. It was after ten o'clock. Photographers and fingerprint men had finished their work. Professor Bronzini's body had been taken to the Questura for further examination by the state pathologist.

The sky was clear and the air was fresh. A host of stars looked down on them as they swung down the wide curving road from San Domenico di Fiesole.

"It's one of the oddest setups I've ever seen," said Lupo. "Why would a man like that take his own life? Always supposing it was suicide."

"There have been persistent allegations," said the Colonel. "I find them over and over again in the papers—in statements from that English naval officer; in comments on the witness Labro; in remarks attributed to Milo Zecchi's widow and his daughter—that the Professor was engaged in faking and selling Etruscan relics. I have been making a few inquiries about him here and in Rome. Twenty years ago he was not a rich man. He was, of course, a recognized authority on Etruscan matters, but learned professors are not necessarily good men of business. A number of commercial enterprises in which he had been concerned had failed. It was at this time that he started to excavate the tombs which lay on his family property near Volterra. Co-incidentally his fortunes began to revive. But how? The relics which he discovered, and presented to the museums, brought him more glory than money."

"You mean that some of the relics, the better ones, may have been smuggled out of the country and sold abroad?"

"I mean more than that. I mean that he would have been ideally situated to *construct* relics. Consider. He had the knowledge and artistry to design them convincingly. He had a ready-made place for them to be found in. And he had a craftsman capable of executing them."

"Milo Zecchi. Of course. And if Milo was threatening to talk, that would be a reason for getting rid of him. But how . . . ?"

"There are still a great many 'buts,'" said the Colonel. "All that I have said is that, if threatened with the exposure of his plot, Professor Bronzini had a comprehensible motive for taking his own life."

"If he did hang himself, who took down the body? In itself, no light task."

"No indeed," said the Colonel. "It would need two ordinary men. Or one very strong one."

"You were thinking, perhaps, of Arturo?"

"It did occur to me to wonder whether his account of how he hurt his arm was entirely candid."

When the car drew up outside carabinieri headquarters a man was waiting for them with a message that had just arrived.

Lupo read it. He said to Colonel Doria, "It doesn't seem that we shall get much sleep tonight. One of our patrols has just found the missing van."

"The truth, please," said Mercurio. "And no more stories about arms being strained in starting up nonexistent tractors. Also, I have spoken to one of the boys. The one who went up to your room at seven o'clock. And I saw the bundle of clothes which you had not had time to destroy. I have placed them, myself, in the large furnace."

Arturo said, "It had not been my intention to conceal anything from you."

"I am sure that is so. But if I am to do what is necessary, I must know exactly what happened."

It took ten minutes to tell. At the end of it Mercurio sat in silence for some time. Then he said, "You did very well. Now I must think clearly, for both of us, so that no harm comes." He was silent again, his brain, a cool and logical instrument, analyzing, considering, rejecting. Arturo stood behind him, also in silence. He had refused to sit. He was the physical force. Mercurio was the intellect. Between them they formed a new and formidable alliance.

Finally Mercurio said, "I can see no weaknesses in the story. Lorenzo, the boy who went to your room, will be sent back to the farm. In any case, he will not speak. If the van has not been completely destroyed, your fingerprints will be on the steering wheel. But what of it? You drive the van daily. You are sure that no one saw you loading up the van?"

"Quite sure."

"Once it was on the road you would not have been visible. And you met no one during your walk home."

248

"I used tracks, not roads. And it was getting dark. Might I ask a question?"

"Of course."

"When I saw the body of my master hanging, and the safe door blown open, I did not stop to think. I assumed that those two men had been responsible for both. But now I have been thinking. *Did* my master take his own life? Why should these men have killed him?"

Mercurio said, "Who can tell what wild beasts will do? But I think you are right. I think he ended his own life. No Etruscan ever feared death, particularly when he felt that his allotted span had been achieved." He thought again for a few minutes. "What is necessary now is to forget the past and think of the future. When does Danilo Ferri return?"

"He comes by train from Milan, and arrives at eleven-forty. He has his own car, and will drive straight back here from the station."

"I hope," said Mercurio with a slight smile, "that he will not have found the business which took him to Switzerland unduly fatiguing."

Arturo smiled back.

It was fifteen minutes past midnight when Danilo Ferri brought his car up the driveway of the Villa Rasenna, between the sentinel cypresses, black and silent, and into the front court.

He parked at the far end of the court and walked slowly back to the house. His southern face, under its neat cap of black hair, was expressionless. No one would have supposed that he had just concluded six hours of bargaining with a circle of suspicious and ruthless men to whom he had been forced to make excuses for delay and firm promises for the future.

It was Arturo who opened the door for him. He said, "What have you done to your arm, Arturo?"

"I fell downstairs, Signor Ferri. I was carrying a heavy vase." He smiled gently. "The vase was not hurt, but my arm was."

"If you are hurt, you should have gone to your bed. One of the boys could have stayed up."

"It is no great matter," said Arturo. He added, "Signor Mercurio would like a word with you. He is in the writing room."

"I'm afraid I'm too tired for more words tonight. Tell him I have gone to bed."

Arturo's giant form was blocking the stairs. He said, "It is very important. I think it would be right to speak to him."

"What do you mean?"

"We have had the police here."

"Does the Professor know about this?"

Arturo said, very gently, "The Professor is dead."

Danilo Ferri stared at him for a long moment, then he swung on his heel and strode off down the passage without another word.

Arturo padded softly after him.

Mercurio was seated at the Professor's writing desk, a huge pile of papers in front of him. It seemed as though he had emptied out every one of the desk drawers.

"Is this true?" said Ferri.

Mercurio said, "Sit down, please. You must be tired."

"Is it true?"

"You cannot make the journey to Switzerland and transact important business and return, all in the same day, without experiencing fatigue."

There was an undertone to Mercurio's speech that Ferri had never heard before. He sat down, and said very quietly, "I demand to know whether what Arturo has just told me is true."

"Much will depend upon what he told you."

"He said that the Professor was dead, and that the police had been here."

"Both those statements are true."

"Is that all you have to say?"

"You asked me a question, and I have answered it." His blue eyes held the black ones for a long moment. In the end it was Ferri who shifted to break the deadlock. He said, "In your own good time, then, perhaps you will be kind enough to tell me about it."

"Perhaps," said Mercurio. He appeared to consider the matter. "Yes, I think it is right that you should know. Particularly since it concerns you. At seven o'clock this evening, the Professor's body was found, by me, in the basement room. It was lying on the stone bench on the far side of the room. Ironical, is it not, that it should have been occupying almost exactly the place which he had always planned that his mortal remains should occupy?"

Ferri said nothing.

"However, I must tell you—and I do so in the full confidence that you will not repeat it—that this was not the first discovery of the body. Nor was it in that position when discovered. Some hours earlier Arturo found the body, hanging from a hook in the ceiling. He also observed that the safe had been blown open."

"What?" The exclamation was forced out of Ferri.

"You are surprised? Why should you be surprised? If you introduce two professional criminals into the house you must expect things like that, surely."

Ferri said, "Go on, please."

"The results were exactly what one might anticipate. Arturo is a Corsican. He was deeply attached to his master. He has no love for Sicilians. He went up to their room, found them packing up the treasure they had stolen, and killed them both. Then he took the bodies, and the treasure, in the small van, drove it into the hills, and burned it. By daylight tomorrow, at the latest, the police will have discovered the remains. They will assume that these two men robbed the safe, were running off with the loot, and, in the darkness and rain, turned the van over the edge, and it caught on fire. Whether they will assume that they killed the Professor, or that they found him hanging and seized the opportunity to rob him, seems to me to be immaterial."

"Why are you telling me this?"

Mercurio said, leaning forward, and speaking very softly, "I tell it to you because you will never dare to repeat it. The police may believe that the killing was an accident. *The organization from which those two men came will not be so credulous.*"

There was a long silence. Danilo Ferri noticed, to his annoyance, that his right hand was shaking very slightly. He put it away in his pocket. He said, in a carefully controlled voice, "I don't understand you."

"You understand me very well," said Mercurio contemptuously. "Those men were of the Mafia. You hired their services. You know the code. It is rigorous. You were responsible to their *capo* for their safe return. Responsible with your own life. You are a marked man. If you get out of Italy quickly, you may live for a little time longer. Where will you go? You cannot go to Switzerland. You have disappointed clients there. Perhaps you have even sold to them, for money in advance, objects which you can no longer produce?"

Mercurio saw that this shot had gone home.

He said, "I think you had better leave tonight. Arturo, who, I have no doubt, is waiting outside the door, will help you to pack, and will drive you to the station."

252

4

The Uses of a Press-Clipping Service

It was ten days, one hot spell, and one thunderstorm later when two significant legal figures, the Procuratore della Repubblica and Avvocato Riccasole, met in the office of the former.

"I was distressed to learn that our promising assistant, Sostituto Procuratore Risso, had been taken ill," said Riccasole.

"He is not really ill. But he is suffering from fatigue."

"His efforts in the municipal election?"

"Exactly."

"I was so sorry that he failed. By such a narrow margin, too. The loss to local politics is a gain to the law, however."

"That is true," said the Procuratore. "Now, about the matter of your client Signor Broke."

"Yes?" said Riccasole. He felt that in forcing the Procuratore to open the suit he was already a trick in hand.

"These developments at the Villa Rasenna have put a different complexion on the matter."

"They have indeed."

"The police have established a certain sequence of events, to their own satisfaction. There are still some points which are obscure, but the main outline is clear. Three people were involved in a trade in imitation Etruscan objects. Professor Bronzini, his steward, Danilo Ferri, and one of his workmen, Milo Zecchi. Two of these are dead, and the third, and possibly the principal criminal, Ferri, has disappeared. It seems that he left for Rome on the night of the Professor's death and traveled by air to Paris. Interpol has been informed, but—" The Procuratore spread his hands.

"I agree," said Riccasole. "On the occasions on which I met him, he struck me as a very slippery sort of customer. Probably we shall not hear of him again."

(Though he did not know it, he was making a prediction that was shortly to be falsified. Less than a month later one of the *Bateaux Mouches,* plying the River Seine, made a sharp turn below the Pont d'Iena and brought to the surface the body of Danilo Ferri, inflated with the gasses of corruption. He was identified by his fingerprints, and the news of his end was transmitted to Florence in due course.)

"But it is not primarily with the affairs of the Villa Rasenna that we must concern ourselves," said the Procuratore. "They are of interest to us at this moment only insofar as they touch the affairs of Signor Broke. It would now seem possible—I go no further—that the involvement occurred in this way. Milo was troubled with his conscience. He had admitted as much. To his employers he thus became a source of danger. The more so since a very large coup, possibly indeed a final and climactic operation, was pending. To guard against this danger Ferri secured the cooperation of two of his countrymen. We have their records. You can see them if you wish. They do not make agreeable reading."

"Such animals have no interest for me."

"I agree. What is clear is that a plot was constructed to kill two birds, if I may so express it, with one motorcar. What is not yet clear is exactly *how* the operation was planned. It seemed to me that this was a matter in which you might be able to help us."

Riccasole pondered. It was a subtle olive branch that was being held out. He said, "I am in some difficulty. It is true that my researches have placed me in possession of certain information which makes it clear how this matter was contrived. It would, of course, be my duty to produce these witnesses, and to lay these facts before the Tribunale in due course. What would not be very sensible"—he smiled disarmingly—"would be to present you with them in advance of the hearing."

"I appreciate fully the delicate position in which you find yourself," said the Procuratore. "May I assure you of this: *If* you can clear up these few outstanding matters, I shall deem it my duty to invoke Article 391 of the Codice di Procedura Penale and to ask that the proceedings be quashed by the Giudice Istruttore. In which case, of course, they will not come to court at all."

"You set my mind at rest," said Riccasole. "On that understanding, then, I will explain to you the matter as it appears to me. You will appreciate, by now, one important point. Professor Bronzini was the master of the Villa Rasenna only in name. Its real head was the steward, Ferri, a much stronger and more ruthless character. The Professor produced the forged relics. But it was Ferri who had the contacts, in the international art world *and* in the criminal world which flourishes on its fringes. He organized the sales and received the money. And when his greatest coup, the culminating operation, was threatened by the mischance of Milo Zecchi developing a conscience, and Robert Broke—who would fully understand the implications of all he said—being cast in the role of his father confessor, then it was Ferri who acted. He had already introduced two professional criminals into the city. The Professor may or may not have known they were there. Now Dindoni was induced, by fear or cupidity, to ally himself with them. He acted as their spy. He installed a microphone in the Zecchi kitchen. Thus, when the moment came, he was able to give them ample warning of how, and when, and where Milo planned to meet Broke. That was the background of the affair. I have no doubt you have much information which I have not got. Does what I have told you fit in with your own ideas?"

"Perfectly," said the Procuratore. "Let us proceed to the night of the killing."

"It is my impression," said Riccasole, "although here I have to admit that I am guessing, that immediately after Milo left his house he was lured into the Tortoni Café. Probably by Dindoni. The woman Calzaletta had been sent away. She had a later part to play. The café was empty. The two men would see to that. You can guess what transpired."

"Yes," said the Procuratore with a slight shudder. "I can picture it quite clearly. Pray proceed."

"Milo was knocked on the head. As coldly as you or I would kill a chicken. In fact the blow, which seems to have caused some bleeding, did not kill Milo. Not quite. He was alive, but unconscious. This was not intentional, I think. The men cared very little whether they killed Milo or not. But I mention it because it produced a subsequent complication. The body was dumped in the back room. One of the men remained behind to clear up the mess. The other stole a motorcar. Not, I am afraid, a very difficult feat in this town at this time of year. In this car he went, first, to the agreed meeting place. It was most necessary to see that Signor Broke *had* actually gone there. If, for any reason, he had not done so the whole plan would have had to be abandoned. Or at least remodeled."

"But Broke *was* there?"

"Yes, and he recollects hearing a car drive up, slow down, and then drive on. Naturally he thought nothing of it. He thought it might be a courting couple. But when he left, the car followed him discreetly, to be sure that he took the expected route home, down the Via Canina. As soon as he was safely in bed, the final stage of the operation was put into train."

Riccasole felt in his pocket for his wallet, and took out of it a faded newspaper clipping, which he smoothed out on the desk. He said, "I must most particularly ask you not to inquire how this came into my possession."

The Procuratore studied it curiously. It was from a Sicilian newspaper, and it was nearly ten years old. It was headed "Mafia Technique" and it said:

A confession extracted from Mafia gangster Toni Perrugino has solved a mystery that has led to the death of one man and the imprisonment of another. Some three years ago in the little township of Adolfi, truck driver Arnolfo Terricini was accused of running down and killing the Mayor of the village, Enrico Caponi. The evidence against him was strong. He was known to be a reckless driver, and his truck had been observed driving fast from the place where Caponi's body was found. The clinching evidence stemmed from a police examination of the front bumper on Terricini's truck, which revealed dried blood, hairs, and fragments of skin, which were scientifically proved to belong to the victim, Caponi.

The Procuratore said, "Interesting."

"You will find the last paragraph even more interesting," said Riccasole dryly.

It now appears that Caponi and Terricini were both victims of the subtle and fiendish vengeance of the Mafia, whom they had offended. Perrugino, when confessing to—nay, boasting of—a number of crimes, admitted that he and two friends, skilled mechanics, had actually unbolted the bumper from the truck and used it as a weapon to beat in Caponi's brains, subsequently replacing it on the truck...

When the Procuratore had finished, he turned back to the beginning and read the clipping all over again. Then he said, "I have promised not to ask you how you obtained this. But perhaps you would allow me to guess where you obtained it. Did it come from the body of one of those two men?"

"The wallet"—Riccasole appeared to be picking his words

with great care—"came from the room in the Villa Rasenna which had been occupied by these two men, and it could well be assumed that it belonged to one of them."

"You are not suggesting that one of these men *was* Perrugino. The details we have make that difficult to believe."

"There is something which makes it more difficult to believe," said Riccasole, "and that is that Perrugino was executed ten years ago. What the clipping suggests to me is that one of the men was, shall I say, an admirer of Perrugino. For a bumper, which on Broke's car would be welded on and almost impossible to remove, he substituted the fog lamp, which was only bolted in position and could easily be detached."

"Do you mean to say . . ."

"I mean exactly what you are thinking. That Milo Zecchi, still unconscious, was brought to the scene of the accident in the stolen car, and was then cold-bloodedly finished off with the metal fog lamp, the blows being carefully delivered, not only to kill him, but also to cover up the marks of the original blow which had rendered him unconscious."

"I see. And that would account for the two-hour interval which the doctors told us had elapsed between unconsciousness and death."

"Precisely. The body was then dumped. It would be half past eleven by then and this would be the car which the cemetery keeper heard arriving and departing. The remains of the fog lamp were replaced. The stolen car was abandoned. The witness Maria gave false evidence of the car number to the police. That was all. It was not even a difficult crime. *Provided they could abstract Signor Broke's fog lamp for the necessary period without attracting the attention of any witness*. Which, with one exception, they did."

"A witness?"

"Unfortunately he will not be able to give evidence for us. He was a dog."

The Procuratore was silent for a whole minute. Then he rose to his feet. He said, "Signor Avvocato, I am infinitely obliged to you for your public-spirited assistance to the authorities in this matter. If I am permitted by you to repeat to the Giudice Istruttore what you have just told me, I think you may rest assured that the case against your client will never come to court."

Riccasole also rose to his feet. He said, "That would be a very satisfactory outcome for my client. And for myself."

The two men of the law bowed to each other in mutual esteem.

5

Finale in A Major

"'*Let no man stop to plunder,'*" roared Commander Comber, "'*but slay, and slay, and slay; the Gods who live for ever are on our side to-day.*' By heaven, Sindaco, I think you've worked a miracle."

"I have done nothing," said the Sindaco. "Except, perhaps, to lend a little weight to the opposition. The credit must go where it belongs. To you three, first. And then, of course, to Avvocato Riccasole."

He had come in person to bring the good news, and had found the committee in full and excited session, following on a cryptic message conveyed to them by Riccasole's wife, Isabella.

"Well, I think it's a miracle, too," said Elizabeth.

"What you have to appreciate," said the Sindaco, "is one simple fact. Where a crime has been committed, Italian justice requires a criminal. In this case you have given them good measure. In place of Broke they have the Professor *and* Danilo Ferri. Moreover, you have saved justice the trouble of convicting them. The suicide of one and the flight of the other are indisputable proof of guilt."

"Do you think they'll let Broke out now?" said the Commander.

"The papers went to the Giudice Istruttore yesterday. The order should be signed quite soon."

"In England," said the Commander, "he'd be able to sue the police and get heavy damages. No chance of that here, I suppose?"

"Certainly not. The police have behaved with complete correctness throughout."

The Commander considered the events of the past month. "I suppose they couldn't have done anything else," he said grudgingly. "In the circumstances. What's their theory about those two thugs? Why did they take to their heels?"

"They were possibly afraid they would be accused of killing the Professor. No doubt they helped themselves to the relics to give themselves funds for their escape. Though they may not have been genuine relics they were quite genuine gold."

"And they *were* the pair who killed Dindoni?"

"Undoubtedly. It is thought that they may have had, if not the active assistance, at least the connivance of one of their compatriots in the carabinieri. Under the new juris-diction—*our* jurisdiction—the matter will not go uninves-tigated. Colonel Doria will see to that, I can assure you."

"I'm sure he'll do what's necessary," said the Com-mander. "But the main thing is to get Broke out, and quick."

"We must go and see Father," said Elizabeth. "He'll know what strings to pull. We'll all go up in my car. What about you, Tina?"

But Tina shook her head. She said, "I will go and tell my mother. I am so happy for Signor Roberto. I desire only to cry." The tears were already streaming down her face. She added, "My mother will feel the same. She will cry, too."

"Curious reaction," said the Commander, as they whirled up the Viale in Elizabeth's open coupé, with the Sindaco wedged between them. "When I feel happy, *I* feel like re-citing. Macaulay meets my mood today.

> *"And nearer fast and nearer*
> *Doth the red whirlwind come;*

> *And louder still, and still more loud,*
> *From underneath that rolling cloud,*
> *Is heard the trumpet's war-note proud,*
> *The trampling and the hum—"*

"Attaboy," said Elizabeth. With her hair streaming out behind her she looked like a Valkyrie.

> *"And plainly and more plainly*
> *Now through the gloom appears,*
> *Far to left and far to right,*
> *In broken gleams of dark-blue light,*
> *The long array of helmets bright,*
> *The long array of spears."*

"That was Miss Plant we just missed," said Elizabeth. "She'll think we're mad."

The authorities were moving faster than the Sindaco had supposed possible. It was at six o'clock that same day, on an evening of hot sun and sudden fierce thunder, that the gates of the Murate prison opened and Broke came out.

He waved away the offer of the green-uniformed *agente di custodia* to fetch him a taxi. His worldly possessions (including the copy of *Paradise Lost,* which did not belong to him but which he could not bring himself to leave behind) went easily in a small haversack slung from his shoulder. He set out to walk home.

Knowing that his photograph had been in all the papers, he half expected passersby to stare at him. No one took any notice. He had been a nine-day wonder and this was the tenth day.

He was well up the Viale when the first big raindrops hit him. He ran the last hundred yards and arrived at his house with the shoulders of his jacket soaked and his hair plastered flat with rain. When he threw the door open, Tina was standing in the hall.

She gave a scream, threw her arms around his neck, and started to kiss him. Broke found himself kissing her back.

She said, "Your coat is all wet, and your hair. You must take it off at once."

"Take my hair off?"

"Your coat, stupid one. I will fetch a dry one."

"Don't bother. Look, the sun is coming out again."

"Give it to me. At once."

Broke, in his shirt sleeves, drifted across to the long window that gave onto the creeper-covered loggia and threw it open. Then he moved slowly across to the cupboard in the corner of the room and took out the battered black violin case, which he had not opened since he came to Florence. In the same dreamlike way he tightened the keys, tensioned the bow, and played a few tuning notes.

Tina, who had been rummaging around in his bedroom, heard them, abandoned her search for a coat, and came running back.

"Better," she said. "That is much better. Now play something."

Broke smiled at her, and began to play.

After the first few notes the door opened quietly and Avvocato Riccasole poked his head in.

He said, "I had heard the news and came to congratulate you. What is that you were playing?"

"I was trying my hand at the A Major Sonata."

"The *Trecentocinque*. Most appropriate. It benefits from a pianoforte accompaniment. I see that we have an instrument. No doubt it is vilely out of tune." He flung open the lid, ran his stubby fingers up and down the keys, said, "Not so bad," and started to play.

Stumblingly and quietly at first, but with growing clarity

and confidence as lawyer and client found themselves in sympathy, the notes of Mozart's most beautiful sonata filled the stuffy room, filled the heart of Tina, as she sat on the edge of the sofa with tears streaming down her nose and dropping, unchecked, onto her chin, floated out of the open window, and filled the garden beyond.

Elizabeth, who had driven down at dangerous speed from her house when her father told her the news, heard the music. She came around from the front of the house, and stood for a moment on the veranda, staring into the room. No one saw her. Broke had eyes only for Tina, and Tina for him.

Elizabeth tiptoed back, climbed into her car, and drove home. Her father said, "Well! Did you see him? Was he happy?"

"Very happy," said Elizabeth, in a stifled voice.

"And what will be the outcome of it all, my clever little man?" said Isabella Riccasole.

She and her husband were lying side by side in bed. Outside, a full moon shone through the half-open shutters, painting black bars on their bedroom wall. Bernado was snoring on the warm stones of the courtyard. A nightingale had taken a short lease of the lime tree.

"I have no doubt," said Riccasole, "that as soon as I left the house, Signor Broke and Tina went straight up to the bedroom, took off their clothes, jumped into bed, and—"

"There is no need to be coarse," said his wife. "Pray let us leave some things to the imagination. Will he marry her?"

"Being a scrupulous English gentleman, he will offer to do so, in a frenzy of self-condemnation, tomorrow morning. Being a sensible Florentine girl, Tina will certainly refuse."

"And who will prevail?"

"The girl, of course. Women always win their arguments." He gave his wife's ear a provocative nip.

264

"Take you hands off me, you monster of depravity. What will happen next?"

"As soon as he has got over his feelings of remorse, and has realized that what he needed at that psychological moment was a woman, not a wife, he will propose marriage to that very sensible and perfectly suitable English girl Elizabeth Weighill. She will accept him, and they will have four children—possibly five."

"Then poor Tina will be left out in the cold."

Avvocato Riccasole settled himself more comfortably in bed and said, sleepily, "Far from it. She will marry Mercurio."

"You mean Mercurio will marry her."

"I mean what I say, my dove. She will have to make all the running. But she will achieve it. Don't doubt it. Indeed, he will make quite a passable husband, when he learns to pay more attention to her body than to his own."

"Your coarseness revolts me," said his wife mendaciously.